AMBUSHED!

The dog was chewing a branch of a dead bush that he had taken a fancy to, when all at once he dropped flat on the ground.

I dropped, too, hitting the ground as flat as Barney was himself. Oh, bless that dog and his bad nerves! If he had been a brave pup, he would have stood up and growled. Then the bright idea of dropping for that ground would never had occurred to me. I would have stood up. At the best I would have been able to turn around and get a rifle bullet through my breast, instead of through my back. Yes, sir, for the trigger finger of that murderer was already crooked around the trigger of that gun so hard that he turned the bullet loose even while I was dropping. I heard it bite past me with a whiz. Looking to the side, I saw a man jump behind a tree.

You might say that I *expected* a man.

What beat me was that it was not Bill or his pal, Jerry, that I saw, but an olive-skinned Mexican.

MAX BRAND®

THE RANGE FINDER

LEISURE BOOKS   NEW YORK CITY

TABLE OF CONTENTS

THE WHISPERER...1

FLAMING FORTUNE..................................79

THE RANGE FINDER...............................195

THE WHISPERER

"The Whisperer" made its appearance early in Frederick Faust's writing career, just as a few of his stories were beginning to appear in Street & Smith's *Western Story Magazine*. It was published in the August 21, 1920, issue of *Argosy/All-Story Weekly*, where, that year, five of his seven short stories and five of his six serials appeared. This story of revenge relies on concealed identity—Who is the Whisperer?—one of Faust's favorite plot devices. What is unusual about the story is Faust's use of a woman, Patricia Lauriston, as his point of view character at the story's opening. Its inclusion in this collection marks its first appearance in paperback since its original publication.

I

PATRICIA FINDS WORK

Unquestionably the average man considers that woman's God-given vocation is the rearing of children. One may even go so far as to say that the average woman concurs in this judgment.

Which prepared the stage for the entrance of Patricia Lauriston, who was not average. Although she admitted that fate and the ways of the world condemned the majority of her sex to marriage, this admission only made her stamp along in shoes a little broader of toe and a little lower of heel. Not that she wished to be mannish. She was not. All she desired escape from was that femininity which bounds its world with children on the one side and a husband on the other.

Neither should it be understood that Patricia disliked men. On the contrary, she frankly preferred them to her own sex. Her whole struggle, in fact, was to be accepted by men as a friend, and it cut her to the heart to watch the antics of fellows who had courage enough to woo her. She noted that men among men were frank, open of hand and heart and eye, generous, brave, good humored; she noted that the same men among women became simpering, smirking fantastic fools. A man among men tried to be himself; a man among women dreaded nothing so much as the exposure of his own innate simplicity and manhood. All this Patricia had discovered by long and patient experiment.

There was the case of Steven Worth, for instance. Steve was the best friend of her brother Hal Lauriston, and Steve was almost another member of the family. Until, on a day, Patricia came home from school in long skirts. Instead of picking her up by the elbows and throwing her ceilingward, as had been his custom in the past, Steve shook hands, blushed, and suggested a walk in the garden. Patricia was only sixteen at the time, but she knew what was coming; a girl of sixteen is at least equal to a man of twenty-six, plus certain instinctive knowledge that has never left the blood of woman since that sunshiny day in the garden when Eve ate the apple and whispered with the serpent.

Therefore Patricia knew exactly what was coming, but she allowed the disease to develop and take hold on Steven Worth. She let him hold her hand; she let him look into her eyes and smile in a peculiarly asinine manner interspersed with occasional glances toward the stars. Three days and nights of this, and then Steve fell on his knees and asked her to be his wife. It didn't thrill Patricia. It merely disgusted her and made her feel very lonely. She told Steve just how she felt and went back into the house.

The next morning Hal Lauriston came to her room and swore that she had broken the heart of his dearest friend and that she was a devilish little cat; the next noon Steven Worth, she learned, had purchased a ticket for South America. Patricia went to Steve and told him—well, she told him many things, and in the end Steve Worth declared that she was the "bulliest little scout in the world" and that he was "no end of an ass." Patricia concurred silently in the last remark. The end of it was that Steve did not go to South America to die of swamp fever, but both he and Patricia knew that they could never be friends again.

The point of all this is that Patricia did not, certainly, miss Steve as a husband, but she regretted him mightily as a friend. She went abroad among the world of men, thereafter, and tried to make other friends to take the place of Steve, but she discovered that after friendship had progressed to a certain point the finest of men began to grow silent and thoughtful and a certain hungry look came in their eyes. The bitter truth came home to Patricia that she was too beautiful to have a single friend; many a time she bowed her head before her mirror and wept because her eyes were of a certain blackness and her hair of a certain dark and silken length. This sounds like fiction, but to Patricia it was a grim and heart-breaking truth.

Now, an average woman of this temperament, at a certain point in her life, would have taken u⁻ woman suffrage or prohibition—or Greek. Patric⁻

however, was not average. She refused to believe that all men are weak-kneed sentimentalists; she looked abroad, like Alexander, to a new world, and new battles.

It followed, quite naturally, that Patricia should go West. For she had heard sundry tales of a breed of men who inhabit the mountain desert, men stronger than adversity and hard of hand and of heart, men too bitterly trained in the battle of existence to pay any heed to the silken side of life. She hoped to find among them at least some few who would look first for a human being, and afterward for a sex.

This would have been enough to send Patricia to the mountain desert. There was another reason sufficiently unfeminine to interest her. One year before Mortimer Lauriston, a second cousin who bore her family name, had been shot in the town of Eagles in the mountain desert by a man named Vincent St. Gore. St. Gore had been tried, but the jury had always disagreed. Patricia Lauriston decided that it would be her work to tear the blindfold from the eyes of justice and bring an overdue fate upon this Vincent St. Gore. She could live not exactly in the town of Eagles, but at the ranch formerly owned by Mortimer Lauriston, and now operated by another cousin, Joseph Gregory. Having made up her mind, Patricia packed her trunk, kissed her mother good-bye, and from the train sent back postcards of farewell to her more intimate friends.

Which brings us to Eagles, a white-hot day in y, the hills spotted with mesquite, and below ʰills the illimitable plains, the stopping of the stage with its six dripping horses, and the entrance of Patricia into the mountain desert.

She was not disappointed. She liked everything she saw—the fierce heat of the day—the unshaven men—the buckboard of Joseph Gregory waiting to meet her. Even Joseph himself was not displeasing to her, although in a population where none was overly attractive Joseph was commonly called Ugly Joe. His forehead was so low and slanting that his dirty-white sombrero had to be pulled literally over his eyebrows—otherwise it would have blown off. His eyes were small and a very pale blue. His nose was both diminutive and sprawling, as if it had been battered out of shape in fistic battles. Below the nose his face ceased and his mustache began. It was the pride of Ugly Joe. The stiff hairs descended like a host of scimitar-shaped bristles far past his lower lip and at either side the mustache jagged down in points that swept far below his chin. If he had shaved, not even his wife would have known him. Patricia, however, was undismayed. She advanced with her suitcase and claimed relationship.

Ugly Joe parted his mustache, spat over the forward wheel of the buckboard, considered her a silent moment, and then touched the brim of his sombrero by way of salutation.

" 'Evening," said Ugly Joe, "throw up your grip and climb in."

"But I have a trunk," said Patricia. "Isn't there room for that behind?"

"Sure! Is that your trunk?"

He pointed to a wardrobe trunk that was being rolled onto the "hotel" verandah. She nodded and offered to get help for the handling of the trunk, for she remembered how two expressmen had sweated and grunted over that trunk, but Cousin Joe shook his head and climbed down from the buckboard. He was a short man, bent from riding horseback, and he walked with the shuffling hobble of the old cattleman, putting his weight on his toes. He was short, but exceedingly broad, and, when a couple of men had helped him to shoulder the trunk, he came back, hobbling along with it and showing no apparent discomfort. He dumped it in the back of the buckboard, which heaved and groaned under the burden.

"Might I ask," said Ugly Joe, as they climbed up to the front seat, "if them are all clothes you got in that trunk?"

"Mostly," answered Patricia.

"*Hmm!*" remarked Cousin Joe, and started his ponies over the homeward path.

For half an hour they jolted along in silence over what might have been a road.

"Maybe," said Ugly Joe at length, "you figure on starting a store with that many clothes?"

Now Patricia had prided herself on traveling light into the wilderness. There were only a few negligees, some house dresses, morning gowns, and several riding and walking outfits, as well as one or two tailored suits. She had not brought a single evening dress! Accordingly she stared at Ugly Joe in some surprise, but, before she could reply, he went on: "You're considerable well fixed for clothes and a name, eh? What's your name again?"

"Patricia," she answered.

"Patricia? And what do folks call you for short?"

"Nothing else. Personally I don't believe in nicknames."

"D'you mean to say," said Ugly Joe, much moved, "that, when your ma or your pa speaks to you, they always take that much tongue-trouble and spend that much air? Patricia!" He did not repeat it scoffingly, but rather with much wonder.

Patricia decided that being in Rome she must adapt herself to the customs of the country. "I suppose," she said, "that it could be shortened."

"Between you and me," confided Ugly Joe, "it'll *have* to be shortened. Long names ain't popular much around here. Look at them hosses. S'pose I give them fancy names, how'd I ever handle 'em? S'pose I wanted 'em to stop and I had to say . . . 'Whoa, Elizabeth Virginia, the first, and Johnny Payne, the third.' Nope, you can see for yourself that wouldn't do. A long name is as much in the way as a long barrel on a shotgun when you want to shoot quick."

"What do you call your horses?" asked Patricia.

"The nigh one is Spit and the off one is Fire. I just say . . . 'Giddap, Spit-Fire!' . . . and we're off. See?"

"Oh"—Patricia smiled—"and what will you call me?"

"I'll leave off the fancy part. Pat is a good enough name. What say?"

"That," said Patricia, "will be fine."

"Sure. I'll call you Pat and you call me Joe. Simple, easy to remember, saves lots of wind and talking. Talking ain't popular none with me."

And he proved it by maintaining a resolute silence for the next fifteen minutes. As for Patricia, she was too busy sweeping the plains with a critical eye to wish for talk. Moreover, the silence was pleasing. That was a way men had with each other. She began to feel, also, that she had at last reached a country where a pretty face was not a passport to all hearts; she would have to prove herself before she would be accepted.

II

THE KILLING OF LAURISTON

Not that this was in the least discouraging to Patricia. She was, indeed, rather excited and stimulated by the prospect, as an athlete feels himself keyed to the highest point of efficiency by a contest with a rival of unquestioned prowess. She swept the country with a critical eye; she glimpsed the massive, rounded shoulders of Ugly Joe with a side glance; the mesquite-dotted hills, the white-hot plains, the man who lived in them—all were good in the eye of Patricia. She would have accepted the silence of her companion and persisted in it, but she came to this place for a purpose and talk was necessary before she could accomplish it.

"I suppose," said Patricia, "that everyone wonders why I've come out here?"

Ugly Joe had caught the reins between his knees while he rolled a cigarette. Now he finished licking the paper smooth and bent a meditative eye upon Patricia while he lighted his cigarette and inhaled the first puff. "Don't know that I've heard any remarks," he responded at length. "Giddap, Spit-Fire!"

They jolted over a particularly uneven stretch of the trail. When Patricia had caught her breath, again she said: "Nevertheless, I'll tell you, Cousin Joe. I've come out here to run down the murderer of Mortimer Lauriston."

She waited for this verbal bull's-eye to take effect, but Ugly Joe seemed not a whit interested.

"That ain't hard," he answered. "You can pick him up mostly any day in Eagles."

"I," said Patricia, "am going to have him tried . . . and hung."

"*Hmm!*" grunted Ugly Joe. "Where you going to get a jury to convict him?"

"Is it hard to do that?"

"I'll say it's hard!"

"Does he bribe the jurors?"

"Nope, not exactly."

"Is this murderer too popular to be convicted?"

"Him?" Ugly Joe grinned for the first time. "Nope, it'd be a hard job to find a feller less popular than this Goggles."

"Goggles? I thought his name is Vincent Saint Gore?"

"Maybe it is, but who can remember a word as long as that? We call him Goggles because of the funny glasses he wears . . . big ones with black rims. Makes him look like a frog. Goggles popular? Not around here, Pat. Nope, he's just a plain, damned dude, that's what he is. Out here for a couple of years for his health. Little, skinny feller who goes around in fancy, shined-up riding boots and trousers baggy above the knees. Lives over to Widow Morgan's house, where he got a piano moved in and he just sits around and tickles the keys, or mosies out and rides a fine, foreign, high-steppin' hoss around. Never talks much to anybody. He forgets everybody as quick as he's introduced to 'em. Popular? Hell, no! Excuse me."

The description was a distant shock to Patricia. She had pictured, quite naturally, a tall, gaunt, swarthy rider of the mountain desert, black-browed, black-eyed, fierce, silent. Instead, here was a man who fitted his name—Vincent St. Gore—possibly some disinherited second son, the black sheep of some honorable family.

"But if he doesn't bribe the jurors, and if he isn't popular," she queried, "how in the world does he manage to escape scot-free? Is it because Mortimer Lauriston was disliked . . . because the people of Eagles were glad to get rid of him?"

"Nope, everybody liked old Mort. He never did no harm, except when he was full of red-eye."

"Then," Patricia said desperately, "was it because Saint Gore . . . your man Goggles . . . killed Mortimer in self-defense?"

"Pat," said Ugly Joe, grinning again, "the more I hear you talk, the more I see that you are the cousin of my wife, Martha. She does just the same way. Get her talking about anything and she hangs on like a bulldog till she's got out of me all I know. I can see you're the same way, and I'll be savin' myself if I tell you the whole yarn right here and now."

"Good," said Patricia, unabashed.

"It was in Langley's saloon," said Ugly Joe. "'S a matter of fact most of these hell-raisin's begin with red-eye and end with guns. Well, it was along about the middle of the afternoon. I was in there, so was about twenty more. And there was Goggles standin' at one end of the bar, sipping whiskey mixed up with seltzer water out of a high glass. He never would drink whiskey straight like a regular honest man. There he stood, staring straight in front of him that way he has and never seeming to see nothing that happened near him.

"About that time in come Mort Lauriston. He was lit to the eyes, was old Mort, and, when he got drunk, he was some noisy. Which everybody knew he didn't mean nothing and they let him go along pounding 'em on the back. He ordered up drinks for the crowd, and everybody accepted but Goggles. Nobody ever included him in anything. He was just part of the landscape, like one of them hills over there. He was there, but he didn't mean nothing . . . but Mort seen him and he got mad. He goes up and says . . . 'Partner, whiskey wasn't never meant to be spoiled by mixing with water.' Then he grabs Goggles's high glass and spills the mixture out on the floor.

" 'Hey, Pete,' he says to the bartender, 'give this feller Goggles a man-size drink of man-size booze.'

"Everybody laughed. They was all tickled at the thought of Goggles drinking straight red-eye. Pete put up a whiskey glass filled to the brim.

"Goggles was standing there pretty quiet. He just fixed the glasses different on his nose and stands there staring at Mort. The whiskey has splashed pretty liberal across them fine riding boots of his, but he didn't make an ugly move.

"He says . . . 'Mister Lauriston, I'm sure that you have carried your little game far enough. You certainly don't intend to make me drink that glass of vile bar whiskey.'

" 'Don't I?' says Mort, and the rest of us laughed. 'Bud, you're going to drink every drop of it!'

"Goggles takes off his glasses and wipes them careful on his handkerchief, puts them back, and studies Mort like a rock hound looking at a new kind of ore. He says in that soft, low voice of his . . . 'You are apparently very drunk, Mister Lauriston. What if I refuse to drink this liquor?'

"Out comes Mort with two big gats. He shoves them under the nose of Goggles. 'Drink, you damned foreign English dude!' he says.

" 'Sir,' says Goggles, 'I'm going to drink this under compulsion, not because I fear you, but because I don't want to harm a drunken man. But the next time we meet, Mister Lauriston, I'm going to kill you.' With that he picks up the glass of booze careful, without spilling a drop, and says . . . 'Here is to our early meeting, sir.' And he drinks the glass down without batting an eye, bows to Mort, and walks out of the saloon.

" 'Well, I'll be damned,' says Mort. 'What d'you think of that?'

"Herb Fisher speaks up and says . . . 'I dunno how you figure it, Mort, but, if I was you, I'd keep my guns ready for a fast draw the next time I seen Goggles. He don't look none too dangerous, but looks is deceiving.'

"Mort, he took that to heart. He left town pretty hurried, and it was about ten days before he come back. At least, he started back, and afterward they found his body on the road near Eagles. He'd been shot fair and square between the eyes and his guns was lying near him with a bullet fired out of each of them, showing that he'd had a chance to fight for his life. He wasn't shot down from no ambush.

"Of course, they arrested Goggles. The sheriff took half a dozen deputies along to help out in case of a muss, but Goggles didn't turn a hair. He walked right into the jail, give a big bond, and never made a move to get away before the trial.

"At the trial he didn't have a chance, it looked like. Everybody knew that Mort was a harmless, noisy sort of gent. Maybe he done wrong in making Goggles drink, but there wasn't no call for any gun play. That was what the district attorney kept pumping into the jury all through the trial and they were all set to hang Goggles. Everybody knew that. But when the last day of the trial came along, right when the district attorney was making his last big spiel, a little piece of paper come fluttering like a white bird through the window right behind Goggles, and over his shoulder, and into the lap of one of the gents in the jury box."

III

THE PASSING OF KENNEDY

"He unfolded it sort of absent-minded and read what was on it, and then he stood up slow, like he was being pulled up by the hair of the head. And he says . . . 'God!' . . . just once, soft and easy, but it cut off the speech of the district attorney like a hot knife going through a piece of cheese.

" 'What's there?' said the district attorney.

"But the gent that got the paper, he just passed it on to the gent next to him, and that one turned sort of green and sick looking and moved it on to the next. And so it went all through the jury box.

"The district attorney finished up, the jury went out and came back in five minutes, saying . . . 'Not guilty!' Yep, it was a unanimous verdict, and afterward everyone on that jury went around telling the boys in a loud voice that he had voted to acquit Goggles, and that he'd like to have the word passed on."

"It was the paper?" asked Patricia.

"It sure was. There was writ on it . . . 'Boys, I've got all your names. If you hang Goggles, you'll have to tell me why later on.'

"And underneath, the paper was signed . . . 'The Whisperer.' Now you know why Goggles ain't been touched by the law and why it ain't possible to get a jury in these parts to convict him. Here's the paper. I got a hold on it, and I've always kept it with me."

He drew it from a vest pocket and handed it to Patricia—a little scrap torn roughly from a larger sheet, and the words on it were scrawled clumsily in backhand, like the writing of a child of seven.

"The Whisperer!" Patricia frowned. "Who is he?"

"Don't you even know that?" Ugly Joe asked in disgust. "Well, you'll hear a pile about him before you been in these parts long. He's a lone rider who hangs out somewhere in them hills. Nobody knows just where . . . about umpteen posses have hunted for him and never got on his trail. They lay a lot of things to the Whisperer . . . some of them may be lies, but a pile of them ain't. I *know!* He's a sort of a ghost, the Whisperer is. He rides a white horse that can go like the wind, and he wears light-gray clothes, and a white handkerchief all over his face like a mask. Nobody has ever seen his face, but when he shows up, he's known by his voice. It ain't any common voice. It's a sort of a husky hissing, like something had gone wrong with his throat. It takes the heart out of a man just to hear that voice."

"Yes," murmured Patricia, "it's ghostly . . . it's horrible. But are you sure that it was really the

Whisperer who threw that paper through the window?"

"That's what a lot of people wanted to know, and particularly Lew Lauriston . . . you know him . . . old Mort's brother. He didn't think the Whisperer had anything to do with the case. So he got Porky Kennedy, the two-gun man, to go on the trail of Goggles and put him under the sod. There wasn't much of a secret about it. Everybody in Eagles knew that it was about time for Goggles to move on his way, because Porky Kennedy had a long line of killings to his credit already.

"Porky went to Eagles, but Goggles didn't show no special hurry about leaving. Finally Porky went to Widow Morgan's house for supper one night. Everybody sat around the table scared stiff, because they knew that as soon as Goggles came in there'd be a killing and one foreign English dude less in the world. But Goggles didn't come in. They began to think that the fool dude finally had got some sense behind them glasses of his and left for parts unknown. But about the middle of the meal, while Porky was telling a long story, the door opened and the wind blew the flame jumping up and down in the chimney of the lamp.

"And from the door there was a whisper . . . 'Kennedy!' And when they looked up, there stood the Whisperer with his white mask and his gray clothes and his voiceless voice. Kennedy pulled his gun, but his hand was shaking so that the gun fell out of his hand and rattled onto the floor, and Kennedy dropped on his knees against the wall and covered up his face in his arms, moaning like a sick kid.

"But the Whisperer hadn't come for a killing. He just vanished out the door. Pretty soon in comes Goggles and cocks an eye over to Kennedy as calm as you please. But Kennedy wasn't interested in any killing just then. He ups from his chair and climbed through the door in about two steps. He hasn't been around these parts since. That's one of the good things about the Whisperer. No robber but himself does much flourishing while he's around. There's some say the only ones he picks on is the other crooks. Others say different. I don't know. Well, a couple of days later Lew Lauriston does a fade away. He didn't even stop to tell us whether the Whisperer had paid him a visit or not, but we just took it for granted.

"So, if you want to try your hand, Pat, why, it ain't hard to find Eagles, and in Eagles it ain't hard to find Goggles."

But the arrows of his sarcasm flew harmlessly over the head of Patricia, for she had fallen into a brown study. Certainly it is not easy to understand Patricia, for I suppose that she never really understood herself. I have never known two people, of all who knew her intimately, who could agree about the main points in her character, and I have always attributed the misunderstanding to the fact that she was so unfemininely serious minded. Really there was nothing masculine about her except a desire to prove herself of some significance in the world, and, because she was so pretty, she was confronted with an endless struggle to make the world accept her as something more than a mere ornament. Sometimes the very desperation of her efforts to do strong things in a strong way made her as stern and hard as any man, and for this reason quite a few misjudged her—in fact, she misjudged herself. To me there was always something plaintive in the quest of Patricia for herself. At the moment when Ugly Joe ceased speaking, for instance, Patricia was really not thinking of the avenging of Mortimer Lauriston's death. She was merely working out a way in which she could prove to Ugly Joe that there was in her a profound difference from that of his talkative wife. Surely here was a man-size problem—the apprehension and bringing to justice of a murderer who even the rough-handed dwellers in the mountain desert dared not touch.

She said at length: "Has it ever occurred to you, Cousin Joe, that the killer of Mortimer Lauriston was really not your man Goggles at all, but the Whisperer?"

Ugly Joe chuckled. "Has it taken you all this thinking to get that far? Sure, it's occurred to me, and to everybody else. If you ever seen Goggles, you'd be sure of it. I've seen him handle a gun in a shooting gallery. Say, Pat, he couldn't hit the side of a barn with a rock. And there ain't enough heart in that skinny body of his to hurt a swallow. We all seen that as soon as the Whisperer got mixed up in the case. Mort was fast with his guns and he shot straight. It must've took a man about as good as the Whisperer to beat him on the draw and drill him as clean as that after he'd had a chance to work his shooting irons."

"The real criminal, then," mused Patricia, "is the Whisperer." She shivered a little, but went on: "The other man, this Goggles, is evidently just a harmless little cur. I suppose the Whisperer uses him to collect information, and then robs the people Goggles points out to him."

"I s'pose so." Ugly Joe, who was fast losing interest in the conversation, nodded.

"And yet you allow Goggles to wander about at liberty! I can't understand you people, Cousin Joe."

"You would, Pat, if you'd ever had any dealings with the Whisperer. Maybe he's using Goggles and maybe he isn't. We've never had any proof of that. All we know is that he's Goggles's friend, and as long as that's the case there ain't anybody around here with the courage to mix up with Goggles. You can lay to that."

"I know," Patricia said, in the same musing voice, "this Whisperer is a dangerous fellow, but he has his weak point. And I'm going to *get* him through that weakness."

"What weakness?" asked Ugly Joe, wakening to a new interest in the case.

"Goggles! The Whisperer may be an outlaw, but he's a man. This Goggles is merely a cowardly little sneak who hides in the terror of the name of the Whisperer. That's why he had the courage to face Mortimer Lauriston. He knew that he could send his man-killer after my cousin. But I'm going to set a trap for the Whisperer, bait it with Goggles, and catch your man for you."

"Going to do which?" gasped Ugly Joe.

"Wait," Patricia murmured, and smiled into the contented distance.

IV

A Plan for Trapping

She said after a while: "Cousin Joe, I want you to hire me the four best fighters and straightest shooters you can get. I want four honest men who will . . ."

"Wait a minute, Pat," answered the other, "I can find you four first-class gunmen, and I can find you, maybe, four first-class honest men, but I'll be . . . excuse me . . . if I can get four honest gunmen. They don't come that way. That ain't their brand. It's this way, Patty. Lots of men can shoot straight at anything but another man. It takes something more than a marksman to shoot down a man . . . it takes a natural killer, and a natural killer ain't often honest."

Patricia sat stiffly erect in her place, but she said firmly: "Then if I have to get a gang of cutthroats . . . well, the end justifies the means. Get me the gunmen, Cousin Joe, and I'll ask no questions about their honesty. Can you get me four men who won't be afraid to fight with the Whisperer?"

Ugly Joe meditated. Finally he said: "I see there ain't any use trying to persuade you, Pat. Just like Martha. I can get you four gunmen who'd do any murder for a price. There's Chic Wood. He climbed a tree with a shotgun over at Tomanac and shot a man for fifty dollars. But he'd maybe want fifty thousand for killing the Whisperer. I could get some more like Chic. D'you want to work with men like him, Pat?"

"The end," said Patricia, "justifies the means. Yes, I want any four men . . . as long as they are dangerous."

"Then I guess I can get 'em. None of the crooks has any special liking for the Whisperer. He's run most of them out of range of Eagles. All you'll have to do is to pay the price. Can you do that?"

"Anything you think they're worth."

"And after you get 'em," said Ugly Joe, "I s'pose you're going to ride through the hills with your posse hunting for the Whisperer?"

"Not at all. I'm going to stay right at your house, Cousin Joe, and wait for the Whisperer to come to me."

"Pat," said Joe solemnly, "if you was a man, I'd say you'd been drinking. Wait for the Whisperer to come to *you*?"

"He will," Patricia answered. "Will you have the four men at the house tomorrow?"

Ugly Joe made no reply, but sighed heavily as he rolled another cigarette. He had heard about this type of Eastern woman, as aggressive as a man, but he hardly knew what to make of her now that she sat at his side. A Westerner is singularly helpless in the presence of a woman. He is accustomed to making his way through a purely physical prowess. Against the peculiar strength of a woman, which is fleshly and yet not of the flesh, he has nothing to pit.

So Ugly Joe felt very much like a tongue-tied boy, unable to recite his lesson to the pretty school-ma'am. If he resented the calm appropriation of his house as the trap that was to catch the Whisperer, he felt a counterbalancing excitement that more than made up. He had shot mountain lions in his time, but this would be a rarer sport.

They reached the ranch house. It was formed of great adobe walls from three to four feet in thickness—utterly impervious to the heat of summer or the winds and cold of winter. A one-storied structure, it rambled out in a roomy square around a hexagonal patio in the center. The exterior of that house, dirty-brown with deep-set windows gaping like mouths, was quite in keeping with the exterior of Ugly Joe and with the sweep of rough hills and sordid plain on either side in prospect, but the patio within was the special province of Ugly Joe.

Water, for the internal or external application of which the proprietor had little use, was here lavished upon *flowers*. There were many kinds, and exceedingly bright colors, blended with all the skill with which a Navajo Indian weaves scarlets and yellows into his blanket. About these flowers Martha Gregory wandered with a watering can in one hand and a short-handled hoe in the other. With the one she dealt life to the flowers. With the other she dealt death to the weeds—a faultless justice. She was taller than Ugly Joe, and her face was even homelier, with a cast of the Scandinavian expressed by high cheek bones, small eyes, and a perfectly straight mouth so rigidly set that not the least blood-color showed in the lips.

At sight of Patricia Lauriston, the hostess dropped her watering can and embraced her guest with the liberated arm. There was more strength in that one arm than in any two that Patricia had ever felt, and, when she looked up, somewhat breathless, she surprised a smile on the lips of the Amazon. It was like a warm surprise of sunshine on a cloudy day—there was something generously enveloping about it. And Patricia smiled back. After all, there is only one smile for all women when they are kindly moved and genuine. Patricia and "Mother" Martha cast an arm about each other and wandered into the house, completely forgetful of Ugly Joe.

His wife was called "Mother" throughout 10,000 square miles because she had no children and had to vent her tenderness on flowers and broken-down houses and sick children. They still tell the story of how Mother Martha rode fifty miles in the space of a single night—fifty miles through a sandstorm that whipped her face raw—how her horse dropped—how she went on the last miles on foot—and reached the house of Jim Patrick. She saved three lives that time, for Mrs. Patrick gave birth to twins, and the lives of all three hovered at the brink of death for ten days, and were finally drawn back to life by the strong arm of Mother Martha.

That is only one of the stories they tell about

Mother Martha. And if Patricia did not know these tales when she first saw her hostess, she must have guessed something of them. For when she passed through the door with Mother Martha, Patricia was extremely glad that she had taken her trip to the mountain desert, and, as I have said, her arm was about the waist of the Amazon.

That evening Patricia borrowed one of Mother Martha's gingham dresses, which flapped about her more loosely than a Kanaka woman's *holoku*, and went into the kitchen to assist Martha. For the good wife would not keep a cook. No one, it seemed, could cook to please Ugly Joe except herself.

The master of the house had already dispatched four riders in four various directions, and late that night, while Patricia sat at the piano—the pride of the house—playing everything from "Swanee River" to the "Maple Leaf Rag," the four messengers returned, and they brought with them four others. Now the messengers themselves were hardy cowpunchers, not overly gentle in feature or voice or manner, but they were missionary spirits of surpassing sweetness compared with the four accomplished ruffians they brought with them. The heart of a moving-picture director would have swelled almost to bursting if he could have seen them enter, for they were ideal figures for that episode in the third reel where the gang of villains pursues the innocent girl—the same episode, you know, where the gallant United States troopers in turn pursue the villains and arrive just in time— well, that's the sort our four gunmen were.

Chic Woods came first. His face was built like some great transatlantic liner, chiefly towering hull with diminutive deck works. Upon that massive jaw and swelling jowl, the diminutive nose, little pig eyes, and forehead lost under a descending scrag of black hair, were set rather as a suggestion of how the face might be finished off than as a necessary part of the countenance. All that anyone would ever remember of Chic would be that jaw and the fang-like teeth and the bull-neck made for hanging on.

Behind him came his antithesis, Harry Yale. He was, as nearly as possible, a figure in one dimension—length. Both his breadth and his thickness were not worth consideration. He looked like a man who had gone without food for a month. There was the blaze of famine in his eyes, for instance, and his cheeks were so sunken that they pulled back the lips at the corners and made Harry Yale seem to smile. It seemed to Patricia the most unpleasant smile she had ever seen. She was fascinated by the man and could not take her eyes from him when he spoke, for with every utterance the great Adam's apple rolled up and down his throat, as if he were trying to swallow it and could never quite succeed.

As for Bob Riddle, who came third, he was far less repulsive than the other two. He was a half-breed, however, and he carried with him that suggestion of mysterious and inexhaustible malice that even a tenderfoot apprehends in a thoroughly bad Indian. He was quite dignified and very silent, which made him seem more venomous than ever.

Against the ugly background of the other three, Jack Tucker was a perfect Apollo. In fact, his good looks had been the ruin of him. They had made him a spoiled child, and out of a spoiled childhood he grew into a youth and manhood unable to accept the rebuffs of the world. When the world struck him, he struck back, and, having a heavy hand and a demon temper, he struck to kill. He had been a gambler for some years, but his killings grew greater than his winnings and he had to move on to fresh fields and pastures new. He was one of those fallen figures that excite no pity because his strength was still great enough to defy the world.

V

The Trap is Set

As these worthies filed in, the messengers who had brought them out of the distance vanished through the open door behind them. The gunfighters exchanged no kindly greetings.

"Well?" growled Chic Woods.

"Well?" snarled Harry Yale.

"Well?" grunted Bob Riddle.

"Well?" drawled Jack Tucker.

"Don't all ask me," Ugly Joe said, affable but a little shaken by this terse battery. "Here's the lady that got you brought here."

The piano was in shadow in a corner of the room and the piano itself cast a night-deep, slanting shade over Patricia. She was only visible when she rose to greet the instruments of her will, and, in rising, the light from the lamp fell softly across her face and splashed a little spot of gold on her throat.

"Hell!" snorted Chic Woods at this sudden apparition, and then instantly dragged the hat from his head. The shaggy hair that sprawled in snaky, black locks made him trebly horrible. " 'Scuse me, lady."

"Certainly," Patricia said, hunting through her mind for the words with which she must explain her purpose to these grim knights of the mountain desert.

Here Jack Tucker, smoothing back his long hair and shifting his orange-colored bandanna, stepped forward, hat in hand, as a spokesman more befitting this occasion.

"Me and these other gents," Tucker said graciously, "come here because Ugly Joe sent for us, and he's showed pretty much man to us. But if you want us, you can buy your chips now and start the game. We'll see that it's on the square. I'll be the guy on the stick myself."

The parlance of the gambling house was unfamiliar to Patricia, but she gathered the general meaning.

"Thank you," she said, "my name is Patricia Lauriston . . . but Cousin Joe Gregory, there, says that I'll have to be known by a shorter name. He has suggested Pat."

"Which I'll agree is a good name," said Tucker. "I'm sure glad to know you. I'm Jack Tucker. This is Chic Woods, here's Harry Yale, and this is Bob Riddle."

She managed to keep her smile steady and shook hands with them each in turn.

"Now," she said to Ugly Joe, "shall I explain why we sent for them, or will you?"

"Pat," said Ugly Joe, "first, last, and all the time this is your party, and run by yourself."

"Very well," she answered. "I've come from the

East with a purpose in which I'll need the help of several men who can shoot straight and have the courage to fight. Cousin Joe suggested you. I want to hire you. It may be hard work so that you can practically name your own prices."

"Seeing it's you," said the gallant Tucker, bowing, "I'm here willing to do any of my little specialties at half rates. What about you, boys?"

Their eyes had held like the bright eyes of four birds upon the deadly fascination of a snake. To men who ride alone in the mountain desert, the very name "woman" is synonymous with purity, beauty, and grace; in the presence of Patricia they stood awed, and their admiration—and their grunt of assent—thrilled her more than any tribute from her cultured friends of the East.

"Wait a minute," Ugly Joe announced, "while I horn in a bit. What she wants is for you to get the Whisperer. I thought that would change you a bit!"

The effect of the name had been magical. Bob Riddle leaped back to the door and peered out into the night. Harry Yale and Jack Tucker jumped back to back and stood crouching a little, as though ready to fight a host of foes, while Chic Woods whipped out two guns and stood with them poised. Patricia shrank back against the wall.

"Steady!" called Ugly Joe, after he had enjoyed the full effect of his announcement for an instant. "I said she wanted you to get the Whisperer. I didn't say he was *here*."

They relaxed, but cautiously. Riddle turned only partly from the door. Chic Woods restored his weapons to their holsters, but kept his right hand still in position for a lightning draw.

What Patricia saw, oddly enough, was not the men before her, but him whose name had produced this panic among man-killers. She envisioned him in one swift flare of sure knowledge—big, silent, neither handsome nor ugly, but simply dangerous!

"As a matter of fact," Patricia said, "I am not even going to ask you to expose yourselves by hunting for the Whisperer through the hills. I simply want you to stay here and be ready to fight when the Whisperer comes. For he *shall* come. Will you stay?"

They stayed, and the next day Patricia rode alone toward Eagles. Behind her the trap was ready, a strong trap with four teeth of steel, and more, because in time of need all the cowpunchers of Cousin Joe Gregory could be summoned. What she needed to make that trap effective was to secure the efficient bait, and already she was tasting the joys of victory. She had no difficulty in finding the house of the Widow Morgan, and there, on the front verandah, sat Goggles. She was at a little distance when she spied him and knew him at once by the description. He wore riding boots so highly polished that from the distance they glittered like mirrors, and his riding trousers were of a mouse-colored whipcord, buttoned snugly below the narrow knees. His loose pongee shirt fluttered with the puff of wind, and he lay easily back in his chair, with his slender hands locked behind his head.

Patricia was irritated, and chiefly by the fact that he seemed so cool. She herself was very hot from the keenness of the sun and labor of the hard ride. She swung from her horse and mounted to the verandah. The nearer view merely proved what she had surmised from the distance. His face was very lean and pale, and behind the great, black-rimmed spectacles, large and pathetic eyes of soft brown stared out at the world. He was finished by a dapper little mustache. It did not extend clear across the upper lip, but was merely a decorative dab in the center. At her approach, he turned his head carelessly, and she noted that his face did not light as the faces of most men did when she came near.

With her whole heart Patricia despised him. If he had been himself a slayer of men, she would almost have admired him—there is a place of esteem for a dangerous man—but at this decorative, smooth, lithe sneak, who lived in the shadow of a great outlaw's protection and like a jackal preyed on the leavings of the lion's meal, her disgust stormed up strongly in her throat. It made her face hard, indeed.

Seeing her pause by him, Goggles arose with just that touch of lingering hesitancy that indicates the courtesy of habit and breeding rather than the attention of natural kindliness. He rose, smiled automatically, and offered his chair. Without the slightest hesitancy Patricia slipped into it and sat calmly, staring up at him.

If she had hoped to irritate him, however, she was totally disappointed. He did not even seem surprised, but leaned against the rail of the verandah, brushing his little mustache with a very slender fingertip and looking for all the world as if he had been merely keeping the chair in trust for her. Patricia was quite sure that the man's blood was no warmer than that of a fish. She pictured him, in one of those quick visions of hers, fawning and cringing in the presence of the Whisperer. Indeed, being the servant of such a grim master gave the fellow a sort of dignity. She had to admit it unwillingly. She could only wonder that a lone rider of the mountain desert could choose so despicable a tool. The man was hardly taller than herself and certainly not a great deal heavier. The only admirable physical characteristic about him was a certain suggestion of lightness for speed. She had seen famous sprinters who had the same delicate, almost perfectly round wrists and ankles, the same marvelously slender hands and feet. His feet, in fact, although they were somewhat longer, were hardly a jot wider than her own. These details Patricia gathered in that first steady, rather insolent stare.

Then she said: "Thank you for the chair, Mister Saint Gore. I've just come in from a long ride . . . very hot, you know, and a little tired."

"Ah!" drawled St. Gore without the slightest meaning in his voice, and then, acting upon sudden inspiration: "By Jove, the Widow Morgan has just made a pitcher of delightfully cool lemonade. May I bring you a glass?'

"Thanks," said Patricia. "No."

"No? It's really very palatable lemonade . . . not made with the wretched extract."

"Indeed?" said Patricia.

"Quite so," babbled Goggles, "and the pitcher is so cold . . . well, there's frost on it, you know."

The description sent a burning pang of thirst down Patricia's throat and plunging hotly into her vitals, but now that she had first refused she could not well change her mind. Unquestionably she hated the fellow with her whole soul.

"My name," she broke in, "is Patricia Lauriston."

She waited for the name to take effect—waited for the guilty start—the flush—the pallor of the coward. Instead, he merely stared curiously—a faint curiosity—toward her, and then past her, as if he were lost at the instant in the drifting of a pale, far-off cloud.

"Really," murmured Goggles, "I'm so happy to know you, Miss Lauriston."

Patricia leaned forward to give the first sharp home stroke.

VI

BAIT FOR THE TRAP

"I am the cousin," she said, "of that Lauriston whose murder you accomplished through the Whisperer."

At this he started. Not sharply, it was merely a sudden and rather hurt glance down at her face, studying her as if he wondered what manner of creature she might be.

"Oh, dear," Goggles sighed at last. "*You* are not going to bring up that hideous old affair?"

"I have come several thousand miles for that exact purpose," Patricia advised, and the rage that she had been controlling took her by the throat like a gripping hand, so that her voice trembled and went small. For her whole soul revolted at the thought of that stalwart cousin of hers done to death through this paltry cur. She concluded: "And having come so far, I'm certainly going to do my best to bring matters to a crisis."

Goggles sank back against the rail and trailed

slender fingers across that broad, pale forehead. "Everyone," he complained drearily, "has been simply wretched to me since the death of that vulgar fellow, and now you come. Well, I'm very glad that you know it was the Whisperer, and not I, who committed the murder."

"No," said Patricia with a fine disdain, "all your part was to call on the bloodhound and set him on the trail of a man you did not have the heart to face by yourself."

"Oh!" Goggles said, and shrank a little away from her. "You don't seem to like me, do you?"

She could not help laughing. The inanity of the fellow was both disgusting and comic. Her laugh jarred to an abrupt stop. "Do you think it strange, Mister Saint Gore?"

"Really, you know," said St. Gore, "I've tried most awfully not to offend you. If my manners have been bad, I know you will excuse me. You see I'm a little troubled with absentmindedness."

"*Hmm,*" grumbled Patricia, and she seemed very masculine and formidable as she frowned thoughtfully down at him. "The more I see of you, Mister Saint Gore, I wish that I could do to you what I am going to do the Whisperer."

He was frankly, guilelessly interested at once. "Oh, are you going to do something to the Whisperer?"

"I am going to see him captured," Patricia stated smoothly, "and either shot down or else hanged from the highest cottonwood tree on the ranch."

"Dear me!" cried Goggles, distressed, "you're such a violent person, aren't you?"

"And I'm almost sorry to have it done," went on

Patricia, "because something in me admires the man in spite of his crimes. At least he has strength and courage and power of action. I wish . . . I wish that someone of your nature were to be in his place."

"Like me!" poor Goggles gasped, and he edged farther away along the rail.

"Stand where you are!" Patricia cried sternly.

He stopped with a jerk, and his eyes widened.

"But I can't do that," she went on, and paused to meditate.

"I wonder," began St. Gore timidly, as if he feared that she would snap at him in the middle of his question, "I wonder how you will attack the Whisperer. He has never killed a woman . . . but, I suppose, he would . . . he's such a terrible fellow. Quite uncontrollable, you know."

"Perhaps," said Patricia, "you have heard of Chic Woods, Harry Yale, Jack Tucker, and Bob Riddle?"

"Oh, yes," Goggles murmured, "and I don't think you could have named four rougher men. Really, you know, they are the sort one doesn't mention . . . in certain places."

"I have hired them," Patricia said calmly, "to do the work that the law could not or would not perform." She considered him again, thoughtfully. "And in some way I'm going to use you, Mister Saint Gore, but just how I can't tell."

The man seemed to have a special talent for asinine expression of face—utter emptiness of eye. But now a dawn of intelligence lighted his eyes. "By Jove!" he cried, and, straightening, he clapped his hands together and laughed with soft glee to himself. "I have it!"

"Have what?" asked Patricia.

"You see," explained Goggles eagerly, "it's been useful now and then, but on the whole an awful nuisance to have the Whisperer trailing me about. I'd give almost anything to have the rude fellow . . . er . . . disappear!"

"You would?"

"So, suppose I go out to your ranch and act . . . well, as a sort of bait for your trap. The Whisperer is sure to follow me. He's like my shadow, in fact."

"Do you mean to say," Patricia said slowly, "that you would actually help to betray him . . . your friend . . . your benefactor . . . no matter what he has been to the rest of the world?"

"Now," Goggles said deprecatingly, "you are thinking hard things of me again, aren't you? But the Whisperer is an awful burden for anyone . . . and I'm quite too nervous to have him always around. It would be a most enormous relief to get rid of him."

She closed her eyes and drew a deep breath. The shameless ingratitude and treachery of the fellow blinded her.

"But how," she said, when she could speak again, "could I be sure that once on the ranch you would not sneak away the first time the Whisperer approached you?"

"That's very simple," Goggles answered brightly. "I'll give you my word not to leave until you say that I may go."

"And you won't ride out and tell the Whisperer all of our plan? Hah! He would wring it out of you through fear."

"Well," Goggles said thoughtfully, "I suppose he might, but that would only make him stay the closer. He doesn't fear anything, you know, and he would laugh at the thought of any four men taking him. Even such men as you have. Did you say Jack Tucker is one of them?"

"He is," Patricia said, and in spite of herself she began to almost admire the catlike cunning of the dapper little Easterner. "I see your plan, and I suppose that a man like the Whisperer would take the challenge of my . . . trap . . . as a sort of sporting proposition. Being your friend, he would try to make me release you . . . try to make me give you your freedom." She straightened, her eyes shining. "And that would bring him at last face to face with me. I don't ask anything more."

"You take my breath . . . you really do," said Goggles, "but, if the plan suits you, suppose I go pack my grip? I'm all ready to start."

"Certainly," Patricia said, and her scornful glance followed him through the door.

He reappeared, carrying a bulky suitcase, tightly wrapped and bulging at the sides. His horse was led around at the same time, and the suitcase strapped behind the saddle securely.

On the way out he had little to say. He seemed more amazed than intimidated, and at this she wondered, until she was able to explain it to herself through the fact that the man trusted all things implicitly to the Whisperer and had grown so accustomed to the infallibility of the outlaw that he did not dream of worrying over any predicament. In fact, there seemed no place for worry in the mindlessness of the fellow. Worry, after all, suggests thought, and that was something, apparently, that never burdened the brain of Mr. St. Gore. Once he brought his horse, a fine animal, to a sharp halt in order that he might gape upon a cloud of singular shape that floated down the western sky. Now and then he broke his silence to speak to his horse in a conversational manner, as one might speak to any rational being.

To Patricia, in fact, looking from the fine, high-held head of the horse to the bespectacled face of the rider, it seemed that the brute was by far the higher type of animal. They were in sight of Ugly Joe's place before the fop directly addressed her.

He said: "I presume that I shall have protection against these . . . er . . . ruffians of yours, Miss Lauriston?"

"I shall personally," she answered, "be your guarantee."

"Will you really?" he queried gratefully. "Awfully thrilling to have your interest, you know!"

She looked at him sharply. In almost any other man the speech would have been a subtle jest, but his face was more blankly serious than she had seen it, as yet. They dismounted at the central entrance, opening on the patio. Here Goggles cried out sharply and ran forward a few steps with his arms out-thrown. He whirled sharply on Patricia, his face ecstatic.

"Miss Lauriston!" he cried. "I've been thinking it rather queer of you to bring me away out here, but now I thank you . . . I positively do! I haven't seen flowers like these since I left . . ." His arms dropped—his face grew grave and almost drawn.

"I beg your pardon?" Patricia queried lightly.

"I beg yours," answered Vincent St. Gore, and he bowed with something that almost approached a gentleman's quiet dignity. "I shouldn't have commenced a sentence which I may not finish."

To Patricia it was as if a cloth of bright, simple colors were suddenly reversed, and on the other side she saw some marvelously intricate design; so much one touch of gravity did to all her preconceptions of the man, and all her knowledge of him as she had seen him this day.

Ugly Joe, crossing from one side of the patio to the other, stopped short. "Hello!" he called. "You got your bird, eh, Pat?"

"You see him," she answered.

Ugly Joe approached to within reaching distance of Goggles, who adjusted his spectacles and leaned forward to peer at the newcomer.

Ugly Joe grew ugly, indeed. "Listen to me, my hearty," snarled the rancher, who had been at sea in his time and whose walk still oddly suggested, at times, the heaving deck of an imaginary ship. "Listen to me . . . you're out here because the lass wants you here for reasons of her own. Maybe she's told you about them. Now I'll tell you one other thing. Don't be lingering around when you find me alone. I can stand the sight of you, maybe, when there's witnesses nearby, but, when I see you alone, I want to fix my fingers in that skinny windpipe of yours. Understand? You damned sneaking cutthroat!" And Ugly Joe turned on his heel, after a farewell glare, and stalked on toward the nearest door with his wobbly stride, lifting high to meet the imaginary deck.

VII

Goggles Talks

"My word!" sighed Goggles. "Who is that person?"

"That," Patricia said coldly, "is my cousin, Joe Gregory."

"Isn't he the rough chap, though?"

"Ah!" she cried with a sudden, overwhelming burst of disgust. "Can you call yourself a man? You would shame a dog . . . a creeping, whining . . . dog." She turned and ran from him. She was shuddering with shame and horror in the thought that such a craven, such a spineless cur, could be a man, could walk and talk and think like a man, and yet at heart be such a travesty on all noble qualities of a man. More sickening, because his admiration of the flowers a moment before had made him almost akin to her—had brought a sudden softening and sympathy into her heart. She despised herself for it now—loathed herself, as though she had touched the face of a leper, and the touch had made her unclean forever.

By contrast she drew the figure of the Whisperer. Perhaps at some time in his career a service had been rendered him by this cravenly scoundrel, St. Gore, and now, to pay the debt, he constituted himself a strong and invisible shield between the craven and the world. More and more details of the Whisperer's character were creeping up strongly in her imagination. He was large, undoubtedly, since so many tales were told of his prowess. And that whispering voice, so horrible to hear, was undoubtedly the result of some incurable affliction. She had heard of men with consumption of the throat, which affected their vocal chords so that their voices became like that ascribed to the Whisperer.

Without doubt the man had come to the Southwest to be cured of his affliction by the purer, drier air. To support himself he had been forced into a life of outlawry. Then this sneaking dapper fiend, St. Gore, tracked the man who he had befriended in some small thing years before, and lived off the earnings of the Whisperer's daredevil depredations. In the meantime, the outlaw was dying slowly of his malady, but would be terrible until the end.

This was the story that grew up of itself in her thoughts, until it seemed to her that she could not bear to face St. Gore again. The temptation to shoot him down—kill him like a snake—would be too great.

It was into this stormy mood of hers that harmonious music ran. In fact, it was so akin to her thoughts of the moment that she hardly noticed it at first, and only gradually it grew out distinctly upon her. It was someone playing on the piano in the distant room, the "Revolutionary" *Étude* by

Chopin, and playing it with consummate strength and mastery. Not an easy thing to do, as she knew by experience, but this musician played with easy perfection. The difficult bass, which must roll but not thunder, swept by in a vast rhythm like great ground swells that roll along and toss the ship, and in turn block out either horizon and tower darkly into the heart of the sky. She had seen such waves, and she saw them again in the music. The treble darted across the scheme of harmony like sharp, stabbing bursts of lightning, illuminating the whole scene. The "Revolutionary" *Étude*—a study in conflict, in an ominous and rising danger like the passion that had held her a moment before.

She left her room and wandered toward the place from which the music came, paused at the door, and then went sick with disgusted disappointment. It was Vincent St. Gore who sat at the piano. He turned a blank face upon her, finished his passage faultlessly, and then rose.

"The bass," he said, "is in good shape, but the whole upper register is a shade out of tune . . . flat."

She merely stared helplessly at him. He had passed to an Indian basket suspended from the ceiling near a window and holding a flower pot full of crimson blossoms marked with streaks of jet. The large petals were like velvet. Now he turned the basket so that the sunshine in turn streamed softly over each flower—turned it with a lingering delight, and the expression on his face was such as she had seen when he first saw the flowers in the patio.

"Isn't it strange?" he said, turning to her, "that

such a rough creature as your cousin Gregory should keep flowers. Or perhaps it's his wife?"

"I think," Patricia responded dryly, "that they are both capable of appreciating flowers."

"Really?" he said, and as usual, when aroused, he shifted his spectacles and peered through them at her. "Very odd, though, isn't it, that they should have the passion?"

"Why?" she asked. It was a burden even to listen to him, and a trial of patience.

"Because," he answered, "it's out of harmony. They love one beautiful thing, and all the rest is discord."

"Perhaps," said Patricia, "they have other qualities just as important."

"Impossible," said Goggles, and shook his head decisively. "There are no others as important as the love of beauty."

"If you feel that way," Patricia said, "I wonder that you can tolerate these people."

"Quite right," answered Goggles, nodding seriously, "but I don't tolerate them, you see. I see no more of them than I do of individual clouds when all the sky is dark. I don't talk like this to them . . . oh, never!"

"It would be unhealthy for you if you did, perhaps," Patricia stated scornfully.

"Would it?" Goggles mused, and canted his head thoughtfully to one side. "Yes, I suppose these creatures would resent criticism with physical violence." He shrugged his shoulders; it was a shudder of aversion that shook his entire body. "However," he said, "I have never bothered talking with them about these things. It would be like sowing the wind, don't you think?"

"Exactly," said Patricia, "and like reaping the whirlwind afterward, eh?"

"I don't quite follow you there," Goggles said, "unless you mean that they might actually strike me? Dear me! I suppose that is possible. One never knows what to expect. Not in these wilds. However, with you there is some difference."

"Hope for me?" asked Patricia.

He considered her with that thoughtfully canted head. "I should really warn you"—he smiled—"that I've acquired a brutal frankness out here in the mountain desert."

"I'm so glad," Patricia stated. "It's the one. . . ." She stopped, but Goggles finished the sentence smoothly for her.

"The one manly characteristic you've found in me? Quite so! Oh, I don't in the least mind people saying such things to me. I've grown quite used to them." And he smirked at her.

She had to grip her hands to keep from striking him across the thin-lipped mouth. "You were saying," she remarked, "that there may be a hope for me?"

"Did I say that? I didn't mean to. No, a woman rarely develops. She is, on the whole, a fixed quantity, and only varies in vanity. You don't mind, do you? I'm quite impersonal."

"My dear Mister Saint Gore," Patricia replied, sighing, "nothing you can say can possibly offend me. Go on."

"Now isn't that comfortable?" breathed the little man. "I foresee some charming chats with you.

You have possibilities, I should say, rather of appreciation than of execution. You would not in the least surprise me, for instance, if I heard you discuss an art with intelligence, but I should be much astounded if you performed anything with distinction. You follow me?"

"*Hmm,*" said Patricia.

"You will attempt to remedy this defect since I have called it to your attention, but after a few years you will see that I am right about it . . . a woman never varies, except in degree. You will abandon the effort to create."

She was beginning to forget what the man looked like. She was hearing only the light, smooth voice. She was drifting away into the sea of the discussion.

"There are other things," Patricia said desperately. "There are other things I can do. There is a world of action."

"A world of action," said the little man serenely. "You can give birth to children, love your husband because he provides the food for yourself and your offspring, and rock a cradle. Within those limits, there is almost nothing to which you may not aspire in the world of action. That must be quite clear to you."

"*Hmm,*" Patricia responded again.

"But, after all," went on Goggles, "what is the world of action? What becomes of it? What do we know of the great financiers and bridge builders and lawmakers and statesmen? You can number on your two hands the few to whom certain poets have deigned to give immortality. No, your practical man, your man of action, rots away into oblivion as rapidly as his name rots away on the headstones of his grave.

"What is left of Egypt? The mind that conceived the Sphinx and the author of the story of 'Cinderella'? What of the heroes of Greece, her captains of industry? They are gone except as some poet names them on a random page. And the poets of Greece? You can run the list into scores. We read them as we read Milton and Shakespeare. Well, to get down to modern days, consider Shakespeare. Now, can you tell me, offhand, who commanded the English fleet against the Armada?"

"No," said Patricia, "I can't."

"It was a certain Lord Howard, I think. But surely in his day he was considered much greater than the obscure fellow who pushed a pen and acted the part of a ghost and finally settled down in a pleasant little village to die like a commonplace farmer. Yes, in those days, no man would have hesitated to choose between the fate of a Lord Howard and that of a Shakespeare. But time is the acid test. Time rusts away all your strong iron and leaves only the good untouched . . . only the gold . . . only the beauty. It is the one thing you cannot resist.

"For instance, I called you out of a distant part of the house with music. Because I play that *étude* in a certain way you despise me, d'you see? After I've gone on, you'll think over what I've said, though you're too proud to ask more questions now."

She slumped into a chair. "I'm not too proud," she said. "I do despise you . . . but I want to listen."

"Well," Goggles said, "I like to talk, for that matter. Almost any audience will do for me when I get started. Even my horse!" He smiled, and, musing upon this absurdity, he drew out a monogrammed cigarette case and offered it to her. She refused sharply. "Ah," said Goggles, withdrawing the case and selecting and lighting his smoke, "you don't smoke? Now, that's rarely stupid of you. You miss a great opportunity, nothing like smoking to set off hands like yours."

She folded her arms to conceal those hands.

"Now," he said, "you wish to seem angry, but secretly you're a little pleased, aren't you?"

"Yes," said the girl. "I like appreciation, no matter from whom it comes."

"Not so well said," answered the dictator of tastes. "Injudicious appreciation is worse than useless. It clogs the mind with inaccuracies. The common herd, for instance, thought much of both Tennyson and Browning in their day."

"But you dislike them?"

"Dislike them? No. When I was a boy, I rather enjoyed them. Then I discovered that Tennyson had nothing to say and knew exceedingly well how to say it, while Browning had a great deal to say, but was never able to utter a single sustained rhythm. Now, in your remark of a moment ago, you were trying to make a hit at my comment about audiences. You missed my point. One talks *with* a companion . . . one talks *at* an audience."

"You are certainly very clear," said the girl.

"Insultingly so?"

"You could never insult me."

"Only weary you, I suppose. And now?"

"I'm immensely interested. Because you pay some attention to the subject that most fascinates me . . . myself."

The eyes of Goggles flashed with enjoyment. "That's bully." He chuckled. "Simply bully! You *are* interesting, but not in the way men have told you."

"Oh?" said Patricia. He was like a dissector, cutting toward the heart of her being, naming each muscle as he passed it.

"You have," said the merciless critic, "the three most important qualities for a woman, their importance ranking in the order named . . . a sound body . . . apparently . . . a beautiful face, and a receptive mind. You have also, in the order named, the three greatest vices of modern woman . . . ambition, discontent, and respect for your *mind*. You are interesting through the clash of qualities."

"And you are under the impression that I will become. . . ."

"Either a virtuous wife and the discontented mother of many children, or the mistress of a great man and the discontented mother of barren thoughts."

She sank farther back in her chair, regarding him with awe and aversion. It seemed to Patricia that the book of her future was being read with infallible wisdom.

"Which had you rather be?" Goggles asked, and smiled.

"I had rather die than be either!" cried Patricia.

"Ah," said the little man, and raised a forefinger. "Then there is hope for you."

After that she could not get another word from him.

VIII

A Message from the Night

Oddly enough that interview increased her respect for the Whisperer rather than for St. Gore. She saw another reason now why the outlaw should cling to this dapper little fop and extend over him the dark cloak of his protection. It was because the outlaw had been a man of culture and had been ostracized from the paths of civilized men. All that he saved from the wreckage was the friendship and occasional meetings with this St. Gore, this absurd little dude with his cold, keen mind.

If she did not utterly despise St. Gore now, she looked upon him as men look upon some ingenious mechanism that does the work of a man—and yet is not a man. She felt almost as impersonally as this about St. Gore.

Apparently he had the most complete trust in the protection of the Whisperer. For instance, when he sat opposite the four gunfighters at the table that night, he looked at them rather with curiosity than with fear, and studied them with such an intent look that Patricia wished for the tenth time that he would lay aside those absurd, owl-like spectacles.

Indeed, it was the spectacles that gave most of the folly to the face of Goggles. Without them, it would have been an interesting, intellectually handsome face. With them, it became a mere mask of inanity. However, she had known men with minds, but no bodies—men dead below the brain. A typical product of one phase of the twentieth century.

The gunfighters regarded Goggles with a curiosity fully equal to his own and much more openly expressed. They were like four great hunting dogs surrounding the weak, defenseless cub of the bear, but daring not to touch it for fear of the terrible coming of the dam. They measured Goggles across his broad forehead and his narrow cheeks—they measured him across his slender shoulders and through his thin chest. Once Chic Woods, speaking in an aside like a mutter of thunder to Bob Riddle, stretched out his fingers and then closed them slowly—a suggestive gesture, as if he were crushing some fragile object filled with life. Yet for some time no one directly addressed Goggles; the cloak of his master's awful power fell like an invisible sense of awe about him.

Finally, however, Jack Tucker said: "Maybe you don't know, Goggles, that I've figured out who the Whisperer is?"

"How extremely interesting," Goggles said, and smiled benignly upon the ruffian. "Do you really, though?"

"You're damned right I do . . .'scuse me, lady,"

said Tucker, "and there was one beside me that knew . . . old Mort Lauriston."

"Well, well," said Goggles, "you've no idea how impressed the Whisperer will be when I tell him that his identity has been penetrated."

"Whatever that means," growled Tucker, "but you can tell the old bird that he's known, all right. Maybe you'd like to hear the story?"

"Indeed," drawled Goggles with enthusiasm.

"By all means," Patricia echoed.

"It was back a few years when the first paying ore was struck over by the Muggyon Hills," said Tucker. "I was laying about Eagles when one day old Mort Lauriston came driving up to me and says he'd like to have me slide out into the hills with him to a place where he thought he'd got the right color, but he wanted to get my opinion before he got his claim papers.

"I climbed a hoss and we went out into the hills, and there, right on the place where Mort had been digging, was Pa."

"Pa?" queried Patricia.

"I was coming to that. There was a chap come out to Eagles from the East. Awful green tenderfoot. He said his name was Peter Askworthy Howe, but the initials on his suitcase was P.A.H., so we called him Pa right off the jump.

"Wasn't a bad sort, laying aside the funny way he talked. Anyway, it was Pa who'd come along and seen the marks of Mort's digging. He'd opened up the stuff himself, and, being a rock hound, he seen the first glance that there was plenty of color . . . real stuff. So he staked out a claim. We come down and allowed to him that

Mort had the first jump on that spot. He told us to go to . . . well, not just in them words, him being particular polite, always.

"He allowed that he was going into Eagles to get his papers. Well, we knew that he'd beat us on a ride, because he had a pretty nice piece of hossflesh with him. He climbed into the saddle, and then I shot the hoss.

"Sort of peeved this Pa, because he ups and grabs his gun. Which was some foolish move, considering how fast Mort was with his six-gun. He put three chunks of lead into Pa's chest inside a space the size of your palm. Of course, the tenderfoot didn't have no chance. He didn't die for a minute, and, before he kicked out, he rolls himself over on his back . . . he was a big gent . . . and pulls himself up on his hands."

" 'Lauriston,' he says, 'you and Tucker will never enjoy the money you make out of this mine. My brother will track me, and he'll learn who killed me. He'll kill you, my fine fellows, and, if you started riding now, you could never ride far enough away or hide so well that you could get away from him.'

"With that he kicked out. Now, I got a considerable respect for what a dying man says, and I allow that the Whisperer is the brother of old Pa. Yep, his name is Howe and he's filled one part of his bet by getting Mort Lauriston. The other part is to get me. I knew the Whisperer was on my trail, and that's why I've been so scarce around these parts lately. I figured he'd a good chance of bumping me off while I was alone. But now that I've got these three bunkies, I guess he's out of luck. What say, Chic?"

"I'll tell the world he's out of luck!" growled Chic.

"Damn his eyes!" broke in Ugly Joe. "When he finds them, he finds me with 'em. Listen to the wind, lads! Glad we're in port tonight."

For the gale had risen suddenly, and now made the stanch adobe walls quiver time and again, and little drafts set the flames jumping in the lamps. Mrs. Gregory rose to fasten the shades on the western and windward side of the house, and, opening a window to do this, a piece of paper, evidently inserted under the edge of the window for this very purpose, whipped from the sill and came fluttering across the room like a white bird, settling gently on the center of the table.

Jack Tucker, cursing softly, leaned forward and snatched up the paper, unfolded it, and read aloud, slowly, with a grim-set face:

> *Gents, I've been waiting for you a long time. I never expected to get you all together. Harry Yale, you come first.*
>
> *The Whisperer*

Tucker tossed it down for examination by any who cared to look. Gingerly, like men touching deadly poison, they raised the little paper one by one and examined the clumsy, scrawling handwriting. It was backhand, and the letters were formed with the same crude care that a child of seven uses.

"At least," Patricia said thoughtfully—and she and Goggles were the only calm people in the room, "it proves one thing. The Whisperer is not your man Howe. This is some uneducated man from the mountain desert. Look at his writing! Isn't that a sufficient proof?"

"Ma'am," Chic Woods said hoarsely, "nothing proves anything about the Whisperer. I don't mind a man . . . but a damned ghost . . ."

His eyes traveled across to Harry Yale. The tall man stood like one transfixed, swallowing hard, so that the great Adam's apple jumped up and down his throat. Through that bronze tan he could not show pallor, but his lips seemed to have grown harder set, and they were pulled toward the hollows of his cheeks by the ghastliest of grins. In the silence that followed, every glance turned finally upon Harry Yale. He stood it for a moment, and then in a sudden fury he pushed back his chair, rose, and smashed his great, bony hand down on the table.

"Am I dead already?" he roared. "I ain't any ghost now, am I? Look somewheres else . . . and to hell with you all!" He strode to the door, hesitated with his hand on the knob, and then jerked it suddenly open, and stood tense, staring into the dark beyond. He closed the door, disappearing into the farther room. Chic Woods raised a shaking hand and mopped his forehead.

IX

THE SECOND AND THIRD MESSAGES

Patricia, with her four gunfighters, felt like a general with mighty forces to direct. It was she who planned the campaign for the next day. She schemed in this way: First of all, Goggles was almost certain to use his freedom at once and ride out to meet the Whisperer, who he would supply with accurate information concerning all that went on in the house. Her plan was to trail Goggles when he rode out, using Harry Yale to do that trailing, because Harry had now the most vital reason for wishing to get at the great outlaw. One man could probably trail the inexperienced Goggles very easily, and the other three in turn would follow Yale at a safe distance, scattered out on either side of him. In case Yale were to find the Whisperer, they could gallop in at once to his assistance, enveloping the outlaw.

She disclosed her plan to the four men, and they agreed readily. Any plan was a good plan to them. What they wanted was action, and quick action to get at the common enemy.

She proved a true prophet. Almost immediately after breakfast Goggles sauntered out toward the barn and a few minutes later was riding toward the hills at a brisk gallop. He was not out of sight before Harry Yale, spurring at every stride, raced after him, and behind Harry, at a short interval, came his three companions.

Patricia, from the kitchen door, watched them disappear with a smile of content. The Whisperer, certainly, would expect some dilatoriness in the campaign against him, some waiting for his nearer approach, some elaborately calculated ambuscade. This quick action, nine chances out of ten, would throw him off his guard. And in the presence of four men like Yale and the others, one mistake would be the last. She felt a queer pain, as well, at the thought that through her this wild scourge should be removed from the mountain desert. No matter how terrible he might be, it would be like the shooting of an eagle—a grim thing to see the air robbed of its lord and its tyrant.

By noon the riders had not returned. In the dusk of the evening Woods, Riddle, and Tucker, hot, weary, discomfited, trotted up to the barn and came in silence to the house. In the first wild burst of speed Harry Yale, better mounted than the others and riding without caution, had outstripped the others, and they had lost him in the windings of the hills. All the rest of the day they had stalked him, but could not get his trail again. They told this tale to Ugly Joe. To Patricia they would not speak at all. She had been the general, and she had failed her army in time of need. For her own part, a sense of guilt oppressed her. Somewhere out there in the gathering dark the tall form of Harry Yale must be motionless. Over it the buzzards, perhaps, were already gathering.

In the midst of her despair there was a shout from outside the house, and she ran out to see the form of a horseman rapidly maturing through the dark.

"Hey, Harry!" called the chorus of his bunkies.

But after a moment, a soft, thin voice answered: "Halloo, there."

"Goggles!" groaned Chic Woods.

"Goggles?" Patricia repeated, and she wished him heartily a thousand leagues under the honest earth.

He came, trailing his feet with weariness, having put up his horse in the barn.

"My word," sighed Goggles. "Will you believe that I was lost in those wretched hills? Yes, indeed! I should hardly have found the house if I hadn't seen the lights at last. Think of wandering all night through those hills. I'm going straight to my room." And he went.

The others settled down at the entrance to the patio to visit. They were silent; for an hour the only sound and sigh was the occasional scratch and blue spurt of a match. They were thinking of Harry Yale, and they were thinking of death.

But at the very moment that Ugly Joe finally rose and turned toward the house, they caught the patter of trotting hoofs through the night, hoofs that clapped the earth more loudly, chugging, at last, in the sand directly before the house as the horse came to a halt. They were too excited to challenge the rider.

"Halloo!" called the voice of Harry Yale.

A happy cheer answered him. Woods and Riddle ran toward him.

"Stay where y'are!" barked Harry Yale. "I got an oath not to stop with you."

"You met him?" called Patricia.

"I'm saying nothin' except this thing," answered Harry Yale. "Bob Riddle, you're the next to go. That's straight from the Whisperer."

"Wait!" called Chic Woods. "Yale, y'ain't going to leave us up in the air like this?"

"Chic, if you come near me, I'll start a gun play. I'm under 'n oath higher'n heaven and deeper'n hell. S'long."

The hoofs started again and chugged softly away through the night, fainter, fainter, until the last patter died out. As for the men, none of them stirred, but Patricia fled back into the house and found Mother Martha.

"I want to stay with you tonight," she pleaded. "I'm afraid!"

"Of what, honey?" asked Mother Martha.

"Of ghosts!" said Patricia. "Of ghosts!"

"I'm older'n you, Patty," Martha stated, "and I've seen a pile more of the ways of the mountain desert. You'll never get the Whisperer this way. He'll hunt down men one by one, just the way he did Harry Yale today. Poor Harry Yale. He's done for. Tomorrow he'll take water from a Chinaman. That's the way of the Whisperer. If he don't kill the body of a man, he kills the heart, which is worse, a lot."

"I won't give it up," said Patricia. "I daren't give it up."

"Why not, honey? Who elected you a man-hunter?"

"It's the first thing I've tried by myself . . . the first real work. I've got to win! And I *will* win, because he can't beat me until I release Saint Gore from his parole with my own lips."

"Patty," Mother Martha assured, "I've seen stranger things than that happen on the mountain desert."

Not a comforting thought for Patricia to carry away to her bed. She lay awake long, considering it. For how, after all, could the Whisperer force her against her will to retract the parole of St. Gore? Perhaps at the point of his revolver, perhaps by striking down Ugly Joe—and even Mother Martha. Yes, to the Whisperer, neither man nor woman made a difference.

When she finally slept, it was only to dream of a great weight that pressed down on her, an invisible burden that beat against her out of the thin air like the wings of some tremendous, ethereal moth, suffocating her, pressing her, resistlessly, to the ground, killing her in the very sight of her friends.

She woke the next morning with little violet circles painted beneath her eyes, and in her throat a steady burning. The rest of the household was already at the breakfast table, in silence, and, when she entered, everyone looked up, but no one spoke, except Goggles. He was more dapper than ever, and seemed to have perfectly recuperated from the effects of his long ride of the day before. There was even a little touch of pink in his usually colorless cheeks.

He rose blithely at the sight of Patricia, and pulled back her chair. Her loathing of him rose to a physical horror. She could not sit down while the man stood behind the chair.

"Thank you," she said heavily, at last. "Won't you take your chair again?"

"Oh," said Goggles, "of course, if you wish."

She looked across to Ugly Joe and met a scowl in reply. "What is it?" she asked.

No one would speak, at first. Then she noted for the first time that Bob Riddle was not there.

"The Whisperer," she gasped. "Last night?"

There came a peculiar, hysterical laugh from Chic Woods, and his little pig-eyes wandered wildly. He tossed a scrap of paper across to her. "I found that tied on the horn of my saddle this morning. Maybe you can make it out for yourself."

She read:

Gents, I'm gone. Nothing this side of hell can bring me back, so don't try. All I can say is: Chic Woods, your turn comes next, and God help you.
Bob Riddle

She read it again, and this time aloud, and, as she finished, Chic Woods sprang up, cursing hideously. He was plainly hysterical with fear.

"I start myself," he cried. "Tucker, if you're wise, you start with me. Any man I'll fight, but this damned ghost . . ."

He turned and fled through the doorway. He was never seen again, it is said, in the mountain desert. Whether he met the Whisperer and death on his flight, or whether he simply left forever his old haunts will never be known.

X

THE MESSAGE TO PATRICIA

As for Jack Tucker, he leaned forward heavily on the table and followed the flight of Chic Woods with haunted eyes.

"For me, there ain't no use in running," he said slowly. "I can see that plain. I can see why the Whisperer didn't shoot up the rest, but just scared 'em off. He didn't want 'em ... he was wanting only me. He *is* Howe, by God, and first he got Mort and now he'll get me! He's cleared out the rest ... well, if he gets me, he'll get me in this house ... d'ye hear? Nobody'll make me leave it. I got two guns that shoot straight and clean, and from now on I eat in my room ... d'ye hear?"

To his glowering eyes everyone who sat at the table apparently had that moment become an enemy. He pushed back his chair, and backed from the room with his hands dropped to the butts of his guns, and through the rest of the day nothing could induce him to leave his room, until the supper hour. It was Mother Martha who finally brought him down. The day of self-imprisonment had changed him. He came down with a soft and cautious step, like some beast of prey, and he fixed on Ugly Joe, who passed him, a curious stare. Joe said afterward that he thought for an instant that Jack Tucker had lost his mind. At any rate, the gun-fighter went down quietly to the dining room and accepted the chair that Mother Martha pulled back for him, and ate the food she placed before him.

No one but Mother Martha is responsible for the story of what followed in the next few minutes, but the word of Mother Martha, hitherto, has been more easily passed than current gold.

She was much worried about Tucker, she said, for when a man shuts himself up with a worry or a fear, he's very apt to lose his mind. It was for that reason that she persuaded him to come down to the dining room. The man was apparently in a panic of wild, soul-consuming fear. Not the sort of fear that makes men run, but the kind that makes them more dangerous than maniacs. She tried to encourage him at first, telling him that he was afraid of nothing. She assured him, finally, that the Whisperer had not a reason to injure him any more than the outlaw had already injured the other three gunmen. For the bullets that killed the man, Howe, had been fired by Mort Lauriston. She had scarcely finished this assurance, when Tucker leaned across the table toward her and said in a ghastly murmur: "You fool! D'you think I'd've told the truth before Goggles, that damned spy of the Whisperer? Nope, this is the way Howe died. He was standing by his claim, and Mort and I rode up, and dismounted. Mort asked him for the makings, and, while Mort was rolling a cigarette, I come behind and stabbed Howe in the back. He dropped, but, being a big man, he died hard. While he was lying there, he told us that he had a brother who'd kill us both . . . a brother we couldn't get away from. Mort laughed at him, pulled out his gun, and shot him three times through the breast. That's how he died! But me . . . I used the knife first . . . and by the knife . . . God knows, but I'm afraid . . . by the knife the Whisperer'll kill me . . . cold steel . . . a sharp edge . . ."

Then, according to Mother Martha, she heard the most horrible sound of her life, something between a moan and a whisper, like the sound of a wind, far off and yet near. She could not tell where the sound came from—the open door, the window, or the ceiling above them. It took the shape of a voice—a voiceless voice, which said: "Jack Tucker, you come next!"

Tucker jumped up with a scream and fired two shots through the open door and another through the window. Then he turned and damned Mother Martha, saying this wouldn't have happened if he'd stayed in his room. So he ran, cursing and shuddering, to his room.

Mother Martha had Ugly Joe call in four cowpunchers from the bunkhouse, and they searched all the vicinity of the house and particularly the sand outside the dining room window, but not a trace of a man's foot was revealed by their lanterns. It was decided, then, to place a guard over the house throughout the night; the next day they would bring out a posse from Eagles. Four men were posted, one at each corner of the house, and at a distance of about fifty feet, so as to command a full sweep of the surrounding ground. It was a dark night, and for this reason each man had a small fire of mesquite wood. The purpose was not to entrap the Whisperer, but simply to warn him away.

Afterward each of the guards swore that he had remained awake and on the alert, not wishing to fall asleep and have a knife slipped between his ribs by the Whisperer before he awoke. Each of the four was equally vehement in the defense of his individual vigilance. For it was known that all four had worked hard that day, and there were many possibilities that they drowsed beside the fires.

What actually happened, at any rate, was that shortly after midnight the household of Joe Gregory wakened with a scream tingling in their ears. With one accord those inside the house and the guarding cowboys outside rushed for the room of Jack Tucker. Ugly Joe himself called out a challenge and was the first to enter, a lantern in one hand and a revolver in the other.

Behind him came his wife, Patricia, and then Goggles, his lean, trembling limbs wrapped in a dressing gown of linen, stamped with a pattern of gay Japanese flowers. They found Jack Tucker lying face downward in a rapidly widening pool of blood. As they turned him on his back, they found that he had been stabbed three times in the breast, each wound enough to cause death. His own jack-knife was still gripped in his hand, showing that he had died fighting, and not, at least, surprised from behind. There was still a lingering life in him.

When he opened his eyes, the first thing that they encountered was the horrified face of Patricia leaning close above him.

His lips writhed, parted, and he said: "You . . . come next . . . he . . . told . . . me."

"Told you that she . . . that the girl . . . comes next?" cried Goggles in horror, and he leaned close to the dying man.

Tucker screamed, struck at the face above him, and died.

XI

THE FOLLY OF WOMEN

Patricia, heartsick and weak, did not wait to help care for the body of the dead man, but went back to her room. Ugly Joe stopped at her door a moment later to say that he had placed eight men on guard, instead of four, and that there would be no more trouble that night, at least. The next day he would take her to Eagles.

Nevertheless, she arranged the lamp on the little table at the head of her bed, so that, by striking a match, she could have a light in a second. The wick of the lamp was turned high, and she made sure that the supply of oil was sufficient. After that she lay in the dark, certain that she would stay awake until the dawn. But the very violence of the succession of grim pictures that passed across her mind wearied her. Her last consciousness was that of shifting the revolver under her pillow so that it would be easier to grasp.

When she woke again, it was with the suffocating consciousness that there was another living, breathing presence in the room. It struck upon her as vividly as a flood of light. She knew that from somewhere in the dark, eyes were upon her. She was as conscious of it as a man may be of the sound of his beating heart, although that may be audible to no ear but his own. At length she made it out—not a shape or any suggestion of a form—it was merely a certain lightening of the utter black near the window and toward the corner of the room. It did not move, but she knew.

Then Patricia was glad, very glad, for there was no fear in her. She was perfectly calm, her hand perfectly steady as she drew out the revolver steadily, softly from beneath the pillow. She had never been so happy in her life, for she knew that she was meeting a test from which the strongest of brave men might have shrunk. She was about to meet the Whisperer face to face.

It must be understood, in order to follow what Patricia did next, that the little table rose almost a foot above the level of the bed. When the lamp on it was lighted, therefore, a thick shadow fell directly on the bed, through the rest of the room, and particularly the ceiling was well lighted. First she flattened herself on the bed—next she trained the revolver on the gray shadow of the corner. Finally she took a match, scratched it, lighted the lamp—and then gripped the revolver hard, her finger on the trigger. All that could have been seen of her, indeed, would have been the first flash of the light on her hand and wrist as she lighted the lamp. Instantly afterward she was lost in the black shadow that swam across the bed in waves, because the unsheltered flame from the lampwick tossed up and down.

But what Patricia saw in the corner of the room, leaping suddenly out of the dark, was the figure of a man in gray clothes, wearing a tall, gray sombrero, with a long white mask across his face, and two dark holes where the eyes must be. She saw his hands; there was no weapon in them.

"Stand perfectly still," said Patricia, "I have you covered with a revolver. I shoot well, and at the first move of your hands I'll press the trigger."

Then came the sound that she had heard Mother Martha describe earlier in the evening, but far more terrible than any description—a voiceless voice—something between a whisper and a moan, ghastly, unnerving. At the sound her arm and hand shook—her very brain reeled.

"I have not come to harm you," said the Whisperer, "I have come only to make you give Saint Gore his freedom. You have only to speak a word, and I shall be gone again. Say it."

"You will only leave in the power of the law," said Patricia. "I have you now . . . I have only to press the trigger. . . ."

"But you cannot," said the Whisperer. "You were cool a moment ago, but now your voice shakes . . . you dare not raise it so that others in the house might hear . . . your hand is growing cold. . . ."

"You lie," said Patricia. "Help! Cousin Joe!"

But even as he had warned her, her voice was only a dry whisper. The hysteria of blind fear seized her at the throat. She knew that in another second he would be complete master—she could feel her strength slipping from her.

He raised an arm and advanced a pace. "I am waiting," he said. "Be brave . . . I have not come to harm you . . . you have only to speak and I will disappear. . . ."

Then she fired.

It seemed as if the Whisperer sat down, shoved abruptly toward a chair, and then he collapsed along the floor.

She leaped from the bed. In the distance she heard many voices—shouts—running steps. Over the prostrate figure she leaned, tore away the mask, and looked into the calm, steady eyes of Goggles. She could not conceive it at first; it was like the miracle that surpasses belief. The revolver clicked on the floor, fallen from her nerveless hand.

"You . . . you . . . you!" she could only stammer.

"I," Goggles said faintly, and smiled up at her. "The game's up, but it was jolly while it lasted."

There came a banging at her door—the shout of Ugly Joe. She leaned, picked up the revolver, and ran to the door, which she set a little ajar and peeked out.

"I can't let you in . . . I'm undressed. I was handling the revolver . . . and it went off . . . I'm not in the least hurt."

"Thank God!" groaned Ugly Joe, and voices behind him echoed heavily: "Thank God!"

She closed the door, barred it again, and ran to Goggles. He had struggled to a half sitting posture, and, as she leaned over him, his eyes widened with a sort of fascinated horror.

"You don't understand," he said. "Open the door . . . call them in. I am the Whisperer."

"Hush!" she said. "Little fool, be still."

She leaned and picked him up. He was hardly heavier than she, and she bore his weight without great difficulty. With her strong young arms, she felt the frailty of the outlaw who the whole mountain desert had feared. For an instant his head lay helpless against her bare shoulder; the nervous right hand that had dealt death once that night hung limply down. She felt the quick, shuddering intake of his breath against her throat.

Only an instant, and then she laid him on her bed. There she tore open his shirt.

"The left side," he said. "You meant well, but the bullet must have glanced . . . on the ribs. A fraction of an inch closer in, and. . . ." He set his teeth with a light click and closed his eyes against the pain.

Then she found the wound. It was bleeding profusely, but she saw at a glance that it was not serious. It had glanced, apparently, from a rib, as he suggested, and had furrowed through the flesh along his side—a grisly painful wound, but not mortal. She ran to her suitcase, ripped a linen shirt into narrow strips, ran back, and made the pack and bandage. She had studied a little of first aid, although she had never before had occasion to make use of it.

He helped her as well as he could, rolling from side to side, although the pain sent the sweat out upon his forehead. When she was finished, he leaned heavily back on the pillows. His face was almost as white as the bedding, and the hand that lay across his breast was marvelously fragile, almost transparent.

"In a moment," he said, "I'll be able to go." He opened his eyes. "But you," he said, "I don't understand . . . why. . . ."

"I don't understand, either," she said. "I don't want to understand . . . I don't want to think . . . except to get you safe and well again."

"And you won't turn me in . . . the Whisperer? Think of the name of it? Think of the fame of it. Think of what it would mean to you."

"Do you really expect me to?" she asked.

"I don't know. I thought I knew . . . a good many things . . . about you . . . and other women . . . but I've been a fool, I guess . . . a great fool. Most men are . . . I guess . . . about women."

"And I, too," she answered. "I've been a great fool, but I think I've found myself in time."

For the conclusion of the story we may as well take the version of Ugly Joe Gregory, as he told it many times in the saloons of Eagles, for every stranger had to hear the story of the last appearance of the Whisperer, and Ugly Joe had the only authentic version.

In ending the story, he always said: "No, I never seen him, but my wife heard his whisper. And while I'm spreading on the talk, I might as well tell you something else damn' near as queer as the things the Whisperer done them three days.

"There was a dude out here . . . a no-account damned dude we called Goggles from his funny glasses. Most of the boys around here remember him. He was a sort of go-between for the Whisperer. And he was the one, maybe, that brought all the hell to poor Tucker and the rest of 'em. He was at the house, you know.

"Well, the dude must have been pretty badly shook up by the bad way Tucker died, because the next day he come down with a fever and stayed in bed off and on about three weeks.

"The funny part was that this girl . . . this Pat I been telling you about . . . got a pile interested in the dude when he was sick. You couldn't pry her away from his bed. Women are queer that way, but she was the queerest of the lot. Day and night she stuck by him like she was his sister. Wouldn't even let Mother Martha, who knew a pile more about nursing than she ever did, help her once in a while.

"Martha, she pretended to be pretty wise about something, but it was all Indian to me. But in the end, well, sir, the dude went back to Eagles, and Pat went with him. And right over there in Widow Morgan's boarding house, in the front parlor downstairs, they was married. Can you beat that? You can't. I'll bet you can't!

"I s'pose she got so used to taking care of the poor dude that she couldn't get along without him. That's the way Martha explained it. Martha was that way herself at one time. She took care of a calf that got cut bad in barbed wire, and afterward she wouldn't never let me sell that calf or market him, but just kept him hangin' around, useless, till he got to be a steer and died of old age. Yep, women are sure fools about some things.

"There was one funnier thing, too, that come out after Pat married that gent. It seemed that Vincent Saint Gore was only part of his name. The whole of his name was Vincent Saint Gore Howe."

FLAMING FORTUNE

The issue of Street & Smith's *Western Story Maga-zine* dated February 19, 1927, marked the first ap-pearance of "Flaming Fortune." George Owen Baxter was the Faust penname under which it was published, as were six other short stories and three serials that year. Additionally, 1927 saw the publi-cation of two short stories under Faust's John Fred-erick byline and five serials and three short stories under the Max Brand byline. "Flaming Fortune" is a wonderful tale of love and greed in which an at-tempt is made to break the spirit of the hard-working, honest protagonist, Henry Ireton.

I

A FIGHT FOR PROSPERITY

When Henry Ireton went courting, he called on the father and the mother of his lady. Henry had always been a dutiful child, and he expected to find nothing but duty in others. So he sat in the parlor and talked to Mr. and Mrs. Corbett Lawes. In the meantime, Rosaline Lawes sat under the fig tree in the yard, admiring the black pattern of the leaf shadows on the moon-silver of the ground, and admiring, also, the handsome bold face of her sweetheart, Oliver Christy. Through the open windows, she and Oliver could hear the heavy voice of the youth her parents preferred.

"I paid five hundred and eighty dollars to the bank, today. That clears all the buildings."

There was an exclamation of pleasure from Mr. Lawes. "How long has it taken you, Henry?"

"Five years, sir."

"A long time . . . the way you've worked."

"Well, I haven't rested none."

"But I'll bet that the bank was pretty surprised, the way you took hold of things."

"Well, the president had me into his office."

"He did! Why didn't you tell us that right away?"

"It would have sounded like boasting, maybe."

"Oh, not a bit!"

"Well, President van Zandt said that he'd been keeping an eye on me ever since I took over the place, when father died. He said that at that time the ranch was mortgaged for a lot more than it was worth. That the ground was wore out, and everything was falling to pieces, and the rolling stock was broken down. And everything was at wrong ends. He wondered how I had made anything come around right."

"He well might wonder," said the thin, sharp voice of Mrs. Lawes. "I hope you told him, Henry dear, that it wasn't owing to no help that you got from him."

"That wouldn't be just," said Henry Ireton. "The bank could have closed down on me any day. But they let me go along and work the thing out my own way. They never pressed me. A couple of times they let the interest run over a whole six weeks."

"Stuff!" Mrs. Lawes said. "Mighty glad they were to see their investment secured. Go on, Henry. You've no idea how interested I am."

"Me, too," said Corbett Lawes. "Dog-gone me if it ain't like a fairy tale, what you've done with the old place!"

"Well," said Henry Ireton, "I just explained things to Mister van Zandt. That was all."

"Go on and explain the same things to us. I've

never really understood just what you've done to make that ranch come to life."

There was a little pause after this.

"Now listen to him blow, will you?" Oliver Christy chuckled.

"Well," said the girl, "it's better to hear him talk about something than it is not to hear him talk at all. He's always been like a wooden Indian, every other time. Just plain dumb."

"Your old man likes him pretty well?"

"Dad says he's a safe man for any girl to marry, and Ma, she agrees."

"In the beginning," said the heavy voice of young Henry Ireton, "everything was pretty much gone to pot, you know."

"Don't I know, though! The fences was all rotten, and the house and the barns and the sheds was all falling down!" Mr. Lawes announced.

"Yes," broke in Mrs. Lawes, "and I had a peep into the kitchen, and such a place I never seen in my life! There was a hole rusted clean through the bottoms of all those kitchen pans, I do declare."

"There was a hole rusted clean through the bottom of the whole place," said young Ireton with a heart-felt warmth. "It was all gone. Three sacks to the acre was about the best wheat crop we'd have in ten years. The barley wouldn't thrive none. Oats would do no good. Every bit of the tools and the rolling stock had been sold to pay the expenses of Dad's funeral."

There was another brief pause.

"It was really pretty bad for Henry to face a thing like that," Rosaline said, in the shadow of the fig tree.

"It's what he was made for . . . buckling down and pulling the plow. Why, he's *built* more like a plow horse than a man! Ever watch him dancing?"

"No," sighed Rosaline, "but I've danced with him, and that's worse than watching him."

The voice within the house resumed: "Well, I had to work the ground. I mortgaged my soul, sold off the cows, and got together enough money to go around and buy implements at sales all over the country. I got the stuff together and brought it back and patched up the plows and the broken-down wagons and the rakes in my blacksmith shop. I even learned how to fix the insides of a mowing machine if it went wrong. Fact is, I think that I could pretty near make a whole mowing machine, folks, just with crude iron, a forge, and a hammer, with fire to help me out." He said it not boastfully, but seriously, soberly, after the fashion of one who is thinking back to the actual facts and stating them without exaggeration.

There was an exclamation, and then Corbett Lawes said: "I've seen you working in your blacksmith shop. I believe that you could make an *adding* machine there, if you set your mind to it."

"Maybe," serious Henry Ireton agreed, "if I had to. But I'm awfully glad that I don't. Anyway, that winter I got the tools together, and I sold off the three good horses on the place, and got eight ratty things in their place. But those eight rats did the work of eight real horses. I used to rub 'em down by hand, curry 'em deep and hard, feed 'em by hand, too, pretty near. And I made them snake the plow along nearly as good as Charley Crosswitch's big eight!"

"Well, you got the work done, and that was the main thing," said Mr. Lawes.

"Then I put in that potato crop that everybody laughed at so much."

"I remember smiling a bit myself, son. It did look queer to see a potato patch on a real ranch, where nothing but grain had ever been raised as far back as people could remember."

"I know that it looked queer. But it was the raising of the grain that had killed the land. And that was why I put in potatoes, and then sowed alfalfa. After I paid for the alfalfa seed, I was clean broke and didn't have a penny for food."

Another pause.

"Why, lad, how in the world did you live? Borrow more from the bank?"

"Borrow more? The bank would have had me arrested if I'd had the nerve to borrow more money. No, I couldn't borrow. But I had a gun. That old Colt that Dad owned. And there was plenty of powder and lead."

"You mean that you hunted for a living? But you never been any hand for a gun or for hunting, Henry!"

"No, I sure wasn't. But I had to, so I did."

"You didn't have the price of cartridges, though."

"I made my own cartridges at home. There was powder and lead. I've told you that. I nearly blew the gun to bits, toward the start. But I'd already learned how to repair things. And I fixed it up so that it would shoot."

"Well, but what could you get?"

"Squirrels and rabbits, all the year 'round."

"Hold on! Hold on! Squirrels and rabbits . . . with a Colt . . . and you not any practiced shot?"

"I'll tell you, Mister Lawes, when you get hungry enough, you *have* to shoot straight. And I learned quick. Before I had pulled up my belt three notches, I could knock over a squirrel nearly every time if I was within a decent distance of it. Anyway, it was a cheap meat market. And when I learned how to find the rabbits, I had them for a change. So I got through the year. The alfalfa didn't do well. Not the first year, you remember. But the potatoes, they saved my life. I had the crop ready before anything else was on the market, and I got all the real top-hole, fancy prices. It was wonderful the money that I took out of that ground from the potatoes. That carried me through to the second year and gave me seed money and a little extra money after I'd paid off the interest at the bank. But the first year was the worst. After that, I began to make a little progress."

"Don't skip anything, Henry. We want it all, my boy!" called Lawes.

"Well, then, the second year we had the floods. They washed out a lot of the crops, but they made my alfalfa wonderful, and I cut four crops and got nearly six ton to the acre. The potatoes were good, too. But the alfalfa was the best. If I'd been able to seed the whole place, I would have cleaned out every cent of the whole mortgage, that year, y'understand? But I'd only been able to put in a bit. Well, I got more than twenty dollars an acre, and, as for the expenses, there wasn't many, because I done most of the work myself. That crop was my big boost. It let me pay off the interest, that year, and a slice off the mortgage, and fix up some of the fences, and get some better horses, though I still kept the old broken-down string of eight. I worked 'em hard, but I never broke them down, and, after that, I always had two men working on the place for me. Beans and potatoes and alfalfa was the trick for the third year. The alfalfa and the potatoes didn't amount to much, but the beans did amazingly well.

"The next year, I saw that alfalfa was too big a gamble. But those crops had done what I hoped for. They'd refreshed the soil and put the nitrates back into it . . . the nitrates that fifty years of grain farming had taken out. I learned all about them from a smart college man. So I worked along till the fifth year, and now things are really pretty well fixed. And the mortgage is pared down to a reasonable size."

"Oh, you've wiped it almost out, Henry. It's not as big as it was."

"No, it's about a half of what it was. But as the bank said, the place was away over-mortgaged. But in another three years I'll have it wiped out. Because I've got what I need to work with, now."

"Tell me what you've got, Henry," Mr. Lawes said. "Add up the list."

"I'll tell you, then. Every fence post is sound, and the wire is new. All the sheds is better than new, and the house is rebuilt from the cellar to the garret. And the barns are loaded to the gills with good first-class hay. And the stalls are holding three eight-horse teams not second to none in the county. And I have first-rate rolling stock. Plenty of plows and wagons. The house is furnished all through. And best of all, I've got first-rate credit at the bank. They'll trust me. They believe in me. And that's why, Mister Lawes, I've come over special this morning, to ask you if my marriage with Rosaline could be set right soon."

II

An Eye of Red

In the darkness beneath the fig tree, Rosaline caught the hand of Oliver Christy and stood bolt upright, with a gasp.

Then they heard the voice of Mr. Lawes, strong and exultant: "Lad, there ain't a man in the county that I'd rather have in the family than you. Furthermore, the day that you marry Rosaline, I'm gonna clear off the remainder of that mortgage!"

"Oh, Oliver!" breathed the girl. "What am I going to do?"

Said the voice of Ireton within: "Thanks. But I don't want no help. I've started this job, and I'm going to bulldog it through. I'd rather. It'll take a few years more, but I want the fun all for myself."

"I understand," said Lawes. "Well, let it be that way. You know that my wife and me have always favored you for Rosaline. There's only one thing that we've set our hearts on . . . to have you get yourself clear of the woods."

"I remember," said Ireton. "You said that if I could ever go to the bank and get another five thousand dollar mortgage, then you'd know that I'd succeeded. Well, sir, I milked Mister van Zandt today. All I have to do is to ride in tomorrow and sign the papers."

"Henry, I congratulate you!"

"Thank you, sir. And what about Rosaline? How does she feel?"

"Leave me to handle Rosaline," said the father. "I've raised her right, and she won't dare to disobey me, no matter what ideas she may have."

Mrs. Lawes put in a little timidly: "Only . . . you think that you could make my girl happy, Henry? You think that you could make her love you?"

There was another little pause.

"That clodhopper," murmured Oliver Christy, beneath the fig tree, and he laughed silently and briefly.

"I'll tell you," Henry Ireton declared, "when I first met her, she was in the third grade, and I was out of school. I set my heart on her then. I ain't a flashy fellow, but I'm tolerable sure and steady. I set my heart on having her, and I'll never stop till I do. Is that straight? Or does it sound like bragging? Well, I never bothered trying to make love to her, because the words for that ain't handy to the tip of my tongue, you see?"

"I see, of course. Still. . . ."

"Well, once I have her, I'll start in winning her by showing her that I love her and that I value her. I think that I'll convince her. I've had lots of dogs, Missus Lawes. I never had one that didn't come to love me."

Rosaline clapped her hands over her ears and bolted away from the tree, and Oliver Christy followed her.

"Hey, Rosie. Don't act like that. You ain't married to the dub yet."

She stood wringing her hands, stamping, very pretty in the moonlight, which made the outer fluff of her yellow hair like a pale mist of fire.

"Then stop him, stop him!" she cried. "Oh, Oliver, if you love me, do something!"

"Well, I'll do something. I tell you, I will."

"Oh, can I trust you?"

"Yes. But if I stop him . . ."

"Yes, then I'll marry you. I don't care when. I'll . . . I'll even run away and marry you. I won't care what Father says."

"You promise that?"

"I do!"

"Kiss me, Rosaline."

"I . . . no, but after you've stopped Henry. Then I will, and marry you."

"I'm going to do it."

"But how? How?"

"There are ways of doing everything. I've got to think this here out."

"Then go think now . . . quickly, dear Oliver."

When he was on his horse, Oliver Christy could not help wondering why it was that he felt more like a loser than like one who had been victorious. But he rode up the moon-whitened way with increasingly high spirits until he came to the crossroads. Lights gleamed from the Ireton house, just up the fields. The barns and the sheds of the Ireton

place loomed vast and dark before him. From the
dust there arose nearby a slender, shadowy figure,
and a rusty, croaking voice said: "God bless you,
Mister Christy."

"Hello!" Christy shouted, reining his horse
aside. "Where the devil did you come from?"

"Not from the devil, Mister Christy," said the
beggar, his two canes wobbling back and forth under his weight. "Not from the devil. God keeps
some of the poor and the afflicted wandering
around this world of His so that the best people
can have a chance to show their charity, dear Mister Christy."

Mr. Christy was the smoothest of dancers, and
the softest of whisperers in the ears of pretty girls.
But among men, he could be as stern as the next
one. Now he pointed the butt of his quirt like a
gun at the head of the beggar. "Cut out that whining," he remarked. "It don't buy you anything
from me. I'll tell you what. A beggar is no more to
me than a weed. No more than the tarweed in the
field, yonder."

For a puff of wind had brought the pungent, half
fragrant odor of the tarweed to their nostrils.

"Tarweed leaves a stain," said the beggar in his
broken voice, his rusty, untuned voice. "It stains
the cuffs of your trousers and it stains your
hands."

"What do you mean by that?"

"Why, Mister Christy, charity is the thing that
washes the stains away again."

"You're more than half crazy, old man."

"Not crazy. Only, I see the truth. And the truth
always looks like madness to those who don't

know it. I tell you, charity is the finest cleanser in the world. It launders things cleaner than soap powder ever could. It takes even a black soul, dear Mister Christy, and makes it as fresh and crisp and white as a best Sunday shirt. Would you believe that?"

"I'd believe," Mr. Christy said, "that you're partly brave and partly a plain old fool. Now get out of my way."

"Oh, dear Mr. Christy," said the beggar, "I wouldn't ask you for much. You see, I never ask for much, and that's why I have to ask so often. Twenty-five cents would make me happy for the night and give me a meal."

"Twenty-five cents? Look here. You go to the poorhouse. That's the place for people like you. Keeps you from being a public nuisance. You hear?"

"Well, I hear you. But I hope that I shall forget what you say. I to the poorhouse?" He shook his ancient head.

"What good are you, then? Tell me that . . . what good are you?"

"Well, sir, I'm around and see things. I tell them when the underproppings of the bridges are getting rotten and unsafe. I tell them when the fences are getting weak. And I tell them a lot of other things. I watch the whole countryside the way that a mother will watch her household, you understand?"

"Who asks for your watching? Who wants your watching? Have the supervisors of the county ever asked you to take on this sort of work for them? No, they haven't, and, what's more, they never will. Now, you get out of my way, and keep out. I'm going to have a talk with the sheriff, and see if he'll let an old vagabond like you go about being a public nuisance the rest of your life."

He turned the head of his horse and galloped up the road that led past the Ireton house. But when he came still closer, he stopped the horse again. He looked back, but in the moonlight there was no sign of old Tom Elky, the beggar. Perhaps he had crawled back under some culvert to sleep there until the sound of hoofs brought him out to stop some other traveler with his whining voice. Christy was glad that the old man was out of sight. Although why he should be glad, he hardly knew.

Glancing across the glistening field of wheat toward the Ireton house, he could not help shaking his head in wonder. He lighted a cigarette and smoked it with a frown. For he felt that the very outline of that house was, in a manner, a reproach to him. He could remember that, in other days, that outline had been no more than a low, broken-backed hulk shouldering at the sky, hardly to be seen on a rainy night. But in the last year it had risen high and spread out its arms like a dead thing come to life.

Yes, and life was certainly here. On this nearest forty acres, long famous for the poverty of its soil and usually used as a pasture only, Henry Ireton had raised his celebrated crops of potatoes at which the whole county had laughed so heartily. Now that field was put out in potatoes no longer, and such a crop of wheat as stood here Christy had never seen before. He judged that it might run twenty-five sacks to the acre, or even more. The straw was long, and it seemed that they had been packed in by hand, and arranged all at one level. And this crop from the old pasture! The broken-down forty acres!

The whole affair seemed to Oliver Christy like a living miracle. In Henry Ireton, he vaguely sensed a prodigious strength that would go on expanding and expanding. Another two or three years, and all his mortgage would be swept away. He would be married to lovely Rosaline Lawes, and by that act he would cease to be partly ridiculous and partly horrible. For all of the Iretons had been unsocial, undesirable people—big-limbed, dark-faced people, loving fights, drinking much beer, throwing their money away, and totally inefficient and dangerous members of society. Half a dozen of the line had died with pistol bullets through their bodies, and others had been ended by drink and wild ways. Out of that muck the form of Henry Ireton had risen. A brutally powerful body was his, but a face more open, a forehead more expansive than theirs had been. More mind and less beast—and mind and beast-strength together had built the new big Ireton house and put up those vast barns, where now, some thirty draft horses were housed, all with fine new harness, and pullers of brightly painted wagons, so that the teams of Henry Ireton were showpieces, so to speak, admired by the entire county. There were other silhouettes to take the eye of Christy. He threw away his cigarette and scanned the great humpbacked stacks of straw and the higher stacks of hay.

What, after all, had Oliver Christy to show in all his life that would compare with this achievement?

He sighed and bit his lip, and that moment, smelling smoke, he looked downward and saw a growing eye of red opening upon the ground.

The cigarette that he had thrown so carelessly into the dead grass of the roadside.

III

A CROOKED SHADOW

He swung down from his horse anxiously and snatched his slicker from behind the saddle. Then he saw that two or three blows would easily put out the blaze, and he rested easier. It would be very odd, he thought, if such a fire should suddenly sweep away the five years of labor that young Ireton had invested in the place. What would Ireton do then? Begin over once more like a slave bending at a wheel?

His laugh was short and fierce, and suddenly he looked over his shoulder and down the road. There was no one in sight—not even the bent form of the beggar. And the wind—it was blowing softly but surely straight toward the house of Ireton. Straight toward five years of slavery and misery and accomplishment.

Oliver Christy, with an oath, flung himself back into the saddle. At the same instant, there was a loud crackling and a long arm of yellow tossed twenty feet into the air beside the fence. Christy, frightened and startled, leaped his horse aside and into the deep ditch that ran along the other side of the road. From that point, only his head and shoulders were visible. He could not be seen, but he could very well watch. Taking out his handkerchief, he mopped the cold beads from his forehead and studied this wave of destruction.

It was hardly a thing to be believed. First the flames ran like a creeping serpent, growing broader at the head, across the strip of short stubble that had been cut in the spring to make a way for the harvester that autumn. The head of the serpent of fire reached the standing ranks of grain, thoroughly dried out and seasoned perfectly by the sun of many weeks. Then there was a distinct crash, as though something had fallen. The flames, exploding upward, cast a wide shower of sparks and flaming bits of wheat stalk as far back as the place where Christy sat his saddle. Then, with the growing wind behind, cuffing them along, the flames raced across the field for the Ireton house, exactly as a sprinter leaps from the mark and then settles quickly into a driving stride. Throwing out its arms on both sides and rushing forward, the fire threw its head a hundred feet in the air. All the ground over which it hurled itself was left black, covered with slender snakes of dying crimson.

Before the blast, a loud shouting rose from the house of Ireton, and Christy saw forms of men, looking ridiculously small and stripped of strength, come out of the house and rush away toward the barn. He had forgotten the barn and the horses in it. And now even the blood of Oliver

Christy curdled. But he set his teeth. Better wipe out the whole thing. For give such a fellow as this Henry Ireton his thirty fine draft horses, only, and he would use them as a seed out of which all of his fortunes would be swiftly rebuilt. Like the hundred-headed Hydra, he would quickly be more formidable than ever.

He saw the mass of fire strike the house like so much volleyed musketry. Windows smashed. Every room was flooded with a living river of fire, and a cloud of smoke shot up above the stricken and doomed house of Ireton. Past the house instantly ran the long arms of the flame. At a stride it reached the barns. A freshly made stack of straw became in an instant a bright crimson pyramided against the night sky. And the whole side of the barn smoked the instant it was touched, and in another instant it was tufted and tasseled with flames. The dwelling house, in the meantime, was belching fire and darkness from every window. The sheds were going up with a roar. Then from the barn Christy heard the human-like scream of a tortured horse.

He had steady nerves, had Oliver Christy. Being an only son of a wealthy man, he had spent most of his life thinking about himself and his personal comfort, but now he found that a new idea was foisted into his mind. He shut it away.

"To him that hath, it shall be given; from him that hath not shall be taken away. . . ." That phrase leaped through his mind, and he smiled grimly. Fire on the ranch of Ireton, fire in his sheds, his haystacks, his house, and fire in the soul of Ireton himself. What would come of it?

The entire side of the barn that faced that way

was now writhing red with fire, but he could see the southern face of the building, and through that face men began to break, working fiercely with axes, cleaving a pass out from inside the barn. Now a man struggled out, and led behind him a horse. But the wild confusion outside maddened the poor beast. It reared, turned, and, neighing wildly, ran back into the doomed barn. Another horse was led out, but now the stubble around the barn was a living sheet of flame, and the poor beast could not be saved. All the rest were lost, unless, perhaps, a way could be found through another part of the barn to freedom.

No, it was far too late! All around the barn, sheds and shocks of hay and rubbish were aflame, and now the fire had curled around all four walls of the big building where most of the wealth of Henry Ireton was concentrated.

Mr. Christy had seen enough. It was too bad. He told himself that he was very sorry for poor Ireton, but, after all, is not all fair in love? And he, Oliver Christy, a son of the old and honorable Christy family, had chosen lovely Rosaline Lawes for his wife. What right, therefore, had a clodhopper to come between him and his will? So thought Mr. Christy, and, galloping his horse up the big ditch, he was soon away from danger—danger of being spotted in that neighborhood—and so he came on to his home.

He found that the whole neighborhood had become alarmed by this time. He himself joined the volunteers rushing to the fire, and he arrived there in time to see the smoldering heaps of ruins of barn and house and smoking stacks, with now and then a long hand of fire shooting up from a jumble of wreckage. It made an oddly interesting picture. It made him feel that he had looked at a scene of war. He himself had worked this magnificent destruction!

But, most interesting of all, as he was walking along, his father caught his arm very suddenly and checked him. "Not that way, Oliver," he said. "The poor fellow is there. We mustn't bother him."

It was Henry Ireton, standing with folded arms, viewing the red-hot ashes that remained to him out of five years of hard labor and mighty hopes.

"Has he said anything?" asked Oliver Christy of someone nearby.

"It was a funny thing," he who was asked answered. "When Ireton seen what had happened, he walked around as calm as you please. Telling people not to work, because everything was too far gone. I thought sure that he had everything more than covered by insurance, the way that he was acting. But he didn't. Seems that his thrifty nature didn't want to pay out good hard cash for insurance, and the result of it was that he is cleaned out. He ain't even got timber left to make the fence posts."

"And he made no complaints?"

"Only one. 'I wish that they could have saved the gray gelding,' says Ireton. "That was his best near leader, you know. The first good horse that he ever bought, and a jim-dandy, you can bet."

Afterward, Oliver Christy rode slowly home with his father.

"I hope that doesn't break the spirit of young Ireton," said the elder Christy. "That fellow has steel in him, but a disaster like this would take the temper out of the best sort of steel, you know."

"He'll go to the devil," Oliver hissed sharply. "I know that fellow. I knew him long ago. Besides, the bad blood has to break out in him some of these days."

"Do you think so? I used to think so, too. But perhaps he used up all the devil in him, fighting his way through poverty and misery. He put his strength into his plow and his blacksmith's hammer. And perhaps you'll see him starting again. For my part, I intend to advance that boy some money. I have faith in him."

"In Ireton?"

"Yes."

"Why, sir, I think that you'd be throwing your money away. I'd never risk a red cent on people of bad blood."

"Well, perhaps you're right . . . I remember seeing old Champ Ireton run amuck with a pick, one day, and nearly kill three men. I've seen other Iretons go wrong. Perhaps this lad would go the same way, sooner or later. But still . . . what a stroke of bad luck."

"I've heard you say, sir, that the right sort of a man compels the right sort of luck to follow him."

"Well, that's true, too. You seem to have a head on your shoulders tonight, my boy. Perhaps you're getting out of your foolish ways. I wonder, Oliver, if you're actually coming into your manhood at last."

Oliver said nothing, but he could have laughed to himself. After all, it was the first really important act of his life, and what quick results it was bringing to him. For he knew that his father had al-

ways looked down at him as a sort of weakling—
not weak in the fist or slow with the gun, but weak
in heart and character. Now the elder Christy was
talking to him as to an equal. To an equal! Perhaps,
before long, he would be able to see those rare and
wonderful qualities that Oliver Christy had always
sensed in himself. It was like the dawning of a new
and better life.

They rode into the yard of the house, gave the
horses to the Negro stableboy, and, as they were
sauntering toward the dwelling, a crooked shadow
walked out from beneath the chestnut tree.

"God bless you, Mister Christy, father and son.
Is there any charity for an old man, tonight?"

It was old Tom, the beggar, leaning upon his two
crutches.

"Here's ten cents," said the elder Christy. "Send
the old pest away, my boy."

"Get out!" thundered Oliver Christy.

"Oh, Mister Oliver," the beggar said, "ain't you
going to let me talk to you a minute . . . alone . . .
about something special . . . important?"

"What?"

"Something, Mister Oliver, that I seen this very
night."

IV

A Beggar Bargains

Oliver Christy twitched the quirt between his fingers. He was not one of those who allow a foolishly romantic respect for years to influence him in his actions. Rather, he felt that an old fool was infinitely worse than a young fool and should be treated with an according contempt. But now he hesitated. There was a certain amount of meaning in the words and in the attitude of the old vagrant.

"Go ahead, sir," he said to his father. "I'll see what's on the mind of this old scoundrel."

Mr. Christy went on into his house, and his son remained behind.

"I knew you were an obliging gentleman," said the beggar. "I knew that you'd finally stop and talk with me."

"You knew nothing of the kind," said the other. "As a matter of fact, I haven't three words for you. If you can tell me something of real interest, do it at once. Otherwise, you get this quirt right on your infernal shoulders."

Tom Elky swayed back and forth upon his canes, shaking his head. "Well, well," he said, "I suppose that you would hardly take the time to consider that remark of yours . . . you're so hasty, Mister Christy."

"Look here, Tom, I won't waste time on you. Have you anything to say or not?"

The beggar shrugged his shoulders. "No, sir. I haven't a thing to say."

The quirt whirled up in the hand of the youth. "By fury!" he cried. "I've a great mind to thrash you for your impertinence! But I think that you're a little mad."

"No, sir, not a bit. Besides, speech isn't the best thing in the world."

"What do you mean by that?"

"Speech at the best, sir, is only silver. But you know the old saying, that silence is golden?"

Mr. Christy dropped the hand that held the quirt. "Silence is golden?" he repeated with a snarl. "Silence is golden?"

"Exactly, sir. I knew that you'd understand."

The young rancher remained a moment, stiffly attentive. "Come over here away from the house," he said, and he led the way to a bridge that spanned the creek nearby, a foaming, dashing little stream that poured out its hoarse voice continually in the ear of the ranch house.

"Now tell me what you mean . . . silence about what?" asked Christy.

"I don't like to say, sir, even here."

"You don't? Come, you'll have to talk out . . . to me."

"Well, sir, fires don't start from no cause at all."

Oliver Christy bowed his head a little, and waited. Then he controlled himself and said: "I don't understand what you mean by that."

"I'll tell you then," answered the cripple. "I mean the fire that wiped out young Henry Ireton tonight. Just after you passed that way."

The quirt shuddered under the convulsive grip of the youth. "Now I begin to follow you," he said. "You'd accuse me of that?"

"No accusing, Mister Christy."

"Will you stop whining? We're alone here. Say what's in your mind."

"Well, sir, after you passed, the fire began."

"Tell me this, Tom. Do you think that a single soul in the county would believe that I burned out Henry Ireton?"

"Why, sir, the fact is that I think they would."

"Tell me how you make that out?"

"Why, I'm an observer, sir, as I told you earlier in the evening. . . ."

"Confound you and your observations. What have they to do with the case?"

"I mean, sir, that I pick up trifles that other folks don't pay much attention to. So I've come to know that both you and Henry Ireton like the same girl . . . like her a good deal."

Christy recoiled a little and set his teeth. "But how could Ireton, burned out and penniless, marry her?" Oliver Christy cast a glance at the boiling face of the creek. He cast another glance over his shoulder at the house, and then he made a stealthy, long stride forward. "Come closer, Tom," he said, "and we'll talk this over in a friendly fashion. . . ."

He reached out his hand to the shoulder of the cripple. He advanced the other hand, and then stopped convulsively, for old Tom had shifted both his canes into one hand, and with the right he now jerked a short-barreled, old-fashioned Derringer from his coat pocket.

"It don't look much, but it shoots straight, sir," Tom said. "I wouldn't take any chances with it, if I were you."

"You'd murder me?" Oliver Christy cried, springing back.

"If I did, sir, the creek would soon roll your body away. And there'd be nobody the wiser, for a long time. When they were wiser, who would ever think of suspecting poor old Tom Elky? Who in the whole country, sir?"

They remained for a moment staring at each other. There was still a bright moonlight from the western part of the sky, and by that moon they studied one another.

At length, Christy said: "I think that we'd better be amicable, Tom."

"There's nothing that I want more, sir. I can't be hostile to Mister Christy's son. I can't afford to be."

"I understand that."

"Thank you, Mister Oliver."

"You want money."

"I haven't any great expenses, sir, but a man needs something to hold body and soul together."

"Well, tell me what you want?"

"You have a rich father, Mister Oliver."

"My father is rich, but I'm not."

"He trusts you, though. He's very fond of you. What's his is yours, in the long run, I suppose?"

"As a matter of fact, you're wrong. He's tight as the devil with me."

"Too bad! Too bad! I was going to suggest ten thousand dollars. . . ."

"You old scoundrel! Ten thousand dollars?"

Tom Elky hastened to add: "But I'm not grasping, and now that you've explained the way that things are, I'll cut the claim way down. I'll make it only five thousand."

"Five thousand! You might as well ask for diamonds! How can I get you five thousand?"

"Well, sir, I wouldn't press you for the whole thing at once. I'd just take your note. Payable on demand. That's the way to write it out. Say . . . five hundred down, and the rest payable on demand. That would do very nicely."

"Why, you idiot, that's a small fortune!"

"Very small. Very small to a rich man like you, sir. I know that you handle greater sums than that every month."

"Tom," said the other, "if you turned in my check for that amount, I'd simply be disowned. And there would be an end of me, and of your claim, too."

"Well, sir, perhaps you're right. So you could make out say ten checks, for five hundred apiece. Then I'd turn them in one at a time. Money lasts me for a long while. You wouldn't be rushed any."

"Oh, Tom, I curse the day that I ever saw your ugly face!"

"I'm very sorry, sir. But a body has to pick up a living. What can an old man do except to stay about and observe matters . . . pick up little things, here and there?"

"You hypocrite! You whining old dog!"

"Six thousand, sir, will be about the right amount."

"You're putting your claim up higher? Let me tell you in plain common sense that I'll give you five hundred dollars, and not a penny more. Not a penny! You can make up your mind to that, or to nothing."

"Sorry, sir. Good night, then." He began to back clumsily away.

Oliver Christy followed, in great anxiety, so that his face glistened in the moonlight with cold moisture as though it were covered with grease.

"Wait a minute, Tom."

"Well, sir?"

"We'll split the difference. We'll call it twenty-five hundred. Heaven knows where I'll get it. But we'll put the sum at that, eh? Be a good fellow and see reason, will you?"

"I've stood here and been insulted . . . called a dog and a scoundrel and a hypocrite," said Tom Elky, "and I don't mind having those names thrown at me, except that, after they've been called, they have to be paid for. I only asked you five thousand, but now the price has gone up to six thousand, and there it sticks."

"Tom, Tom, it'll simply ruin me, and be no good to you. For mercy's sake, give me a chance on this."

"I'm giving you your chance. You've got more than six thousand dollars in the bank, in bonds."

"The devil! How did you know that?"

"An old man has got to go around observing the trifles, and remembering what he sees and what he hears. And putting the information away in his mind. I have shelves and shelves filled with information tucked away in my mind, sir. I ruffle up the whole lot and get out the name of Oliver Christy, and you'd be surprised at what I know about you, sir."

"You've surprised me enough, already. I don't want to know any more. But suppose that my father asks to have a look at those bonds . . . as he does every month or so?"

"Why, sir, you'd have to find a new plan, I suppose. There are ways for a rich young man to get money."

"Tell me how?"

"Why, you could go to old man Sackstein. He lends money."

"Yes, at twenty percent."

"That's only a fifth. He would give you money, I'm sure. He knows that the whole great estate of Mister Christy will come to you someday. Why, he'd be glad to lend you money, I'm sure. So let me have your notes, Mister Christy."

"Oh," groaned Oliver Christy, "this thing is just beginning to take me by the throat."

V

A MAN OF RUBBER

The worse the medicine, the sooner it should it be taken. So thought Oliver Christy, and after he had brooded for a few days, he went straight to the office of Israel Sackstein, the money-lender. In the hands of the beggar, Tom Elky, there were twelve notes for five hundred dollars. To be sure, there was a verbal understanding that Tom Elky was not to present those notes for collection before the lapse of a year. That is, they were not to come in faster than once a month. But, in the meantime, who could tell what freak might take the fancy of the old man? Or who might wheedle the notes away from him and suddenly present them?

It would be ruin. The elder Mr. Christy had stood a great deal from the fancies of his boy. Many a thousand he had spent, and he had declared that he had had enough. Thereafter, if Oliver could not demonstrate that he was capable of acting like a sensible grown-up man, he could get out in the world and shift for himself. That prospect Oliver hated. Not that he was too stupid or too weak to work, but he felt that work would degrade him utterly. Work was for slaves and for slavish spirits, not for masters of men like himself.

There was, more than this, a vein of bitter sternness in the soul of the elder Christy, and if the older man were to learn the nature of the hold that Tom Elky possessed over his son, nothing could prevent Mr. Christy from disowning and disinheriting the boy. Of this, Oliver was shrewdly aware, for all of his life he had made a study of his father—a study that was of infinite value to him in teaching him just how far he could go.

He knew that he was now walking along the dizzy edge of the precipice, and one false step would ruin him. The Christy fortune would go entirely into the hands of charity, and Oliver would be left destitute, with a great number of expensive habits and no means of gratifying them.

He was very irritated by this affair, and he cast the blame upon two people—Rosaline Lawes and big Henry Ireton. He was very fond of the girl, of course, but certainly he had never contemplated such a danger as this for her sake. To crush Ireton with the butt of a cigarette was a pleasant idea. But to be pauperized for the sake of Rosaline was simply ridiculous.

So, as his bosom swelled, he remembered that for the past year and a half he had been watching himself with a scrupulous care, taking heed that his expenditures should not pass a definite mark. He had gained much in this manner. He had made sure of the inheritance, unless some accursed freak of chance should throw him off the track. In the meantime, there had been the growing hope that the elder Christy would die. He was afflicted with a mortal disease. The doctor had thrice told Oliver that the sad day was rapidly approaching. If only what must happen, would happen soon.

Devoutly, Oliver Christy turned up his eyes and breathed forth what was almost the first truly ardent prayer of his life. Let the days of his father end. For what good could the man do now? He had labored, lived, loved, been happy. It was high time that he should step aside and permit a gentleman to take the reins of the fortune in hand.

"The generation which makes the money rarely has the slightest idea how it should be handled," Oliver was fond of saying.

At least, no doubt as to how money should be spent troubled the broad bosom of Oliver. So, on this day, he mounted his best horse and swept off down the road for town. He was in somewhat of a hurry, but he did not mind swinging to the side so as to pass the black face of the ruined farm of big Henry Ireton. For one thing, it had become a sort of gathering place for gossip, for people came from far and near to see the wreckage of the brightly promising farm. A score of insurance representatives had come out to take pictures and hear the story told of all that the farm had been. It was just such a tale as brought them business.

Henry Ireton was ruined, beaten into the ground, and his heart broken. Mr. Oliver Christy was very sure of that, and he was not sorry. The wretched business had cost him so much peril and mental discomfort that it would have been a fine state of affairs if Ireton had not, in fact, been utterly destroyed.

On the way, he met none other than Mr. Lawes, and the heartiness of the latter's greeting was a story in itself.

"Why, Oliver, you haven't been to see us for a long time. What keeps you away?"

Very different from the old days, when Oliver was the unwelcome suitor, and Henry Ireton the favored fellow. Christy smiled to himself. He understood very well what the change meant.

"I'm going to see the remains of poor Ireton's place," he told Mr. Lawes.

"Poor lad," Mr. Lawes said a little shortly. "But, after all, when a young man knows too much to take the advice of his elders, and will go ahead on his way in spite of everything that can be said . . . the punishment be on his own head." He added, looking dourly upward: "The punishment be on his own head!"

"I've often thought that there might be something in that very idea," admitted Oliver Christy.

"There is! There is!" Lawes declared, growing more excited. "Fine a fellow as ever lived . . . but would a man want to trust too much to such a headstrong young chap who is always risking everything on one throw of the dice? I hope not!"

Oliver said pointedly: "Does Missus Lawes agree with you, sir?"

"She does," Lawes said, growing a little red. "She absolutely agrees with me, you may be surprised to know. But there's nothing to keep people from changing their minds when the truth is offered to them, is there?"

But even this was not enough for Oliver. He wanted an unconditional surrender. So he said: "I wonder if you exactly mean that the engagement of Rosie has been broken off?"

"I mean exactly that and nothing else!" declared Lawes. "Why, sir, I shudder when I think of what might have happened, if she'd been committed to the hands of a headlong headstrong man such as Ireton. Besides, he's below her! You realize that?"

It was perfectly obvious that he wished to draw on his roadside companion to commit himself still further. But Oliver merely said: "There's no credit left to him, I suppose?"

"Not a cent's worth!" declared Mr. Lawes. "What happened to him in the bank . . . well, I'll repeat it to you in his own words. He told me about it. I must say that the poor boy is honest. He went to Mister van Zandt, and told him what had happened, and that the face of the farm was swept as bare as his hand, and he wanted to know if Van Zandt would advance him money on a fresh mortgage. What answer did Van Zandt make, do you think?"

"What was it?"

"He simply said . . . 'My boy, Stonewall Jackson was a good man and a religious man, but, when he found an officer who failed, he didn't much care whether the officer was foolish or simply unlucky. He changed the officer for another. Now, I know that you have worked hard for five years, and you're done very well up to this time. I'm glad to see that you don't want to surrender even now. But, from my point of view, I'm no longer interested. You can't force fortune to change her ways. She has her favorites, and she has those that she doesn't care to favor. You understand me? I don't want to put more money into your hands.'"

"That's rather straight talk," Mr. Oliver Christy commented, "but though I'm sorry for Henry, I can't help agreeing with Mister van Zandt."

"He's a sound man, is Van Zandt," said Lawes. "Very sound. Knows business and knows men. I'm sorry for Ireton, too. Very sorry. I want in the worst way to see him succeed. But I'm afraid that he's nothing but a bulldog. A plain bulldog. And bull-dogs can't win the greatest prizes. Not in this world of ours, constituted as it is."

"*Humph!*" said Oliver Christy. "I should say not."

"You'd think that the poor boy would give up, though, wouldn't you?"

"What?" young Christy cried. "Hasn't he?"

"Not a bit. Wait till you see."

Oliver was stricken with amazement—and a sort of perverse fury. Was it possible that this fellow could still win out? Then he added: "Well, perhaps he'll pull through, after all."

"Not a chance in the world, unless he can get a loan of money right away. Not a chance in the world. And who'll loan him money?"

"The same people who would try to carry water in a sieve, I suppose."

"Exactly! You have a penetration, Oliver. I'm glad to see that you understand these matters so well."

"Thank you."

They turned into the last lane.

"Look, Oliver. There's a crowd yonder. What's happened?"

They galloped hastily ahead and found some half dozen buggies gathered along the fence, where men and women going to and from town were staring across the fields of Henry Ireton. Where the black heaps of the house lay there was now a little ragged tent standing, and an open-air fireplace just outside. Farther on, there was a hayrack, a broken-down affair, with some remains of hay in it, at which four rattle-boned horses were eating, and a few bales of hay lay upon the ground. A red-rusted gang plow was not far off, and in the distance was what was left of the blacksmith shop, and particularly the anvil and the forge, which had remained intact. More than all that, to show that the place was under control, a fence was being run down on one side of the burned wheat field.

"What in the world is it all about?"

"Don't you see, Oliver? The queer man is going to sink in his teeth and not let go. He's worse off than ever . . . well, really not worse off than he was five years ago. People can hardly believe their eyes. And no wonder. There's no heart in that man, otherwise, it would certainly be broken."

They made hurried inquiries, and soon the story was told, and they discovered that by using patches of credit and money owing, here and there about the countryside, Henry Ireton had managed to get together these horses and the rest that was seen. He was plowing a vegetable patch by the creek bottom now. And he was fencing the burned wheat field, because even half-charred wheat has its value. It will fatten pigs handsomely, and Ireton intended to use it for that purpose.

The man was of rubber. The harder he was floored, the more quickly he bounced back to his feet.

VI

THE MONEY-LENDERS

"His luck has run out," Mr. Lawes observed, when his companion at last turned away with him. "And it will never turn back to him. He succeeded for a while. But there's a flaw in the Iretons, as other men have found out before me. A big flaw. They can't win out in the finish."

It cheered Oliver Christy to hear this. He had almost felt that his masterstroke, which had involved him in such difficulties, had been struck in vain. It had given him Rosaline, it seemed. He had only to ask for her, and she was his. But she was not enough. He was not even sure that he wanted her at all. But now, it seemed, public opinion sided with him in downing this man. Disaster had struck down Henry Ireton, and the entire countryside enjoyed the spectacle of his fall. They would not let him rise again, no matter how he might struggle to that end.

So thought honest Oliver.

In the meantime, since the Lawes' place was on the way toward town, he turned in to visit Rosaline. He stayed on the front porch long enough to bask in the bright, welcoming smile of Mrs. Lawes. Then he went off to find Rosaline.

He saw her coming down from the dairy, carrying a bucket, her sleeves rolled up to her elbows. The moment he saw the sun sparkling in her hair and glistening along her round throat, he knew that he wanted her, indeed. Wanted her with all his heart! He hastened to take the bucket of grain and scraps.

"What in the world are you doing, Rosaline?"

"I'm going out to feed the chickens."

"Why, you silly dear, isn't there a hired man to do that for your father?"

"There's a hired man to help my father. There may not always be a hired man to help me."

"What? Am *I* to turn pauper? And have you changed your mind about marrying me?"

"I told a man this morning," Rosaline said, eying him steadily, "that I wouldn't be in a hurry to marry you."

"The deuce you did! Who did you tell, Rosie dear?"

"Henry."

"Henry who? Camden?"

"No. Henry Ireton."

"What the devil? Has that fellow been showing up here to beg for sympathy after he was burned out?"

Rosaline looked deeply into the eye of Christy. "Don't talk like that, Oliver," she said. "I tell you,

I've never seen such a man as Henry Ireton was this morning. You would have wondered at him. You would have stopped hating him."

"I don't hate him. I despise the poor clod, and that's all."

"He's not a clod."

"I've heard you call him worse than that a thousand times."

She said illogically: "Father and Mother haven't the least use for him now that he's been broken. At least, now that they think he's broken."

"By my word, Rosie, you've fallen in love with him!"

"No. I don't think so." She became a little pensive, and then went on: "I wish that you'd seen him coming down the path there, Oliver. His tattered old clothes, all baggy at the knees, and his hollow eyes."

"And his grimy whiskers," added Oliver with a sneer.

"He was clean as a whistle," said the girl a little hotly. "You mustn't talk about him like that. He's a man."

Sharp, hot words rose to the tongue of Mr. Christy. But this girl seemed so crystal clear and lovely in his eyes this morning that he could not take chances by opposing her. He listened to what she had to say further.

"He came to talk to me," she went on. "I didn't want to see him. Mother didn't want me to. She met Henry at the gate and told him he mustn't have any more hopes of me. I couldn't afford to wait another five years. That was so brutal! I came out and met him. I told him that I was glad to see him. I wish that you could have heard him talk, Oliver . . . so gently and, yet, so steadily. He said that he was afraid that it was only pity that was working in me. And he said that he would get on without the pity, but that he realized that he had made a great fool of himself in working directly for dollars and thinking that a wife would come on the side, so to speak. And he wanted to know if I could possibly give him a few months, or even a few days to work some sort of a miracle, and come to me again. He wanted to try to work the miracle, and try to make me love him, you see."

"What's so fine about that, Rosaline?"

"You don't think so? Well, I thought so."

"What did you say?"

"That I had never cared about him. That I liked him better that minute better than I'd ever liked him before. And that if I loved him, I'd marry him in five seconds. No matter whether he had five cents or not."

"You didn't mean that!"

"Didn't I? You just bet that I did."

"Rosie, I think that the scoundrel turned your head."

"I don't know. I do know that from that minute I began to think seriously. I always thought that I wanted an easy life. Now I don't know. All at once I knew that I would have to be at least *prepared* for anything. Prepared to marry a pauper."

"But what about me? Have you forgotten your promise to me? If anything stopped your marriage with him?"

"No matter what I promised you, I wouldn't marry you if I didn't love you, dear Oliver. You can always know that, because it's the plain truth. Oh, I wouldn't dream of marrying the best man in the world, no matter how well I had sworn to do it, if I found the day before the marriage that I didn't love him."

"And you definitely don't care a whit for me?"

"No. I didn't say that. I'll tell you, Oliver, that you've always been so handsome, and so much desired at the dances, that I've just taken it for granted that I loved you . . . because all of the other girls mostly did. Don't simper like that and look so silly, Oliver. I'm not saying it to flatter you. I'm just telling you what's been in my mind. If I let you hold my hand, yes . . . and kiss me a few times . . . I don't know whether it was because I cared a lot for you, or just because I thought that it was really the thing to do."

"Tell me one definite thing?"

"If I can."

"Are you engaged to me or not?"

"Most decidedly not. I wouldn't trample on Henry's soul like that. I told him that he could have some time, you know."

Oliver Christy remained staring at the ground and biting his lip. And then he flashed a quick glance up at her. "You're really a great girl, Rosaline. I don't blame you for not wanting to grind him into the dirt. I don't want you to, not for a minute. Let that go. Give me time, Rosie. Will you do that?"

"I will. And . . . I wish that you'd give poor Henry a hand. If he'll let you."

"If he'll let me?" Oliver laughed hollowly and bitterly. "That *is* a bit of a joke, old dear!"

"Well, you go and try it. Tell him that you want your father to arrange a five thousand dollar credit for him. And then see what happens. Because you'll be . . . oh, so terribly surprised, I think. I don't think that he'd take a penny from you. You go and try. Oh, that would be a fine thing for you to try, Oliver dear!"

Her shining face dismissed him. He went off and took his horse and went slowly down the road. He had permitted himself to say one sharp thing to Mrs. Lawes: "I don't think that Rosaline has much time for me, Missus Lawes. She's too busy with the chickens, you know."

That would bring Rosaline a talking-to from her mother who looked a sensible person, to say the least. It might even inspire the authoritative hand of Mr. Lawes, and Oliver grinned a little at the thought. But, between them, they should be able to bring the silly creature to her senses. Ah!—to be able to listen in at that talk.

He went straight on toward town. Rosaline— and Ireton—and the Lawes—and the destroyed farm became of less and less import to him. He began to think more and more of the greater climax that lay before him. He was to try to get money—lots of money—six thousand dollars in cash. And he was to try to get it from the formidably famous Sackstein. Just how he would persuade the gloomy Sackstein he did not know. But, at least, he was reasonably sure that even Sackstein would hesitate before refusing anything to the son of Christy, the millionaire. The more he dwelt upon the power of his father, the more secure he felt, and so he went into the town with a better nerve, and straight on to the office of Mr. Sackstein.

It was hardly to be called an office. Over the livery stable there were three or four rooms, and there dwelt Mr. Sackstein. There he conducted his business without a secretary, just as he lived without wife or child or servant. Men said that as much as a $100,000 in cash often was held within the capacious arms of Mr. Sackstein's old-fashioned safe. Half a dozen times clever robbers had raided the premises. There they always learned that Mr. Sackstein possessed other old-fashioned articles, notably old-fashioned Colts of a ridiculous date and pattern. However, from his hand the bullets from these guns flew straight to the mark.

At various times, five men had given up their lifeblood upon the naked floors of Mr. Sackstein. Recently it was beginning to be understood, even by the boldest and the greediest, that he who took the Sackstein fortune would probably have to pay down more than even that fortune was worth.

Sackstein never dreamed of a different address. He was known in his place above the livery stable. Men traveled 500 miles to come to him and make him strange proposals—for he had an ear for everybody. He was a court of last resort. He was the goal of desperate missions. It was well known that he would risk $50,000 in a cause from which a bank would shrink instantly. Many were the fortunes that he had lost for these wild ventures, these truly lost causes. But many and vaster fortunes he had made in the same manner.

Young Oliver Christy, looking at the battered, sagging door that gave entrance to the stairway, wondered how many lost souls had entered by this means before. Then he pulled the door open, and climbed safely up the steps, until, at the upper landing, he heard a loud voice, its words muffled a bit by distance and intervening partitions—the voice of none other than big Henry Ireton, who it seemed had come, also, to this court of last resort.

VII

If the Dead Rise!

A sneer touched the lips of Oliver Christy, and yet there was complacence in his eye, also. For this was the result of his own handicraft, that had brought Ireton to such a pass. Mounting a step or so higher, he could hear all that passed, for the voice of the money-lender was as piercing as a steel drill, and the loud, rumbling of Ireton echoed all through the building.

Those tones were dying away now, and the last that Christy heard was this: "That's the lay of the land. I've been cleaned out and gutted, but that ground is rich. I've fertilized and rotated crops until I've freshened it up. The fifty years of wear and tear it has received have been made up for. I could put in five wheat crops one after another and always get a good yield. But I don't intend to do that. I tell you, there's a future before that place. All along the creek, there's soil so rich that it will do for truck farming. And with fifteen hundred dollars, I can run a permanent dam across the little creek and hold enough water there through the year to irrigate that low ground. Think what good fresh vegetables would bring in this city where everybody lives out of tins!"

"I don't know," said the money-lender. "Tinned food is the lazy man's habit, and the lazy woman's habit. You can't say how it will change with 'em. Tell me, how many acres have you altogether?"

"Two hundred and eighty-four."

"That's a round bit of land."

"For the truck gardening, there's about forty-five acres of the low ground. That ground is made up of pure river silt. It's so rich that you wouldn't believe it. I can run in some laborers and farm that ground for every kind of vegetable. I'd go halves with them. I give the ground and tools and such. They give the handwork, which is the most important part of the game. We split the profits fifty-fifty. Now, that may not seem very much to you, but I've worked the thing out. I tell you, if I can sell those vegetables at all, every acre of that ground will show at least a thousand dollars in stuff during the course of a year, with any luck at all. Split that thousand two ways. It gives me more than twenty thousand dollars for my share. Twenty thousand dollars a year from that bit of land."

"Not possible," said Sackstein.

"It doesn't sound possible, because you're like the rest of the people around here. You've got your guns sighted for wheat and cattle and such games. But there's other work worthwhile. Nothing looks possible until it's done and finished."

"Just what, in a word, do you want?"

"I want twenty-five thousand dollars from you."

"Twenty-five thousand! How much land?"

"Two hundred and eighty-four acres."

"What's the sale price of that land?"

"With the barns and the house down, and the whole place burned black, I've had an offer of a hundred and fifty dollars an acre for the farm."

"That would be close to forty-five thousand dollars?"

"Yes."

"And what's the mortgage?"

"The mortgage is for thirty-one thousand dollars."

"Let me see. Thirty-one thousand . . . and twenty-five thousand. You want to hold mortgages for fifty-six thousand dollars on land that won't bring you in forty-five thousand dollars at a quick sale!"

"That's what I want."

"For how long do you want the loan?"

"Five years."

"How will you pay?"

"Not a penny of interest the first year. After that, I'll pay you twelve percent for four years. That will give you about ten percent return on your capital."

"You offer me ten percent in a deal where I'm apt to lose the whole capital sum!"

"Put it higher, then. Name your own item, and I'll see if I can stand it."

"I should say, twenty percent."

"You want to double your money in five years?"

"I take a great risk."

"That rate would bleed me to the core," Ireton said after a pause. "It would mean five years of horror for me. Well, I've had five years of horror already, and I'll undertake five years more. Do I get the money?"

"When could you build your dam?"

"Inside of two weeks."

"And get in a crop next spring?"

"No, the fall is coming on late. I'll get in a quick crop of vegetables the minute the water has raised behind the dam. I'll catch the market with some late things and get fancy prices for them. For that matter, if this town won't take the stuff, I can slap it into fast trains and send it express to the nearest city. That would cut down my profits, but still it would leave me a fine margin. I'll raise four crops a year on that land, Sackstein."

"Wait a minute." A chair scraped back.

Oliver Christy snapped his fingers softly and shrugged his shoulders. If Ireton could get money as easily as this, how simple it would be for him, the son of a rich man who was dying. Yet he was irritated. Ireton had been put down once. He would be better pleased to keep the farmer down.

"You want twenty-five thousand dollars?"

"Yes, Sackstein."

"Count that money."

"This is thirty thousand."

"You keep the extra five thousand so that you can live like a man and not like a dog from now on."

Mr. Christy leaned against the wall of the stairway, hardly able to give credence to his senses.

"And sign this note, Ireton."

"Heavens, man," Henry Ireton cried, "you only ask for forty thousand dollars the end of five years . . . and you extend the time at six percent if I am not able to pay then! What do you mean?"

The snarling harsh voice of Sackstein said: "I ain't interested in these deals, Ireton. I ain't a bit interested. I like chances. I like big chances. Chances on men and weather, and dead mines, say. That's the way that I like to venture my money, and make big or lose big. But this deal of yours, it's too small. It's too safe. It's too sure, and I ain't interested."

"But you risk thirty thousand . . . ," began Ireton.

"I don't risk anything," said the other. "I know you. There ain't anything that you couldn't do. If it came to a pinch, I suppose that you could make yourself good weather and turn the hail away. Well, I've followed you. I know you planted potatoes and worked over 'em and got yourself money and elbowroom that way, while the whole county laughed at you. But I didn't laugh, young man. No . . . I knew. And when your place was gutted by the fire, I knew that you wouldn't quit. There isn't any risk for me. Instead of giving my money to a bank to keep for me until something worthwhile turns up to invest in, I give it to you. Within two years, you'll have enough money to pay me back. But don't bother. Keep plugging away, and, by the very end of five years you'll have your house and barns and all rebuilt, and enough to pay me off, and fifty thousand in cash, besides. In the meantime . . . I think I could let you have a little more money, young man, that is, for just one purpose."

"What purpose?" Henry Ireton asked, his voice quite shaken and off key at this singular speech.

"To marry on," said Sackstein.

"What!" cried Ireton. "Marry, when I've been . . ."

"Burned out? Young man, marry that girl poor. Marry her rich, and she'll keep you rich. Let her work. She wants to work. She needs to work. I know women. You believe what I say." And he added: "I'm putting in another twenty-five hundred. That gives you plenty. You go get married. Go quick!"

"But," Ireton exclaimed, "she wouldn't have me! Her father and her mother . . ."

"Her father and her mother ain't her," said Sackstein. "You go and try her. Because I know. You go try her and see what's what. As for her father and mother, just let them know that you've raised thirty thousand dollars. That's all."

Henry Ireton was saying: "I want to say . . ."

"I don't want to hear you!" barked Sackstein. "I'm pleasing myself, not you. I don't often have a chance to put money on a sure thing. Now go back to work. That's where you want to go. Don't wait for nothing, except to pick up the girl on the way. Good-bye. Don't talk back to me. Good-bye!"

Oliver Christy slipped softly down the stairs and around the corner from the door; he stepped in the shelter of a little group of poplars.

From that covert, he watched big Henry Ireton stride out from the money-lender's door and go off up the street, leaning eagerly forward, like a man walking into the teeth of a heavy wind. There was a sway to the shoulders of Ireton that reminded Oliver of the walking beam of a big steam engine. He watched Ireton out of sight, and then he turned in at the door of the money-lender, once more, and went slowly up the stairs. For he was filled with anxious thought. Not twenty-four hours ago, Rosaline Lawes had been a person of no importance— just a grade better than the rest of the pretty girls who could dance well. But now she had stepped far higher, by the operation of the law of supply and demand.

There was only one girl, and two men wanted her. Where he had felt himself invincible with women in the past, he was by no means so sure at the present moment. For this fellow had risen from the ground where he should have remained for the rest of his life. He had found generosity in a man whose heart was supposed to be harder than chilled steel. And if a fellow could work such a miracle as that, might he not, also, work another miracle with Rosaline?

Storm clouds, then, were gathering around the head of Oliver Christy. As he climbed those stairs, he wished fervently that the flames that had scoured the fields of Ireton, bare and black, had also consumed the master.

But as the thing turned out, it seemed that the dead could rise from the grave!

VIII

BURNING VISIONS

However, while Oliver Christy, in a black frame of mind, climbed the steps toward the office of the money-lender, the happiest man in that county was big Henry Ireton, striding up the street toward the spot where he had left his horse. He had his hands filled with such tools of power as he had never dreamed of before. Ready money! It meant nothing to him for its own sake, but because, with it, he would transform his farm into a garden, a bit of fairyland, covered with greenness and richness and capable of pouring out a glorious tribute every year.

He had asked for $25,000, in the first place, because he had wanted to be able to cut down the size of his demand if necessary. He had imagined the hands of Sackstein thrown into the air, and an exclamation of protest and rage breaking from his lips. But, instead, a sort of divine madness seemed to come upon the man. There were extra thousands, and many of them, in the hands of Henry Ireton.

Well, he would use every penny of that money and turn it into a shining account. In the meanwhile, he could not help glancing upward, now and again, and noting the drifting of the white, massive clouds across the face of heaven. He was filled with gratitude. On this rare day, thoughts of God swept through his mind like the passage of the great clouds through the heavens. He determined, with this vague swelling of his heart, to make his life better, and more and more fruitful.

He passed by a school. A throng of children had poured out for the recess, and their shouting and their tumult were stilled, while many hands pointed toward him. He was the man who had worked so vastly hard and from whom misfortune had stripped away the fruits of labor. So in a silence, awed and reverent, they watched him go past.

A fire came into the hollow eyes of big Ireton. One day those children would have cause to know him better, and to know him without pity. Yes, one day he would be rich. He felt the sinews of money, of power. All was his—granted a little time for him to bring his wider schemes into execution. Then he would build such a school as the town had not even dreamed of. He would give them the best teachers. And he would build them a fine high school, too, where boys, such as he himself had been, could receive an excellent education.

The fire still burned in the eyes of Ireton as he went down the street, although no trace of a smile appeared on his lips. He reached his horse, mounted, and turned toward the bank, and then he paused. In that pause, a new resolution came to him.

So he hurried straight to the bank, and, as he entered the front door, he saw President van Zandt turn hastily away. He knew the meaning of that haste. Van Zandt did not care to meet face to face with the man to whom he had recently refused money.

Up to the cashier's window went Ireton. "Hello, Ransome," he said. "What's my account?"

"Six hundred and twenty-two dollars and sixty-three cents," replied the cashier after a moment.

"Close the account for me, will you?"

As he stood with broad back turned at the opposite counter beneath the window, writing his check for that sum, Ireton could hear the murmur go up and down the bank. He was a known man, surely. He could have lived all of a most prosperous life and yet not have sunk into the imaginations of people as deeply as he had through this recent calamity. People looked at him with awe, yes, and with a sort of terror, as though he were a man who had known all of the horrors of hell.

Then a stir, a brisk footfall, and the hand of a man on his shoulder.

It was President van Zandt. "Now, my boy, you're not thinking of closing out your account and carrying on without a banker?"

"D'you think that's foolish?" Ireton asked, controlling himself. But he began, as though automatically, to shuffle in his hands the great sheaf of banknotes that Sackstein had so readily entrusted to him.

That rustling, soft noise caught the attentive ear

of the banker. He could not help looking down. A look of startled wonder shot across his eyes. He almost forgot what he was saying. "Yes, yes, my boy. If you ask my advice, I must tell you that I think a man has cut off his right hand when he gives up a bank where he is known!"

"What good is it to be known here?" asked Ireton. He allowed his voice to swell a little. "I'm going to John J. Rix and let him handle my money for me."

"Rix!" Van Zandt laughed with a broad sneer.

"Rix ain't a fool," Ireton declared. "He started with nothing. He's got a tidy bank, now, because he knows how to back men. He's growing every year."

"It's a small amount," said the president. "I do hope that you're not going to trust a little bank like that with any considerable sum!"

"Only thirty thousand dollars," Ireton said.

"Thirty . . . good heavens! Where did you . . . ?"

"From Sackstein."

"What! Have you lost your soul?"

"Look here. Does that look like selling my soul? I get thirty thousand for five years. And at the end of that time, I pay back forty thousand."

Van Zandt clasped a hand against his forehead. He could not speak, for the nonce, and now, from every part of the bank, attention had been focused upon them.

When Ireton spoke, all could hear, for he could not lower his voice. It would swell out loudly in spite of himself. It had a powerful hum, like the sound of whirring machinery. "I'll tell you what, Mister van Zandt, I banked with you for five years and did a lot of business through you. I've paid you fat interest and premiums on thousands of dollars. I've never missed an interest day. And I've never begged off. You know that. A few days ago, when I came in, you said that my credit was ace high. Then along came a fire and wiped me out. When I came again, you couldn't see that I was the same man. There was soot on me. You thought that the fire had burned my heart out. But it hadn't. I'm the same man that made the old farm pay, and I'm going to make it pay bigger. But I'll not work through you. Rix is square, and he knows men. *He* gets my account."

Mr. van Zandt was still blinking, and he could only cry out: "My boy, my boy, such a sum, in such a bank . . . why, it's unheard of! Rix only carries a few hundreds at a time . . . the cowpunchers put their paltry little savings with him. And . . ."

"That's the kind of a fellow I want," said Ireton. "The sort of a man that wouldn't trim the cowpunchers with their little accounts of ten and twenty dollars. As for his being small, he's growing. But you're shrinking. Five years ago you were bigger than you are now. Five years from today, you'll be shrinking still smaller. And one of these days John J. Rix is going to run you out of the banking business, because he knows how to risk his money on men, and not on acres of ground!"

As he strode through the door, he had a feeling that Van Zandt was curling into a corner, very badly sagged, and that there was something like a cheerful smile sparkling behind the eyes of the clerks. Very plainly they had heard some one speak aloud the things that they had been thinking for many years.

Across the street and into the bank of John J. Rix went Ireton. There were two clerks and Rix himself. That was the entire staff. A burly cowpuncher was telling John Rix how he chased a fine band of wild horses across country but could not get their leader—a matchless pacer.

"Is that band still together, Jerry?"

"Yes."

"You're broke, now, and you want me to fix you up for another run?"

"That's what I'd like."

"Well, this time I'll fix you, but you play to take the wild mares as you run the leader. We'll hope for the leader. But, at any rate, we'll make money on the mares."

"Will you do that, Rix?"

"I will!"

"Man, but you are a square shooter!"

"No, it's just business to me. Have a talk with Mitchell, there, and get it fixed up in detail with him. Hello, Mister Ireton."

"Hello, John Rix. Can I open an account?"

Not a shadow crossed the stern face of Rix. "I'm glad to have you. Gladder to have you than I am to have your money. And I don't suppose that there is much money?"

"Well, not a lot."

"I want you, just the same. You'll raise money for the bank, and, although my resources aren't very big, as you know, I'm going to scrape together what you need."

"You don't know. . . ."

"I do know. You want cash to turn back into that land."

"Hold on, Rix. How would you lend it?"

"Six and a half percent will do for this bank."

Ireton laughed aloud, so great was his joy. This was a man, indeed. "Sit down and tell me what I can expect from you. Then I'll go away and think it over. And tomorrow I'll make my deposit."

Hours later he left Rix. Burning visions had unrolled before their eyes. He knew that he had at last found a man thewed and sinewed like himself. What could stop them, now?

In the dusk he started to ride out from town, and heard a hail from the side of the road.

"Hello, Henry Ireton! What are these wonderful things that we hear about you?"

Aye, that was Corbett Lawes.

"It's late, Henry," he said. "You better plan on having supper with us as you go on out. Wait a minute . . . I'll telephone to the wife to have things ready for you!" He ran back from his buckboard into the store that he had been leaving.

Ireton stared down the road, smiling faintly. It was not Lawes that he was seeing with his mind's eye. It was Rosaline as she had stood before him earlier in the day. She had not failed him. Rix had not failed. What did fires and follies matter when one could find, in a single day, one real woman and one real man!

IX

A FINANCIAL SURGEON

It was long before this hour, of course, that Oliver Christy climbed the stairs to the office of the money-lender. He was received in the usual fashion of Sackstein. That is to say, after he had knocked at the door at the head of the steps, a sharp, bitter voice called: "Who's there?"

"Oliver Christy," he answered.

There was a moment of pause, and then followed several soft clicks that he knew were caused by the moving of the well-oiled bolts. Then the door opened, and before him was an open doorway. He heard a voice saying: "Come in, Mister Christy!"

He strode into a little, dingy room. On the opposite side of it stood Sackstein, a tall, stooping man. He was so broken by age, or by sickness, that his bent attitude gave one continually an impression that he was lost in contemplation. But he was never lost. His keen wits were perpetually working, as Olive Christy well knew. More than once desperate fellows had gained access to this chamber and had attempted to shoot down the old man while pretending to talk business matters over with him. But not one succeeded. The reason lay on the table before Sackstein in the form of two heavy revolvers, not of the latest model, but of an undoubted accuracy and ready condition. You might say that these were the only friends and protectors that Sackstein had in the world. But there could hardly have been any man who wished for less protection and friendship than he. Twice a week a woman came to the rooms and cleaned them thoroughly under the keen eye of the master of the place, and it was said that his entire stock of information concerning the outside world was gained from these visits. An adroit questioner can learn much from even the humblest source.

But it was certain that nothing could induce Sackstein to leave his chambers. There he remained and watched the world from afar—and never missed a significant detail that might affect his own affairs. Up and down through the mountains men ventured on expeditions in which thousands of his money were committed to the hazard. Still he remained behind in the dingy little rooms, and let fortune take care of her own.

Now he said to Oliver Christy: "I first have to ask every man to close that door."

Oliver closed the door.

"And then to sit here."

Oliver took the chair, but since he was facing rather sharply toward the brightness of the window, he strove to hitch it back into the shadow, but found that it was fastened to the floor. He had to remain where he was, partly blinded by the light, and awkwardly uncomfortable before the keen glance of the money-lender. No doubt that was a contrivance on the part of Sackstein that had been carefully thought out before.

"Now," said Sackstein, "what brings you here?"

"Money," said Oliver Christy. "I've come for money, of course."

He could not help speaking rather sharply—it was such a foolish question. As though anything under heaven, except money, could have dragged him to such a house as this.

"You've come for money," said Sackstein. "Well, well, well! And yet I suppose that you have a good deal from your father every year?"

"We are not speaking of that," said Oliver. "The point is that I wish to have money from you. Six thousand dollars."

"That is the point, of course," said Sackstein, "but at the same time one wishes to know. There are ways of throwing money away. Money is my lifeblood. You ask me for six thousand drops of it. Then you are angry when I ask you why you should need that blood . . . you who have so much of it! For your father is a rich man. Quite a rich man. Quite a rich man!"

"Yes, a little more than 'quite,' I presume," Oliver stated, more irritated than before. "I suppose that he's about the richest man in the county."

"In the county? Ah, no, no!" said Sackstein. "By no means as rich as all that."

"Are you sure?"

"Quite."

"That he's not the very richest man in the county?"

"Quite."

Oliver slumped indignantly back in his chair. "I'd like to know who is, then," he said.

"I wouldn't tell you that," Sackstein said impolitely. "But I would name a few who are richer. There's Samuel H. Chandler. He's richer."

"That old scamp?"

"He has just above a million dollars."

"What? My father is worth five or six times that amount!"

"Your father, young man, is worth a shade over six hundred thousand dollars. That is to say, he's worth that much if some of his present investments turn out fairly well. It's a mistake for elderly men to invest too much. Men who are past a certain age, and who are invalids."

Beads of cold moisture stood out on the forehead of Oliver, and his eyes thrust almost from his head. This was a dreadful shock to him. "You've no way of knowing," he gasped.

"I have, though. I never make mistakes about such things. Money is just hard, dirty stuff to you. To me, it is the air I breathe, the food I eat, the drink I taste. So I know all about the money affairs of our neighborhood."

"If you did," said the boy, "you wouldn't tell what you know to me. Not unless you had some distinct purpose. . . ."

"I tell you," said the other gravely, "because your father has not more than ten days to live."

"Ten days!" Oliver gasped, standing transfixed beside his chair. "Ten days! But the doctor said . . ."

"The doctor is a kind man. He lied a little. More than a little."

"But why should he lie?"

"You will see, after a while. But now tell me . . . knowing your father is to die within ten days, do you still wish to get money from me?"

Somehow, one could not doubt the exactness of the information that this man claimed to have. He spoke with a resolute certainty. There was a ring of iron knowledge in his tones. He could not be wrong.

But before ten days passed, long before, he would have to reckon with the first of the notes of the beggar. Yes, the entire lot might be presented at the bank, and then what would happen? One glance at them would ruin him with his father— cut him out from the old man's will. There were only ten days to wait. No matter if the size of the estate were so vastly reduced from his great expectations. Still, there was over half a million, and that would take a good deal of spending. What was six thousand, then, to him, who would inherit so much in a day or so?

"Yes, yes," he said aloud. "I need the money. I'll have to take six thousand dollars at once."

"Six thousand dollars is a great deal of money," said the other.

"Come, come! I happen to know that you've just given thirty thousand dollars to that pauper, that burned-out rat of a fellow . . . Henry Ireton!"

Sackstein whistled. "So, so, so," he said. "You don't like poor Henry Ireton?"

"I? I never think about him. It's not a matter of likes."

"Well, he is a great young man," said Sackstein. "But to provide for him, I had to strip myself. It left me very little, and very soon I expect great demands."

"I know that this is the sort of nonsense that most money-lenders talk."

"You have heard others, I suppose?" Sackstein said.

"Well? Will you talk sense to me?"

"I try to talk sense. I try to tell you that a while ago money was cheap, but now there is a premium on it."

"No! You mean to say that a few minutes ago you were willing to give to Ireton. But now you see a chance of trimming a customer, and so you want to hold me up!"

"Tush, tush. You talk very violently, young man."

"Well, be brief. Tell me what I must sign. I want six thousand at once."

"I prepare the paper . . . at once." He took a blank note from the table drawer and scratched a few words of the statement in a hand that accomplished much with little trouble. "There it is," he said.

Mr. Oliver Christy found himself staring down in bewildered lack of understanding. "Man," he said, "do you realize that for six thousand dollars in hand, you demand twenty-five thousand dollars in three months?"

"That is what I have written down," Sackstein agreed, and he met the enraged stare of Christy with an unfaltering eye.

"Twenty-five thousand damnations!" Oliver cried, leaping to his feet. "Do you mean that . . . ?"

"Hush," said the other. "Hush. I hate loud talk."

There was so much iron of determination and contempt commingled in his voice that Christy suddenly saw in amazement that Sackstein meant exactly what he demanded. Four hundred percent for a three months' loan! It was a usury too dreadful to believe.

"Only tell me," Oliver said, trembling with fury, "what has made you ask such outrageous terms?"

"Because I thought I could get them, and I still think so," Sackstein declared. "You have to pay me for the insolence with which you entered this office, the scorn with which you stared at my poor room, with the disgust with which you eyed me . . . and above all, you have to pay for your self-certainty, and for your knowledge of how I treated the burned rat . . . as you called Ireton. You have to pay for most things. But then, you can afford to. What are a few thousands to a rich-blooded fellow like you, with half a million in hand? Besides, the need is very great . . . the need is very great. I am a financial surgeon. I am only called in on rare emergencies. And then I am at liberty to charge a round fee to a rich patient." He added the last words with a sneer, and a looked so coldly in the face of Oliver Christy that the latter winced.

"Give me the money," he said, "but if there were any other place where I could get it, I wouldn't be here, Sackstein. Perhaps someday I shall be able to take revenge on you."

X

BEGGAR'S PHILOSOPHY

From the office of Sackstein, Oliver Christy came forth in a grim humor. However, once he had paid such enormous price he might as well turn his money to the best advantage. And that was to find Elky and pay off the blackmail as soon as possible. Someone was always sure to know where the old fellow could be met. Now it seemed that he was last observed on the road out of town, wandering toward the old dead town of Sandy Gulch. In that direction, accordingly, rode Oliver Christy, and at a brisk pace.

He was a full three miles from the town when a stumble of his mare brought her down on her knees and sent Christy flying over her head. But he fell without breaking a bone, and, springing up again, he ran back to her and found her well enough. She had not even skinned her knees, and the cause of the trouble was, apparently, that her off foreshoe had wedged neatly between two rocks. For, when he examined that hoof, he found that the

outside of the shoe had snapped squarely off for almost an inch from the point. He mounted and
went on again more slowly, thanking heaven that
his neck had not been broken in the fall.

His spirits rose, after a time. There had been
enough discouraging events within the last few
days, but in the sea of troubles there was one spark
of encouragement, and that was that his father had
not ten days to live. How the old money-lender
could know was certainly beyond the comprehension of Oliver, but it did not enter his mind for a moment to doubt the prescience of Sackstein. Such a
man as he simply could not afford to make mistakes. A moment later, sighting the wavering form
of the cripple before him, he called out in a tone of
positive cheerfulness.

Tom Elky turned and regarded the rider with
some doubt in his mind. He shifted both his canes
into the left hand, leaving the right hand free.
What that movement meant, Oliver Christy could
not help understanding. He had seen the blunt-
nosed weapon produced before. But he had no intention now of attacking the old fellow.

"Tell me, Tom," he said as he came up, "what is
the reason a man can forgive another man after
he's been wronged by him? Because I feel that I
could almost forgive you, Tom."

"Mostly it's that way," said the beggar. "I'll tell
you why. The people we hate are the ones that we
have wronged. We hate them because we know
that they have a right to hate us. They've seen the
devil in us, and therefore we loathe them. But if a
man harms you, on the other hand, you're apt to
respect him. You may be hot against him, but, at

the same time, you cannot help feeling his strength. You'd be glad of his friendship."

"You're a philosopher," Oliver announced, smiling in spite of himself. "You're a philosopher as well as a beggar and blackmailer. Is that it?"

Tom Elky merely smiled. "You've got some sort of a message for me, I suppose," he said.

"I've come to make you a proposal."

"Well, sir, I'll listen to it."

"You have notes of mine for six thousand dollars."

"And I'm a sad man that I had to ask for them."

"I know how sorry you are. But tell me . . . will you do a stroke of business for yourself and sell me those notes at a price?"

"What sort of a price, sir? Suppose that I turned those notes in at the bank? They'd be pretty sure to honor them."

"Not a penny of them! I haven't an account big enough to feed a sparrow."

"Well, well," murmured Tom Elky. "But your father . . . what do you propose, sir? And where is that first five hundred that you promised to me?"

"This is not the day that I promised it to you. But today I could show you something better. I'll compromise with you. For three thousand dollars cash, give me those notes."

"What? Fifty percent of the whole thing?" The cripple laughed excitedly.

"Why not? Three thousand dollars is a fortune."

"Not half as big a fortune as six thousand, sir. No, not for three thousand."

"Well, I'll strain myself and make it thirty-five hundred."

"I'll tell you what I'll do," Tom Elky bargained,

"and that's this . . . I'll take five thousand dollars cash from you on the spot. And then I'll give you the notes."

"Five thousand!" shouted the youth. "Five thousand dollars?"

"Yes."

"Not a penny more than four thousand."

"You're not talking to me, then, Mister Christy."

"Hold on, Elky. I can barely mange forty-five hundred. How is that?"

"Why, sir, I'll make it a gentleman's agreement at that figure, if you can't afford to live up to the terms of your contract with me. Have you got the money?"

"Have you got the notes?"

"Here, sir."

"Let me see them."

"I'd rather see your money, Mister Christy."

"You old, doubting scoundrel. Here it is, then."

"Thank you, sir. I'm very glad of that. Thank you very kindly, sir."

He took the money and passed over the notes, and young Christy touched a match to them and watched them burn.

Afterward, he regarded the old man with a snarling look of dislike. "That money has cost me something," he said, "and I may as well tell you, Tom, that I had the other fifteen hundred here ready to pay you for the notes, if I'd had to. I'm fifteen hundred in on the deal."

"Maybe the forty-five hundred will last me out my time," Tom Elky said with perfect good nature. "I'm not a man to mind a sharp bargain, because I've had to drive some on my own account in the past . . . as you may remember, sir."

"I remember," Christy assured Elky. "I was a fool that night. But I'll never be such a fool again. And it may very well be, Elky, that one of these days you'll run out of coin and remember the old story and come trying for blackmail once more. I warn you now that you'll be risking your wretched head if you do."

"I know that, sir. No, I've played my hand for what it was worth, I suppose. Now I'll have to rest content. And, after all, you'll have to agree that forty-five hundred dollars for the observations of just one night . . . that's not so very bad, sir?"

"You old devil!"

"No hard names, sir. By the way, I think your horse has a broken shoe, by the marks."

"Never mind that," said Christy. "But see that you remember what I told you about blackmail. You caught me the first night and troubled me a little when I was nervous. But that will never happen again."

"All right, all right," said Elky. "I've forgotten all about the Ireton fire. And I suppose that the rest of the people will, too, before long. They say that he's got big backing, and that he's going to be able to open up in grander style than ever. They say that in the very first five years he'll be able to strike out wider than before."

"Do you believe that, Elky?"

"Why, a man could believe anything about a fine young fellow like Ireton. He's proved what there is in him."

"Bah! I'm sick of the talk about him. Suppose that he slips once more. Could he get backing for a third time?"

"If he slipped once more?" Tom Elky, repeating the words, shuddered a little and shook his head.

"What's the matter?" Christy asked.

"Why, if Ireton slipped once more and lost everything the way that he did in the fire . . . if that happened, why, he would never do another lick of work."

"He'd sit down and mourn, eh? Break the heart of the puppy, would it?"

"Break his heart? No, it would start him breaking the hearts of others. If Henry Ireton is ever put down again . . . why, the gent that puts him down had better have the wings of a bird, because unless Ireton is killed, he'll run amuck. I know his nature. If he's checked again, the world will pay for it."

"You think he would go bad?"

"Let me tell you something," said the cripple. "When his supply of chuck was low, he used to kill squirrels. And you know what he used to kill them with?"

"Well?"

"With an old Colt."

"I've heard that yarn."

"You don't believe it?"

"Not a word."

Tom Elky shuddered with a sort of uncanny pleasure, and then he murmured: "I didn't want to believe, either. But then I saw with my own eyes. Just the heads, Mister Christy, just chipping off their heads. A bullet apiece, very neat, and never anything wasted. He says to me . . . 'If only I had a smaller gun, I could save money. Ammunition for a revolver is too expensive to waste on squirrels, Elky.' That was what he said to me. I remember the day well. And him with three days' whiskers on his face, standing behind his forge and whanging a big bar of iron with his hammer. He has a grand right arm. He could make a fortune in the prize ring, if he missed out farming. But no . . . let him fail once more, and he'll take a shortcut to fortune with a gun in his hand."

"You're fairly sure of that, it seems to me."

"Oh, I'm fairly sure, well enough."

"Perhaps he'll have a chance, one of these days. Good-bye, Tom."

"Good-bye, sir. And remember what I said."

"What's that?"

"We hate the men we've wronged, not those that have wronged us."

Oliver Christy turned in the saddle and regarded the grinning old man for a thoughtful moment. Then he rode on. He was beginning to turn a new series of thoughts through his mind, and they were not unpleasant thoughts—so little unpleasant that, in riding, he could not help whistling a little again.

He took the way toward the house of Lawes, for the day was wearing late, and in that house there was always a welcome waiting for him.

XI

STAGED BY THE DEVIL

That the devil had taken charge of the life of young
Oliver Christy will be more than apparent before
we have proceeded much further in the course of
this history. For all that Oliver accomplished can
hardly be placed against him too directly. There
were other affairs to be taken into consideration.
Perhaps he was too sorely tempted to resist. For, as
he jogged his horse through the shadow of the
trees before the house of Mr. Lawes, he did not
have to enter the place in order to see what was
happening.

A big lamp cast a broad glow over the porch of
the house, and on that porch sat Mr. and Mrs.
Lawes, and their daughter Rosaline, and with
them was none other than big Henry Ireton. The
center of the group was indubitably Henry. He
talked, with few gestures, but with an earnest
rumbling in his voice that rolled out to the road-

way and hummed like the sound of hornets in the distempered ears of Oliver Christy. For Mr. and Mrs. Lawes to hang upon the words of that young man seemed bad enough, but worst of all was Rosaline Lawes in person—a shameless and abandoned baggage!

For she leaned a round arm on the back of Henry's chair, and peered over his shoulder, now and then, at the design that he was sketching on a piece of paper that he held. Not many glances for his sketch. Most of the time her head was raised toward her parents, as though she already knew exactly what Ireton was saying, and all his plans.

Oliver Christy sat his horse in the dusk of the trees that shadowed the road and cursed the sight, and cursed the girl, and, above all, he cursed the man who was the central figure of that scene. The girl, perhaps, could be said merely to err. But Henry Ireton was a manifest villain. In what the villainy of Ireton consisted, Oliver Christy did not pause to seek. The fact was that his heart was so tormented by overwhelming jealousy that there was a mist before his eyes. He knew that he hated Ireton. He knew that he wanted to rub out the farmer as a boy rubs out a word on a blackboard. Let no trace be left. But, on the other hand, it would be no easy trick to rub out Henry Ireton. There was enough blood and bone in him to make annihilation a difficult job.

So great was the ache in the heart of Oliver Christy, that for a moment he thought of snatching out a Colt and trying a bullet for the head of Ireton, and it was no sudden compunction of conscience that stopped him. Rather, it was a knowledge that all his muscles were twitching and his body shaken so from head to foot that no gun could be fired accurately from his hand at that moment. So he remained staring hungrily. The beauty of the girl fascinated him because of the very indistinctness on account of the distance. She was not herself, but was all that he had ever hoped or dreamed she might be. She was not Rosaline Lawes. She was simply "beauty of woman." Then she laughed, and the sound made him almost cry aloud.

He turned the head of his horse and rode carefully away, praying that his presence so nearby should never be detected. And, as he swung into the long, twisting lane that started toward the house of his father a scant mile from that spot, the devil who was so apparently managing this affair from beginning to end plunged him into a brand new adventure.

There was a clatter of hoofs behind him, and three riders swept up.

"Hello, stranger. Is this here the way to the Christy house?" called the foremost.

"Yes, and I'm Oliver Christy."

"If that's your name, shove up your hands. I want to talk to you." The stranger then added slowly: "And I dunno that you'll need your hands for your answers. You being an educated man, you don't need gestures."

"Good," Oliver Christy said, nodding at them. "I see you fellows know your business. What do you want of me?" He lifted his hands above his head without any sensation of nervousness or of great anger. Rather, this affair was a soothing thing to him. Compared with the vast irritation of his heart, this hold-up was as nothing whatever.

"You've got six thousand dollars with you," said the spokesman, while the other pair circled rapidly behind Oliver. "You've got six thousand. Now let us know where you carry your wallet, and, when we have the coin, we'll turn you loose and ask you no questions."

Oliver Christy merely laughed.

"You won't tell us?" This came in a more threatening tone.

"Three quarters of that six thousand is gone already."

"What are you kidding us about that for? Where could you have spent that money this side of town?"

"Well, there's my wallet in my inside coat pocket . . . no, on the other side. You count what's in that wallet. Then tell me if I lied to you."

The wallet was snatched out, and the leader growled: "Keep a gun on this bird. He ain't as mild as he talks. I know him." He began counting the money that he had found and cursing between the hundreds. "It's an outrage," he said. "There's ain't more than enough to wet the throat of the three of us, boys, because he's told the truth."

"Unless there's some more money hiding about him," another of the trio said.

"He ain't that kind of a crook," replied the leader. "No, there's no danger that he's got more stuff around him. Fifteen hundred! And we expected enough to get us to . . ." He was checked by a warning word from one of the others.

"What do we do with the big boy now?"

"Aye, what do we do with him?" was echoed by the third.

"There's the roar of the creek, not far off," responded the leader.

The blood of Oliver Christy stopped in full current for the moment, but then he saw the leader shake his head violently.

"Killing before, that ain't so bad," said the leader. "It's got to be done, sometimes. But killing afterward . . . why, that's murder. An' I won't be no murderer. No, sir, I'm gonna keep my hands white."

"I wish," said another, "that we could send to the devil the bird that gave us this bum tip."

"It ain't so bad," said the leader. "We've got something to travel on now. And we'll need it. But I wish that we could take a crack at something really big . . . that's my wish, friend. Christy, if we turn you loose, will you not try to trail us?"

"Boys," said Christy, "there are three pretty good men here. And it's a shame that so much nerve has to be wasted."

The leader chuckled softly. "You ain't grieving one half so much as me and the rest," he said, "and if you know of any little jobs around this part of the world that we could fit our hands to. . . ."

"Not so big as that," Oliver stated, his idea growing fiercely in him.

"How small?"

"Well, there's only one man."

"One? That's neat! How much of a man?"

"He's got an old, rusty Colt. That's the only sign of a gun on his place."

"Aye," said the leader, "this sounds sweet. I take it that there's some gent that you ain't very fond of, Christy?"

"Yes, that's about it."

"What's his name?"

"Never mind his name. You're new to this country?"

"Yes, I'm new to it."

"All of you?"

"Every last one of us."

"Suppose that I take you to thirty thousand dollars in hard cash, my boy?"

"Thirty . . . ten thousand apiece? Why, old son, that would be about man-size for us."

"Hold on," put in a member of the crew, "we don't hold out on a partner, do we?"

"I was talking like a swine," said the leader. "No. We don't hold out. Why you should need money, heaven knows, your old man being as rich as they say he is. But you're due for your quarter of the loot if you put us onto it."

"I don't want the money," said Oliver.

"That's what they all say . . . mostly . . . till they see the coin. And then they change their tune. But where's the lay?"

"The first lane," Christy explained, "there on the right, and then straight onto a main road, where you turn right as far as a broken-backed barn on the left side of the road. . . ."

"Big boy," cut in one of the trio, "showing is better than telling. That's what the teacher used to say when I was a kid. Who is the gent you're sending us after?"

"Never mind his name. You want money, don't you? Or do you want the dope to write a newspaper article about it?" So the leader silenced his too officious follower. "Mister Christy, we'd take it mighty kind if you would show us the way," he went on.

All of this time, Oliver Christy was meditating profoundly. The devil had placed these tools at his service. He would be worse than a fool if he failed to use them.

"Follow me, then," he said.

"Wait a minute, old-timer. You get back the wallet and what was in it, first."

"Thank you."

"And if this deal works, we'll call you the whitest man that we ever met up with."

A white man! Even Christy had to shudder a little as he listened. But presently he touched his horse with the spurs and set off at a round pace. The three followed, and with a dust cloud whirling up behind them and turning the lower horizon stars dim, they galloped down the lane that he had first pointed out, turned onto the broad main road, and sped on through the night until they saw before them the broken-backed barn.

Now they were close, and Oliver drew rein. "You go on into the field beyond this one," he commenced, "and wait till . . ."

"Hold on, big boy. That's too thin. We go over there alone, and, while we wait, you round up some other friends . . . no, we don't doubt you none, but still we ain't fools. You see our reason?"

"I see your reason," said Oliver, "and I'll go with you and see the whole thing through. Why not?"

XII

THREE AGAINST ONE

There are some who say that to conceive is really the same as to plan, and to plan is, vitally, the same as to act. But the advocates of such an idea should have stepped into the heart of Oliver Christy for a moment as he strode across the fields with two of his new companions.

As for the remaining of the trio, he had been left with the horses, because it was always well, in such affairs, to have the means of retreat well secured. Surely three of them, striking by surprise, should be enough to master a single man. For this reason, as the fourth and youngest member of the party remained behind, the three of them went across the fields. The horses were concealed in the shadows of a dry slough. That left them means of retreat near at hand, and at the same time invisible.

The big body of Oliver Christy fairly trembled with delight as the time for action approached. All the other matters of his life seemed nothing whatever. Yet it seemed to him rather strange that he who had sent that field up in smoke—partly by accident—should now be lying in wait in the blackened stubble of his own making and striving to destroy the owner of the field in a new way.

He said: "I'll tell you this. The man that we're waiting for is not such a giant. Not any larger than I am, as a matter of fact. But he's a regular Hercules. Naturally strong, and he's made himself stronger all his days by hard work. Besides that, he's a very good shot."

"What might you mean by that?" asked one of the three. "Will you tell me what you might mean? Some gents can shoot pretty straight at a target . . . rifle or revolver. Some are only good with a rifle. Some can hit a target, but not game. And I've known lots of bang-up hunters that was no good at all when it came to a flurry with other men. What sort of a shot is this here friend of yours that we're laying for?"

"I only know this," Christy advised, "that, when he was low in funds, he used to get his fodder by shooting off the heads of squirrels."

"Hello! That's pretty rare! But I've managed it myself, now and then, with a good rifle that I had. Not often, but I got them now and then, the tricky little devils."

"With a rifle, yes," Christy agreed. "But this fellow was using a revolver."

"What?"

"An old-fashioned revolver that most men couldn't work at all."

This statement was followed by silence for a moment, after which the leader said: "You know that this here yarn is the facts?"

"I know it," said Christy. "I never saw him do it. But I've heard him say what he did, and he isn't the kind of a fellow who would lie."

"Look here," said the leader of the crew, "you have been mentioning a gent that has thirty thousand dollars, and that lives here in that tent in the midst of this burned-down house and sheds and haystacks, and all that. Tell me . . . does he own the land?"

"What's that to you?"

"Questions don't do any harm, but what I was chiefly thinking was that you've been telling us about a gent that was a hard worker . . . strong, and steady with a gun . . . and what's wrong with him, I would like to know? Because I never have hankered to get on the wrong side of a decent gent."

"You never have?"

"No."

"Then get out of here," Christy declared savagely. "I'll take on this job by myself, because I think that I could use thirty thousand dollars." He added after an instant: "Don't start whispering with yourselves, and don't try dirty work, my friends. I have a pair of guns with me, as I don't mind telling you. And I know how to use them, and use them fast. Now put that in your pipe and smoke it. You stay here and work with me and stop asking your asinine questions, or else you cut loose from here and leave me alone. I don't care which."

This stern statement reduced the others to a moment's silence, after which the leader said calmly: "You're a rough bird, I see. Well, I don't mind roughness when I'm making a fair share of money out of it. I don't take lip, but I don't think that you mean this for lip. It's just your way of expressing yourself, I suppose. But look here, *amigo*. You get away with this, just now, but don't try that line of talk again. The bigger they are the harder they fall is my motto."

This, in turn, brought no rejoinder from Oliver Christy. He was, in fact, a little ashamed of his outbreak, and yet, in the speaking, never had words been sweeter on the tongue than these. All the violence in them did not offend, but rather delighted him, and, as he spoke them, he had thrilled and filled with a grim determination to be at least as bad as his threat.

"Hush!" said the third man. "Do be steady. There's someone coming."

Down the road passed the beating of hoofs, and then through the gate into the field came a single rider, who dismounted at the little tent. They watched his outline as he tethered his horse.

"Now," said Oliver Christy. For a savage wave of emotion had risen in him, and he wanted to close on his victim that instant.

"Wait!" the chief cautioned. "Wait, man. There'll be a better time in a moment."

But he strove in vain to hold Oliver Christy down. They had tied handkerchiefs over their faces, and now, as they rose, the three white spots were visible for some distance.

Yet that was no advantage to Henry Ireton. He had turned his back in the act of carrying his saddle toward the tent, and the first he knew of danger was the hard-jabbed muzzle of Christy's revolver poked into the small of his back, while the hoarse, shaken voice of Christy bade him put up his hands.

Up went his arms mechanically—and then jerked almost down again as he remembered the vast prize in cash that he was carrying—and his hope for victory in his labors as well.

"Don't do that again, bo," cautioned the leader. "Go soft and easy, kid. Otherwise, I'll blow you to bits. We're playing this game for something more'n pin money."

"Very good," Ireton said. "I understand. You've beaten me. It's in the belt." He spoke so quietly that one might have thought his heart was not breaking.

Christy ripped the belt away from his victim, and opened it. It was fairly jammed, in the money compartment, with bills of large denominations. A faint cry broke from each of the three. For that instant, their interest in the plunder they had received was greater than their interest in the man from whom they had taken it. Their guns were still pointed in his direction, but their attention had wavered, and, in that instant, Henry Ireton struck.

He had not been afraid from the first—not afraid for himself, but for his money. It was more than life to him. Now, as he saw his ghost of a chance, he used the weight of his fists with glorious effect. The left hand smote the assistant to the chief on the side of the head and staggered him terribly, although he blazed away with his revolver and punched a series of bullets at the sky. His right hand, falling with more effect, nearly dropped the leader. Then he leaped for Oliver Christy, who held the money belt. He leaped blindly—and got the barrel of a Colt slammed squarely between his eyes. The gun exploded at the same moment, and Oliver Christy, standing fairly over his victim, fired straight down at his head.

"You've killed him!" said the leader of the crew, creeping nearer.

"What call had he to cross me?" Oliver Christy asked. "He's taken no more than he deserves. I've no regrets. Is he surely dead?"

"I don't feel any heart action. No . . . and there's blood here between the eyes. You've shot him through the brain!"

"Dead men keep tight lips," Christy said with a grunt of satisfaction. "Now let's clear out of here. The noise of these guns may bring someone. But first . . . have we left any sign behind us?"

"Such as what?"

"Such as they could trace us by?"

"Old son, you been reading books."

"Yes, if you want to put it that way."

"You go home and stop worrying. You're fixed. They'll never find us."

"You haven't dropped anything. And there are no fingerprints on the body?" Christy asked.

"No, I guess not. Come over here. Strike a light, Shorty. Hey, here's Sammy, come with the horses . . . like a good kid. He's never off the job. Sammy, come here. Shorty'll strike a light, while the rest of us split up the boodle on the spot. That's the most satisfactory way, eh?"

"A lot the most," said Shorty obediently making the light.

"Now let's have the stuff, big boy," said the leader.

"One moment," Oliver Christy said. "Who suggested and planned this affair? Who brought you here, and then who was it that pushed the deal through, after Ireton had knocked the pair of you down?"

"I wasn't down!" said one.

"You were done for, though, shooting in the air like a drunk."

"Big boy, wait a minute. How much would you claim?"

"Not claim, but take. I'll take just half of this stuff. That leaves five thousand apiece for the rest of you."

"Ye gods, man," said Shorty, "are you gonna throw your life away?"

"You won't let me have it, then?"

"Are we crazy?"

"Boys, hold on!" gasped Sammy. "He ain't dead!"

"Who? Ireton?"

"Yes. There . . . he's moving . . . he's gone!"

"Who?"

"Ireton!"

For the big shadow of the supposedly dead man had jumped from the ground and lunged for the tent.

Three guns blazed instantly after him. But Christy was already sprinting for dear life. He knew that there was apt to be a rifle in that tent, and he did not care to be standing in shooting distance of a rifle opened on them in the hands of Ireton. So catching his horse by the bridle, he threw himself into the saddle and shot away across the field.

XIII

HONOR AMONG THIEVES

Although Oliver Christy fled fast and first, he was not such a vast distance in front. The other three were not a fraction of a second in following an example so quick and intelligent. They flung themselves headlong at their horses, but they paid the penalty of an instant of delay. Such penalties are constantly paid, the world over, but in no place so often, or at such a terrible price, as in the Western states.

Lying prone, in front of that huddle of a tent, regardless of the crimson that was spreading over his face, Henry Ireton cuddled the butt of his rifle against his shoulder and took aim. He had only starlight for his shooting; otherwise, not even Oliver Christy, head start though he had, would have escaped.

The rifle spoke, and the horse of the leader pitched high in the air and fell down with a human scream of pain. The outlaw himself had landed on his feet, like a cat, still running in the direction of freedom. The rifle spoke again and Sammy threw wide his arms and pitched headlong for the ground. A third time Ireton fired. But, after that, the riders drove into a thick veil of darkness. For some moments there remained vague shapes before the eyes of Ireton, but he knew that he was shooting by guess, rather than by aim.

The leader had reached the body of Sammy, where it lay crumpled on the ground, and, great as was his fear of the deadly marksman in the dark behind him, he was true to his instinct of leadership and crouched beside the fallen man.

"Sammy! Sammy!" he gasped. "Are you gone?"

"I'm done," groaned Sammy. "That hound is a cat. He can see in the dark. So long. Give Sally . . ." So he died.

The leader remembered freckled Sally. Give her what? The golden watch, perhaps, that was Sammy's most precious possession. He wrenched it away, and, starting to his feet, still bending low, he raced away again. Fortune favored him for the good heart he had shown. The horse of Sammy had slowed to a dog-trot. That fine gelding the leader caught, and in another instant he was off on the traces of the fugitives, where their vague outlines were rapidly melting into the night before him.

Fast and furiously he rode. Three times fences rose before him, and three times he recklessly put his mount at them, and cleared them, flying. That brought him up with the other two, for the great weight of Christy in the saddle had brought him back to his companions in mischief. As they came into a road beyond the long fields, a white hand went up through the eastern trees, and a pale moon showed them to one another.

"Sammy dropped!" Shorty exclaimed.

The leader answered gravely: "Poor Sam is dead. God rest him. He was a bunkie."

That was the epitaph of Sammy, but, with a sigh, Shorty added: "It comes high, big money does. Always. And now do we get the coin?"

"You get your half," big Oliver Christy announced.

A twitch of a hand, and Christy found the revolver in the hand of the leader pointed toward him.

"Christy," said the outlaw, "I've been trying to treat you like a man. But I see that there ain't any use. Gimme that belt!"

The hand of Christy had dropped into his coat pocket. "I have you covered from my pocket, man," he said.

"How do I know you have a gun there?" sneered the other.

"You take your chance on it, then, and see what happens."

"Christy," said the outlaw, "they're apt to come swarming around us at any moment now. There's no doubt that, if Ireton was able to shoot that way, he wasn't dead, he was only stunned. He wasn't even badly wounded. Such a man as him will be a hard one to put off the trail."

"You told me he was dead," Christy said bitterly, "and, if I hadn't been sure of that, I would have stopped and finished the hound. But I trusted to your word. Confound him! He'll make trouble for me, until one of us is dead. Tell me one thing before we make the split . . . how did you find out that I had six thousand dollars?"

"Let that rest."

"Sackstein told you," Christy conjectured, "because nobody else could have known. Sackstein told you, and that he would work in company with you to rob me of the money that I had from him. Isn't that a fact?"

"Who is Sackstein?" the leader asked.

A stinging retort almost burst from the lips of Christy, but he controlled himself. "Here's the belt," he said suddenly. "Count the stuff, you. There's ten thousand apiece for us." As he spoke, he flung the belt to Shorty, and the latter greedily opened the money compartment.

"Nobody would accuse you of being in this game for the fun of it," said the leader, as Shorty counted out the money. "But the fact is that I pay the dead men and the living as well. There's no shares lost by going West. Not with my men."

"You mean that you'll pay Sammy a share, too?" Christy asked.

"I mean just that."

"So that you and Shorty can split it up between you as soon as you're out of my sight?"

"Do you think so? You don't know my reputation, if you say that, my friend. Sammy has an old aunt that raised him. She could use seventy-five hundred a lot better than any of the rest of us. And she's going to get it."

"I've got your word for that." Oliver Christy sneered.

"It's good enough authority for you," the leader

replied hotly. "Let it go at that, because you won't get any better chance. Now that I've got the drop on you, I've a mind to croak you . . . you've been so keen to beat the rest of us out of our shares."

"Try it," Oliver Christy challenged. "I invite you to step out and try it, old son. You and me could have a fine party, on the strength of that. You and me and Shorty. I don't ask for trouble, but just one of you start to fade away with that money."

After this a moment of pause followed, the horses stamping and tossing their heads impatiently, and the steam going up from them through the moonlight.

"All right," the leader said at last. "Have you made the split, Shorty?"

"Yes."

"Then count out a share to Christy."

It was done, the bills being shuffled rapidly into the ready palm of Mr. Christy. He received seven thousand five hundred dollars, exactly.

"Now," said the leader, "the time has come for us to quit each other, and I got to say that I'm glad to go. I like to be in strong with my partners, I don't mind saying, but I never before seen a man that I could leave so easy as I can this one here. I'm through with you, Christy. I hope that I never have to lay eyes on you again. For all of the murdering, cold-hearted swine that I ever met, you're the meanest and the worst. Shorty, let's get out of his sight!"

They reined their horses back, whirled them around, and galloped rapidly away.

Behind them, they left Oliver Christy thoughtful and somewhat down-hearted. For he had not yet grown entirely calloused. There was still some room for kindness in him, and still some vanity of gentleness and the desire for the respect of his fellow men. He did not care so much for love. But he wished to be respected. Respected for strength and valor. But even those criminals despised and hated him. And that cut him rather deeply. However, he could not remain foolishly there in the road, waiting to be taken. So he turned the head of his horse and cantered briskly away toward the house of his father.

It was not very late when he arrived in view of the light that shone continually from the lower windows of the front hall. But what amazed him was the glitter behind the windows of his father's bedroom, just above. The elder Christy was in the habit of retiring early, and had been ever since his fatal illness commenced. But here it was nearly eleven, and there were all of these lights. Oliver Christy pushed his horse rapidly ahead, swung down, and strode up the steps. The pale, drawn face of the servant at the front door told him everything.

Up the stairs with a bound, and into the room where there was a hushing of whispers. Figures drew back against the wall. He stood above the white, dead face of his father and wondered at the softness of the dead man's smile that had been so pinched and stern with pain during the last years of his life.

Then he went downstairs again and poured out a drink. He needed to be alone and to meditate and to add up, as it were, his account of the events that had happened on this day. He knew that he had in pocket $9,000. He knew that he had paid off a blackmail debt of $4,500, and the total left him in debt to Sackstein for $25,000. Only $13,500 to show against a deficit of $25,000, and this in spite of the fact that he had used guns, trickery, and the advantage of number, and secret information secured as an eavesdropper. That, too, in spite of the fact that the stain of one man's lifeblood was already upon the money that he held. It began to appear to young Christy that, after all, it might be just as well to avoid sin hereafter. It hardly paid. It was distinctly a losing account.

He finished his drink and extended himself more comfortably in his chair. After all, he had finally spiked the guns of Henry Ireton. He had stamped that man out of his way. Rosaline would become Mrs. Christy. The face of life would smile for Oliver. Yet he could not be sure. He could not be *quite* sure. What was overwhelmingly important was that he had failed to kill Ireton.

The devil had certainly been in that piece of hard luck.

XIV

SLUMBERING GIANT

There is no giant so large that he may not be stunned by a blow that is heavy enough. Henry Ireton was stunned. He knew that he had slaved for many years. He knew that he had conquered, and then chance had wiped out his victory in a cloud of fire. It had not entirely destroyed him, however. No, for he learned that his work had won him the confidence of men and women, and, when he started on the upgrade, the first person to meet him with kindness had been Rosaline Lawes. She had given him heart to try his fortune further. The adventure with the money-lender had been in the nature of a miracle. Then there had been the dealing with John Rix. At the very moment when he was reestablished, the money had been snapped up out of his hands. He had been left empty-handed.

Not quite empty-handed. Yonder in the field lay a dead horse, and near it there was a dead man. He went out and looked at them with vague, regardless eyes, and then he turned sadly back to the tent—no, not so much in sadness as in a daze. There in the tent he sat with fallen head.

The news traveled rapidly up and down the countryside, for when was there a time when the story of tragedy did not leap like lightning?

The sheriff came—big, urbane—a man gentle in speech as he was terrible in action. He touched the shoulder of Henry Ireton.

"Ireton, I'm sorry," he said. "Tell me what's happened?"

Ireton pointed to the field where the dead man lay, and bowed his head.

"But the way it happened . . . I want to know that. And how many of them were there?"

Ireton's head rolled loosely back on his shoulders. "I dunno," he said.

The sheriff looked down for a moment into that blank, stricken face, and then he, too, retired. "Leave that man alone," he ordered. "Wait for a doctor, will you? Leave him alone until a doctor has a chance to get at him."

A doctor was brought. He found a passive patient. The doctor came out from the tent even graver of face than the sheriff had been. "I'll tell you what," he said. "If the poor devil had another house standing here, filled with livestock, I'd advocate putting it on fire at once."

"What do you mean by that?" asked the sheriff.

"I mean that he's in very bad shape. He's fallen into an apathy that may mean any number of things. But for my part, I think that it means a broken heart."

"Broken . . . nonsense," said the sheriff. "That fellow is tough as iron."

"I've had to do with these iron men before," declared the doctor. "These mountains are filled with 'em. They do very well under certain conditions. But usually they're best for work that needs edged tools. Now Ireton is that sort. Give him a mountain to move, and he'll try to move it. But give him a mystery, and he's up in the air."

"I don't follow that drift," the sheriff said, gnawing at the end of a sandy mustache.

"Listen," explained the man of science. "When this chap received for an inheritance a property mouse-eaten with debts, and worn out by stupid management, it was a concrete objective for him . . . and he started marching straight toward his goal. It took him five years. But he beat the game. The whole county knows what punishment he took in turning the trick. It was a grand thing . . . a miracle, I'd say. Then came the fire. Well, that was chance. A bad blow. A sickening blow that would have stopped most men dead in their tracks. But in seven days this fellow Ireton had started the machinery of credit working and was back on his feet . . . more strongly fixed than ever. But just on the heels of that restablishment comes a second attack that wipes him out. He's robbed. And mark what happens, not to his pocketbook, but to his mind. He doesn't mind the money loss. At least he could recover from that. But what destroys his morale is that this blow comes . . . through no fault of his own. It unnerves him. It's a mystery. Why should bad luck pick him out like this and kick him twice? He can't understand, and, being baffled, he's entirely at sea. His will fails him. And inside of two or three weeks . . . we'll bury that iron man, Sheriff."

"Hello! Hello! You haven't been drinking, old man?"

"Not a drop. Except on Saturday nights. Not a drop. When he dies, it'll be a cold, perhaps, that'll turn into pneumonia. Or it'll be from a consumption that will develop and run at a gallop through him. Because, man, he's going to be so weakened by his grief and his bewilderment that the first disease that comes along will kill him as surely and as easily as a bullet planted between his eyes."

"I guess I sort of understand," the sheriff said slowly. "I had an uncle, once . . . by the way, how bad Ireton's face is, eh? Somebody must have fired a gun right into his eyes. He is burned and blackened with the powder burns."

"And yet they missed him," said the other. "Well, and they battered him with some heavy club. I tried to dress the wound between his eyes and clean his face, but he brushed me away. You've no idea of the power of that man's arm, Sheriff."

"I have, though," the sheriff contradicted, smiling grimly. "I remember when young MacMahon ran amuck one day. He'd come down from the lumber camp, filled himself with liquor, and started out to paint the town red. I heard of it and started to get him, but I was ten miles off when the message got to me. When I arrived, I was just in time to see the finish. MacMahon had ridden down the street, a gun in each hand, shooting at the lights on each side, in the homes. Halfway through the town he met Henry Ireton, driving a farm wagon.

He shoved his guns into the holsters and roped Ireton with his lariat. Before the noose was pulled tight, Ireton stood up . . . I saw this . . . and jumped for MacMahon like a tiger cat. He reached the horse of the lumberjack. He pulled MacMahon out of the saddle, and they had it out, hand to hand. MacMahon stood half a foot higher than a tall man. He was a giant. But Ireton folded him in his arms and smashed his ribs like chalk. You could hear the bones snapping in the poor devil's body. MacMahon was a fighting devil. But I heard him scream with the pain of it. He crumpled in the dust, and Ireton left him lying, face down, and got on his wagon, and drove off. No, there's no man in this county that would take chances with that fellow with bare hands. Now you tell me that Hercules is going to die of a broken heart?"

"Yes . . . or go crazy. He has to be brought out of the stupor that he's in at present. Has he any very close friends?"

"No, but there's a girl."

"Good! Get her."

They got Rosaline Lawes. Mr. Lawes was by all means against her coming.

"There's been a friendship between her and big Ireton," he told the sheriff. "But you can't expect a girl to throw herself away on a pauper and. . . ."

Rosaline cut in sharply with: "Friendship? I was engaged to marry him. And I'm still engaged! And I'm going to him as straight as I can."

"Rosaline!" her father shouted sternly.

"I'll be on a horse in two minutes," she said to the sheriff. "Will you go with me?"

"Honey," said the sheriff, "I never done nothing more willingly."

In another moment or two they were on the road, and the sheriff explained as well as he could what the doctor had said. He cautioned: "You'll find him looking awful. They bashed him in the face before he ran them off."

"What do I care how his face looks?" cried the girl. "I know what his heart is, and that's what counts with me. But don't you know who did it?"

"No, we can't even identify the dead man."

"Ah, if he'd only killed them all."

So they swept up to the place. There was a score of people wandering around the field, looking at the spot where the dead man had been found, and at the dead horse whose body had not yet been removed. The sheriff and the girl went past these and to the tent where big Ireton still sat in his stupor.

Nearby, old Tom Elky, the beggar, took off his hat and stretched out his hand to them.

"You scoundrel!" snarled the sheriff at him. "I've a mind to take you to jail for this. Turning the misery of an honest working man like Ireton into capital for your own lazy hide!"

"I've been a working man in my day, Sheriff," whined Tom Elky.

"You have? Tell me one good thing you ever accomplished in your whole worthless life?" He pushed past the beggar to the tent, Rosaline in tow.

There the sheriff waited outside. He merely had a glimpse of the girl falling on her knees at the feet of Henry Ireton, and then he turned his back sharply, but still her broken, choked voice came out to him. He shook his head and breathed hard and moved farther off. "Women," he said huskily. "Well, God bless 'em."

"Aye, aye, sir," said the piping voice of Tom Elky.

The sheriff started and looked askance at his unsought companion. "Bah!" he said. "Get off this land!" And he moved a little father on.

A minute later Rosaline Lawes came out, weeping, terribly shaken. She ran to the sheriff. "Do something! Do something!" she said. "I think he's lost his mind. He just sits there. He didn't seem to know me. When I began to sob, he took my face in his hands and called me little girl, and told me not to cry and to go home to my mother . . . he didn't even know me!"

XV

THE BEGGAR TAKES A HAND

"If she didn't turn the trick, no woman could," said the doctor to the sheriff. "Now what can we try?"

"There's John J. Rix getting out of that buggy, just now. Try Rix. He's Ireton's banker now, they say."

They met Rix at the fence. On the way to the tent, he listened to the doctor with an intent frown.

He looked up with a smile and a nod. "I know," Rix said. "He thinks that he's ruined. I've seen men smashed like that before by money loss. Wait till I have five minutes with him. I'll bring him back to life."

Both the sheriff and the doctor were near enough to overhear most of what John J. Rix said to Henry Ireton on that day in the tent, and their report of it did much to bring to Rix the business and the confidence of the entire county later on.

They heard the banker say: "Ireton, you've had two doses of bad luck. That's your share for the rest of your life. But don't think that I'm through with you. I trust you still for a money-maker, old fellow. Keep your head up. I can't finance you to the tune of thirty thousand dollars, but I can do enough to build barns and sheds for you, livestock and tools can be bought with my money, and I'll keep you going with seed and every other necessity. We'll make a campaign of this together, Ireton. Are you agreed? Do you hear me, man? Well, I'll say it over again and . . ."

And over again he said it. But there was not a ghost of a response from the big farmer. The doctor and the sheriff moved to the road with Rix who was much moved by what he had seen.

"If what you had to say, Rix, couldn't move him," said the doctor, "then nothing could move him. We've tried a man, and we've tried a woman. They've used the two best arguments in the world . . . money and love. And he's still not touched. What can we do?"

"Go deeper still," said the banker, clenching his fist. "The man in him is dead, I tell you. There's only one brute left. He looked straight through me the way a lion looks through you when you stand in front of the bars of the cage in the lion house. I never had such a chill go down my spine. I tell you, Sheriff, that fellow is breaking his heart because he doesn't know how to get at the fellows who robbed him."

"That may be," said the sheriff. "But one of you suggest something, will you?"

Nothing could be suggested. It was the final opinion of the doctor that the big fellow should be left alone, undisturbed by a crowd, and allowed to rest, if he would, until the following morning.

Then if life and activity had not come back to him, he should be removed at once, and cared for in some public institution if there were no friend to take him in. Certainly he was in too strange a situation to be left to roam at large.

So the crowd was driven from the fields of Henry Ireton. The last to go was the old cripple, Tom Elky, hobbling on his canes, and very loath to move, because he had reaped a rich harvest from the people who had come to the place that day.

"Put him in stir, Sheriff!" called a strong, cheerful voice. "Because I don't think the old rascal deserves a penny of charity. Search his pockets, and I'll bet that you find money enough to keep him the rest of his days."

Elky jerked his head around toward the speaker and saw, sitting on a fine horse, in a gray suit with a black, broad band around the upper arm, none other than young Oliver Christy.

"Who would I get lots of money from?" he croaked back. "From you, Mister Christy? And what would make you give money away? Not charity, I'm thinking."

There was a subdued chuckle from the bystanders, and, in the midst of it, Christy rode off in a rage, for he was not celebrated for his generosity.

"Mind you," called the sheriff as he rode away with the rest of the company, "mind you, Elky, you're to keep away from this place and leave poor Ireton in peace!"

"Aye, aye, sir!" But to himself Tom Elky added: "Me that never done no good in my life, eh?" He paused, leaning upon his canes, close to the fence, and, with a grim frown, he thought back over his years of life. No good deeds? He would raise them to his memory one by one. But the triumphant smile began to fade from the lips of ancient Tom. Year by year and decade by decade slipped in review past his mind's eye. Still the great good deed did not appear. There had been many and many a fine hope, and many and many a noble thought. But deeds are the current coin that passes in this world of ours. And what had Tom Elky done? He looked up with a sudden gasp at the pale blue of the sky. He looked down and shook his head, and at that moment he saw something printed on the ground that made his brows pucker.

Only the print of a horse hoof, but it was enough to make Tom Elky gasp, and then glance sharply over either shoulder. He looked again, and, turning about, he retraced his way across the field, studying a trail, until he came to the side of the tent, where all the trail disappeared in a blur of recent sign. Then he drew himself nearer on his sticks and looked through the open flap of the tent into the blank face of the man within.

"Good day, sir," said Tom Elky.

There was not a shadow of understanding on the face of Ireton.

"Good day, sir!" Tom Elky said again, adding: "I was thinking that I might be able to do something for you, sir. Something in the way of getting your money back for you."

"Aye," said Henry Ireton. "I thank you kindly. Good-bye, I thank you. I want to be alone."

"I mean," Tom Elky cried in a sudden passion, "that I want to take you where you'll get the heart's blood of him that robbed you last night!"

As by a miracle, the body of the strong man was filled with life. He rose. He strode forth, and his hand fell on the shoulder of little Tom Elky. The cripple cringed helplessly away.

"You old snake," Ireton said, "you were lying here in the field, watching, and you saw it all, and recognized 'em in spite of their masks. Aye, and you've kept the knowledge until you knew that they were safely away."

"I wasn't here! I wasn't here!" Tom Elky protested. "But I tell you this . . . Oliver Christy was in this field last night or this morning. He wasn't here this morning because I seen him come and go again. And there you are."

"Wait, wait!" cried Ireton. "Christy's a rich man. And what have I ever done to harm him, tell me?"

"You fool!" snarled Tom Elky. "What's right or wrong to a skunk such as Oliver Christy? As for a cause . . . aren't you engaged to the girl that he wants to marry? Isn't that enough for him?"

"Rosaline? Rosaline?" whispered Ireton. "I think she was here this morning."

"Crying at your feet. Yes, she was here."

"Never mind her," Ireton hissed coldly. "I want to know something more about the same fellow Christy. I want your proof that he was here last night. Because if he was . . . if he was. . . ."

"I seen the mark of the shoe of his horse."

"How can you tell a horse by its shoe?" Ireton asked.

"Because his horse yesterday was shod with one broken shoe, and this field has prints of a broken horseshoe in it."

"Ha," Ireton murmured. "I think you know what you're talking about. Do you? Do you, Tom Elky?"

"I know! Go prove it with me. Come . . . look out yonder at the sign of a. . . ."

"I don't want any proof. I want Christy! It's he that I want. I'm going now."

"Where?"

"To find him."

"Not in broad day."

"Aye, in broad day!"

"And what'll you do?"

"I'm going to kill him. I'm going to take him in my hands and kill him, Tom Elky. Stop holding to me, or I'll throw you down!"

"You won't, Ireton. You won't. Listen to me. I only wanted to stir you up and do you good. If there is a murder done, the sin of it'll be on the head of Tom Elky."

"Keep your hand off me!"

"Ireton, dear Henry Ireton, kind lad, listen to me. They've got all the other things against me in heaven. I've been a sneak and a coward and an idler and a traitor. But there's no red mark against me. There's no blood, Henry. Don't you put it against me now."

But Henry Ireton jerked himself rudely away, and Tom Elky fell upon the ground.

He gathered himself up and brushed the dirt and the soot of the black stubble from his face. "God forgive Tom Elky," he said. "God . . . don't count it against me." Then he saw the figure of Ireton striding away, and, scrambling to his feet, he started after it, screaming. But that was quite vain.

He saw Ireton reach the fence and vault across it into the road, and then he was out of sight around the next bend.

There was nothing to be done, and the terrible silence of the naked countryside settled around the heart of Tom.

XVI

IN LAWES' DINING ROOM

That day was one of the great ones, if not the greatest, in the life of Oliver Christy. He had begun in the early morning by discharging on the spot with no extra pay for long service, all of the old retainers who were distasteful to him—and, in the eyes of Oliver, nearly every one who had ever borne a tale to his father about him was an enemy. Then he had given directions to the undertaker to proceed with the arrangements for his father's burial, and he had ridden over himself to arrange at the church for the most magnificent funeral that the town had ever witnessed. By doing such credit to the dead man, he felt that he was very directly doing credit to himself.

When this was done, he had gone here and there, always with a very grave face, collecting little speeches of sympathy, and scoffing at them in his heart. For he felt that any son must rejoice to come into the fortune of a rich father; and he believed that these speeches of confidence were the rankest sort of hypocrisy. That was one of the main charges that Oliver leveled against the world— hypocrisy. He felt that he saw through it and, for his own part, believed that all human actions may be well enough motivated by sheer expediency.

So he came around past the scene of his last night's exploit, and he could not avoid stealing close enough to see Henry Ireton within the tent. It gave him an immense thrill of satisfaction. But then, just as he was riding off, he learned that Rosaline Lawes had come to Ireton that day and attempted to rouse him. It caused a sudden and violent reaction in the heart of young Oliver Christy, and straightway he was flying down the road toward the house of Mr. Lawes. It would be seen what effect the inheritance of a great estate had upon Mr. and Mrs. Lawes, even if a young girl had been so rattle-brained as to lose all sense of proportion.

It was nearing dusk when he reached the house of Lawes, and he was received by Mrs. Lawes at once and with great unction. She was a practical woman, was Mrs. Lawes, and Oliver had recognized that element in her nature long before.

He went straight to the point. "I want Rosaline. I can give her the sort of a home that she should have. Tell me, Missus Lawes, will you back me up with her and with your husband?"

"You'll need precious little backing-up with my husband," said Mrs. Lawes. "He's got an eye in his head, I hope, and can at least tell white from black, poor man. As for Rosaline, she'll come around in time. Just give her a day or two. Let me tell you something, Oliver Christy. All young girls are a little crazy. I know that I was. And when Rosaline had a chance to throw herself away on a bankrupt farmer, it appealed to her romantic self. She wanted to do it terrible bad. You wouldn't believe! However, when she comes to understand that poor Henry Ireton is really quite simpleminded now. . . ."

"He was never much better at any time," Oliver commented coldly.

"Maybe not. Maybe not," Mrs. Lawes responded hastily. "However, he's all broken now."

"I saw him sitting like a great calf," Oliver said. "His spirit is broken."

"Well, Rosaline is in bed. She's cried herself into a fever. But she'll come 'round. There's common sense in her. Now, dear Oliver, you stay here and wait till my husband comes. Well, isn't that his step on the porch now?"

Oliver stayed. He stayed till dinnertime, and the talk was all that he could have wished it to be. There was no question of opposition. All should be as he wished. Only, they must go slowly and softly, for Rosaline was a stubborn girl with the fierceness of a tigress, when she felt that she was in the right.

The telephone began to clamor. But Oliver Christy knew that nothing could come to that house by way of news so important as the things that he had to say to this pair.

"Take the thing off the hook and let it hang," he suggested. "I hate a telephone. I never knew anyone to hear anything of importance over the wire, did you?"

So, when Mr. Lawes could not at once understand the message, he followed that clever suggestion and left the receiver hanging off the hook.

"Couldn't get the name," Mr. Lawes stated. "Anyway, they weren't asking for my name. That's all I was sure of. They must have the wrong number. Listen to it buzz, still, like a hornet."

They finished their coffee. But no sooner was the telephone placed on the hook than it sent a thrilling clangor through the house once more.

"I'll answer it myself," Oliver announced curtly, and he snatched it off the hook. "Hello?"

A hoarse voice shouted dimly back to him: "I want Mister Lawes's house. I want Mister Lawes's house. Is this the right place?"

"Yes," Oliver answered, and he added to his hosts: "Some drunkard on the wire, it seems. I can hardly hear his voice."

"If this is the Lawes' house, then is Mister Christy there?" called the other speaker on the telephone.

"I'm Oliver Christy."

"Thank God!"

"What's wrong?"

"I thought you were a dead man before this. I've been trying to get you. Something wrong with the phone. I sent off fast riders. But I thought that he would beat them. . . ."

"Peters? Is that you?"

"Yes, sir."

"What nonsense are you talking?"

"No nonsense, I'm afraid. He means deadly murder, sir."

"Murder?"

"Yes."

"Who . . . what under heaven . . . who are you talking about?"

"Henry Ireton. He came here with blood on his face. A dreadful sight. He asked for you. When he couldn't get you here, he said that you were probably at Mister Lawes's house, and he took a horse from your stable and started off at a wild gallop without so much as a saddle blanket beneath him to . . ."

"Great heavens!" cried Oliver Christy. He dropped the telephone receiver. "Let the door and the windows be closed, Mister Lawes!" he cried. "Send for all your servants! Call in the men from the bunkhouse. Lose no time. Lose no time in heaven's name, or I'm a dead man! Henry Ireton is coming here to murder me!"

Mrs. Lawes started up with a scream. Lawes himself turned deathly pale, and his face grew flushed.

"I'll . . . I'll send word . . . Ireton has waked up!" gasped Lawes. And he began to rise. He had no time to complete the movement, for a heavy step crossed the porch, and the door to the dining room opened. They saw the lamplight flash far away on the green face of a tree in the garden. Then the shadowy bulk of Ireton entered the room—Ireton with the crusted blood still streaking his face—Ireton with his eyes on fire.

Oliver Christy leaped backward with such a shriek as could never come twice from the throat of any human being. He tugged and pulled a revolver from his clothes. He fired.

But Ireton leaped in. A second bullet seemed to

be fired at him in vain from the shaking hand of Christy. Then Oliver Christy went down with a crash before the charge of the farmer. Twice they rolled back and forth on the floor. Then Ireton rose to his feet. In his hand he held Christy's gun, gripped by the barrel. On the floor lay Christy, not dead, but senseless.

"Now let them come and hang me," Henry Ireton said quietly.

They did not hang Henry Ireton.

In the first place, it was long before Oliver Christy recovered enough to appear in court against the other man. In the second place, when the sheriff sat down one day with the pale-faced, bandaged convalescent, something snapped in Oliver Christy. The whole story of his misdeeds burst from his lips. He could not help talking. He confessed it himself. His nerves were gone from the moment when he first saw the dreadful figure of Henry Ireton stalking toward him through the door of the Lawes' dining room.

But there was no legal punishment for Christy. He was allowed to pay for his double crime as far as money could pay for it. But as for pressing a prison sentence, Henry Ireton relented.

Newly married men are too often foolishly forgiving of their foes.

THE RANGE FINDER

The year 1925 was a prolific one for Frederick Faust in which he saw published seventeen short stories and eight serials. Under the Peter Henry Morland byline, "The Range Finder" appeared late in the year in the November 14th issue of Street & Smith's *Western Story Magazine*, in which all but two of the serials appeared that year. A first person narrative, "The Range Finder" tells the story of James Lang, newcomer to the West, and his adventures while guarding a mine and befriending a dog named Barney. This is the first time the story has been reprinted in paperback.

I

A MAINE MAN'S DEFEAT

My name is James Lang. I am forty-seven years old, but, according to my lights, I've lived only about the last fifteen years. Up to that time I lived in Maine, where my father, my grandfather, great-grandfather, and all the rest back to sixteen-fifty something, have always hung out.

I spent those thirty-two years like most of the other folks in that part of the world. I did my share of schooling, playing, fighting, and squawking. After I got big enough, I used to go out in the woods and do lumbering for the paper mills, cutting down the saplings, I mean, and the other scrub wood that goes to the pulp mills. It is amazing to think of the thousands of miles of newspaper articles and headlines I have cut down with my own axe! If I could be paid for it at a cent a word. . . .

However, to get back to Maine. I say that life was not living, and it really wasn't because I formed a taste for something bigger and better, as I think, later on. In the winter lumbering was bitter hard work. You know, of course, that the thermometer up there thinks nothing of hitting thirty degrees below zero. That is easy to write down, but mighty hard to live through. The days are really not so bad, because then a man is dressed for the cold, and he's usually working and keeping his blood humming. But if you sit down to eat, you're chilled through before you get the first sandwich down your gullet, and it takes a swig of smuggled Jamaica to wake you up. The nights are bad, too. You people who have always lived in a warm climate— or a *decent* climate—have no idea how the cold will come fingering under the thickest blankets, prying down your backbone, and settling in the tips of your toes. It's a fair bet that you don't really get an hour of sound sleep out of every ten that you spend with your eyes closed during Maine nights at a lumber camp in winter.

When we came out in the spring, I was a hunter. Perhaps that sounds a good deal better to you. Of course, there *is* sport in it. But just about the time that the Maine woods get comfortable in temperature for people, they get comfortable for midges, black flies, mosquitoes, and a million other things that fly and crawl.

I was a pretty good hunter. I had the natural gift for trailing, and I loved guns. Which is the main reason why this little confession has to be written—hunting and guns.

Trailing in the Maine woods is a job all by itself. To those who have never been there, I'll say that the country is broken all over with little hills and cut across by creeks, rivers, ponds, and lakes.

Every inch of the land that is solid enough for the purpose is covered with what the Maine folks call a forest. A Westerner would call it overgrown brushwood. Those Maine trees are just big enough to be irritating and just small enough to give you no lumber.

When you track a deer through ground like this, you have to keep your wits about you. A hundred deer can dodge you in every quarter section that you pass over; you have to move along almost smelling your way, because mere eyes and ears will never turn the trick. I mean this literally. A hunter has to have an extra sense. Of course, it really isn't the sense of smell, but I'd as soon call it that. At any rate, I was equipped with an extra lot of that sense. Ever since I was a little youngster, I was known for it.

My father and even my cousins, when they wanted to kill something extra bad, would always try to snake me along with them, even before I could handle a gun well enough to take part in the shooting. I've said a hundred times to some fellow along with me—"There's a deer on the far side of that hill." Or: "There's a deer in those woods, there." Sometimes I was wrong, I admit. But about five times out of ten I was right. I don't know what to call that extra sense. A lot of people have it, more or less. Mostly they don't talk about it a great deal, because it's hard to put it into words.

I could endure black flies or mosquitoes for the sake of enjoying myself with a gun. I used to think that I was about as good a shot as any man ever needed to be, until one day a young fellow came up hunting from New York. He was making a buckboard do cross-country tricks in most amazing style and covering country where even a mountain sheep would have been afraid to trust itself. He dropped in at a camp where I was with half a dozen other men, all hunters.

He said that his name was Cobden, and sat down to eat lunch with us, passing around high-powered cigarettes afterward—the kind that put a tickle in your nose just to *think* about smoking them. After that, somebody began to talk about the fine shooting that his cousin could do, and then about a friend he had in Carolina—I said that I thought Maine men were about as good hands at shooting as anybody in the country.

This Cobden had sat and listened to this for a long time. Here he began to laugh.

"Why," he said, "you fellows have still-hunted up here for so many generations that you can't hit anything more than fifty yards away. I'll put up a target at seventy-five yards and beat the lot of you . . . this revolver against your rifles."

He had a long, snaky-looking .22-caliber revolver. I found out afterward that it was just a target gun. It shot with an extra easy trigger, being very light and especially well balanced for slow, deliberate shooting. However, the idea that any revolver in the world can beat out rifles made us laugh. In another minute, we had laid some bets with this Cobden, and he had paced off seventy-five yards and blazed a chunk off the face of a tree. The place that he shaved off with that stroke of the axe was not more than four inches square. I waited for him to make it bigger, but he didn't. He just turned around and came back to us.

"Now," he said, "we're going to shoot at that target. Each of you shoot in turn, and, after each of you, I'll put in my shot. We'll shoot like this . . . one of you stand off and count one, aim . . . two, fire. Because, of course, you wouldn't ask me to allow you to take a long bead . . . rifle against revolver."

That was fair enough, as anyone could see, but the more we looked at that little blaze on the face of that tree, the more nervous we got. The reason being that at seventy-five whole paces that white spot looked almost like nothing at all. I had used a rifle all my life, and so had the rest of them, but our shooting had been at game that we had still-hunted until we had it dead to rights.

Well, I'm ashamed to say how that shooting match turned out. Just by luck, I hung my own bullet right in the center of that white blaze; one other Maine man got his inside a corner of the white spot. The rest were nowhere. Two others hit the tree and the rest didn't even land on that. But the New Yorker stuck five of his six .22s right in that blaze, and three of his six shots were grouped as close as anybody could ask in the center of the spot.

We paid our bets, but he wouldn't take the money. He only laughed and said that it would have been robbery, because he had spent too much of his time in the West, where men really *have* to shoot if they want to get game.

Beaten, and with our money refused, we listened pretty respectful and didn't sass him back, although we were all fighting mad. There never was a Maine man that wasn't proud of his state, no matter how much he might have to cuss her in spots. I'm no exception to the rule.

However, this Cobden said: "Out yonder, if you can't draw your bead at three hundred yards and shoot pretty accurately, you had better not go out hunting at all. I've done a lot of mighty pleasant shooting at greater ranges than that. A lot bigger! I'd be ashamed to tell you fellows at what a distance I killed an antelope one day, but, after it dropped, I had to walk an hour to get to the body. Though I admit almost all the way I was climbing down one side of a cañon and up the other side of it. . . . the body having fallen on the far side of a ravine from me. However, I'm nothing extra among those fellows. I do fairly well as a hunter with the average run, but I'd never pretend for an instant to stack up against their *real* hunters. Those men simply have long-distance eyes, and they have a wonderful way of judging distance. I can guess my hundreds pretty well, but I've known men who could say . . . 'That's about five hundred and seventy-five yards!'

"Well, you get at the end of five hundred yards and see how much difference a miserable little twenty-five steps makes one way or the other. Not much to your eye, but all the difference between a dead deer and a missed one, or a merely scratched one that you chase for half a day and lose at the end of your chase. No, those old-timers who really hunt, in the West, are jim-dandies. I wouldn't stack up with them at all. But one of them taught me what little I know, both revolver and rifle."

That was all he said. He was a windy youngster, a good deal too proud of what he could do, particularly with a revolver. At that, he was very neat with it. He stood out at thirty good man-size paces and clipped the edge of a dime. He did other things about as good.

"You ought to go on the stage," said one of my friends, "because there's a lot of people that would pay money to see you."

"There's a lot of people that would pay money to laugh at me, too," said Cobden.

That little day's work changed my life—completely. After Cobden left that camp, I spent two years thinking about what he had said to me—and that is no exaggeration. I had been so humiliated that I couldn't get over it. Of course, thinking about it wasn't a remedy. I practiced, too. I fairly lived with a revolver and a rifle during those two years. In the winter, when it was so cold that you had to shoot in gloves, I kept right at the job, even so.

When I tell you that in those two years I just about used up my wages to find myself in powder and lead, you can gather how much tonnage I poured into targets. It was not all shooting, either. I tell you, I put myself through a terrible course of sprouts.

You see, I was thirty years old when I met Cobden. Every man, when he gets to be thirty, likes to be proud of just one thing that he can do pretty well. In my case it was hunting. Shooting, of course, is at least fifty percent of hunting. So Cobden had given me a shock that lasted. I decided that if I were *not* a good hunter, I had to make myself one at once, or else there would be no excuse for my existence.

II

WESTWARD HO!

The biggest part of shooting is to find the target. Granted that a man with good nerves can hold a gun steady, and that a man with a clear eye can hit the mark, the distinction between very good and very bad rifle work, as Cobden had pointed out to us, lies in range finding, of which my still-hunting had never given me the slightest comprehension.

I used to spend hours marking down points around me and making a guess at the yardage, rifle in hand. Then I would go out and pace off the distances. It was devilish work. Some days I would hit off the distances close enough to have made a kill every time. Then there would come a change in atmosphere; the air would get cloudy and I would be thrown clear off in my calculations. Again, there would be a crystal-bright day, and *that* would make a fool of me. Or the glaze from snow, a cold in my head, a headache, almost any little thing would make me fall off—not much in the shorter distances, as I got better and better at that range-finding work. At 300 yards and more I was constantly off.

After I had been working like this for more than a year, I met an Army officer who showed me a lot of practical ways of getting the range, some complicated and some simple, although only the simple ones were of much use to a hunter who has to sight his game, make his guess, and then shoot—all in a second, say.

However, I had my bright moments. I remember calling a tree 590 yards from my post and pacing exactly 589. I was so delighted with myself that I did a war dance on the spot. And the very same afternoon I made a fifty-yard error on the same locality. That is the fortune of the range finder.

Between pacing out distances, wearing out shoe leather, and burning up ammunition, I worked myself thin and got a long-distance squint in my eyes. I'm afraid that I always looked as though I had just lost half my family, and I couldn't sleep well at night.

Then I would see that young Cobden laughing and saying: "You Maine hunters, you can never get the hang of a rifle. You haven't the air for it out here." I always thought that remark was mere mockery, and I couldn't get over it.

Well, I had been working away in this fashion for two years, with rifle and with revolver, getting so improved that I couldn't see any advancement in myself from week to week—but only from month to month I could tell that I was stepping forward. About this time I picked up a paper that advertised excursion rates to the West. It wasn't the rates that interested me. It was the idea of going

West. I never had any idea of saving up seventy or a hundred dollars just for the sake of taking a train ride of few thousand miles in length. For the first time the idea of leaving Maine jumped into my brain with a click. That night I lay awake and studied the darkness, asking myself why I should not go to the land of the good hunters.

I drew down the balance of my wages the next day, and with a rifle, a revolver, a lot of poundage in ammunition, a book of practical range finding, and eighteen dollars in cash, I started, vaguely, West.

Three months later I arrived. I had begged and stolen part of the way. I had worked enough to pay for another section of the ride—but, finally, there I was—in the West. I woke up one morning in an empty boxcar, with my hip and shoulder bones being jolted right through the flesh on the dancing floor of that car. When I edged the door open and looked out, I understood what Cobden meant when he had scoffed at Maine air.

This was different, more different than I could believe. I was swinging up a long grade, with the engine moaning and snorting up ahead of that long line of empties. Off to the north my eye was jumping across twenty miles of hills, maybe fifty miles of open, and huge mountains piled up in browns and purples. Beyond all that were the sky-blue mountains of the horizon.

There had never been a time in Maine when I had been able to see even the firs of these distances with any clearness. This Western air was like a crystal well. Distance simply diminished objects in size—and their outlines remained practically as clear as ever. To me, with my eye muscles trained for focusing quickly through a filtering of mist and wood smoke, this clarity of the air was like a god-send. The only thing that made me squint was to shut out the excess of light, which was more than I needed. I sat there and gaped at the scenery, not noting a single detail of the beauty of color or of form, but only losing myself in dizzy, drunken plunges of the eye.

The next time that train stopped, I did not ask where it was going, or what the country was like in the region. I walked up to the station boss, and said: "Will you tell me what the name of this town is?"

He looked at me, knowing that I was a tramp who had been using a boxcar without paying freight, and his lip curled. Then his eye ran over my rifle and revolver, all strapped on as big as life. He said: "This town is Elmira. Why? Are you going to stay and have a meal with us?"

I laid a hand on his shoulder. He didn't like that much, but I was a good deal too happy to pay any attention to a little thing such as his likes or his dislikes.

"Are you a citizen and a steady liver in this town?" I asked.

He said he was and shrugged my hand off his shoulder. Then he asked why I wanted to know.

"Because this here town looks to me like home, stranger, and I aim to stay here a considerable slice of my life."

"Well," he said, "we welcome all kinds here." Then he turned his back on me.

That was not particularly hospitable, but I was nothing very much as a picture to please the eyes. I am a couple of inches over six feet high. I weigh in speaking distance of 200 pounds. I wear a number twelve shoe, and I've never yet run across a glove that would hold my hand without groaning. My muscles are not big, but I'm stronger than average because, as a smart doctor told me once, my sinews get a good strong leverage on my bones, making a pound of my muscles work just as effectively as *two* pounds of muscles do in another man whose ligaments don't take hold of the bones so far out toward the end. What this means is that on a dead lift, I'm a pretty weak man. I can't carry a load any good at all. But I can hit a hard punch and walk fast, though I'm no good at running.

However, I don't want to give you my idea that I'm a freak. I'm just what even a mother would have to admit was "plain." I have a hinge in the middle of the back of my neck, my nose and my jaw are long and lean, and my mouth was made extra special in width and limberness. Otherwise, my legs are longer than they would have to be, and so are my arms, a good deal.

This ought to give you a pretty good idea of me. I'm ashamed to say that a lot of hundred-and-fifty-pound men could break me in two, if it came to wrestling, but even now—at forty-seven—it takes a licking good young 200-pounder to stand up to me for a single minute with the gloves. Boxing and shooting were the beginning and end of my talents. I had gone through a little schooling. I could read and write and figure, and all that. I didn't have any vice, except plug chewing tobacco and Jamaica rum, and I had never had a real sick day in my life.

So there I was, thirty-two years old, with fifteen

cents in my pocket, a fifteen-dollar hole where my stomach should have been, a rifle, a revolver, and a wish to have a few more looks at these mountains and the shootable things that were in them.

That town of Elmira was not much more worth looking at than I was. Like me, it was chiefly bones. I mean it was stretched out on the shore of a lake, with the big rocks sticking up pretty unsightly here and there. There was a sign painter in that town. You could tell that clear from the railroad, because every sign had been made so that it faced the rails. By the look of those signs and what they said about Elmira, I judged it had a boosters club or a chamber of commerce, or maybe both.

Those signs said that Elmira was a boss place for anybody who had weak lungs, bad heart, troublesome kidneys, failing liver, or an ailing stomach. It said that real-estate investors should wake up and look that way for investments; it also invited the rest of the globe to keep its eye fixed on Elmira in the day and also in the night. It said there were excellent hotel accommodations in Elmira, and it allowed that the bathing in the lake was the finest fresh-water swimming that the world could offer. I could guess that it was about the coldest, because my eye made only about two jumps from the summit snows to the blue-white waters of that shivering lake. Everything except the tops of those mountains was burned and brown-looking, saving the patches of trees—maybe a couple of hundred acres of them here and 500 there.

In spite of the signs and all the good things that was mentioned on them, I decided that maybe I could get along with that town pretty well. So I unlimbered my joints and strolled down toward the town, taking in the details of the surrounding 10,000 square miles!

It was a pleasure to breathe that air, in spite of the alkali sting. It was a pleasure to see the brown shadow of the mountain standing deeply in the waters of the lake. I decided that I would go into the store to get more information. So, into that store I stepped—and into one of the worst tangles that any human being ever found in his whole life.

III

Enter the Hero

It was the rifle and the revolver, of course, and the heavy ammunition belt that made the difference. I looked like a walking arsenal, but I had no idea that was not the ordinary guise of a Westerner. I thought, from the little I had heard and read, that in the West men used guns like friends from whom they never wanted to be parted. When I tramped into that store, I got myself stared at, of course.

There were a couple of cowhands in there just sitting and sunning themselves, as you might say, in the memory of how big they had spent their money that day. Besides that, there were three or four other men—a trapper and several others, all old hands in that part of the country. I suppose that I could not well have fallen in with a less green crowd than these fellows. They were all as hard as nails—real range men. When I saw them flashing side glances at me, it never occurred to me that I looked a bit queer or out of place. As a matter of fact, there wasn't a single man of the lot that had a gun. At least, there was not a single gun that showed—which makes a big difference.

I said "Howdy" to them as I came in, and I went up to the counter to buy some crackers and cheese. It was about the worst cheese that I ever laid hold on in my life, at that. As I sat there in the corner of the room, munching, I said: "This cheese is old enough to talk for itself, storekeeper."

You would think that he would get a little offended at that, but he didn't.

"There is just no way," he said, "to educate that cheese. I agree with you, exactly. That cheese is old enough to walk and talk. But it won't improve itself none. In my father's time and in mine, I've known that cheese for close onto fifteen years, and it don't seem to get sense."

He kept his face very straight, and so did all the rest of them. They just looked at him very sympathetic to have found a cheese as simple as that. I ventured to laugh a little. They all looked quick at me, as if they wondered what it was that I had found to laugh at.

A man of about my own build and looks—tall, broad, and bony—stood up and stretched out his length, saying: "I'll have to be getting along."

"Sit down and rest your feet, Luke," somebody else said. "I ain't had a chance to look at you yet."

Another man remarked: "You being a hunter yourself, Luke, maybe the stranger could tell you some yarns about hunting in his part of the country that would do you good to hear."

As solemn as judges, they all turned, looked me over, and nodded. Luke said: "I see you always keep your guns right with you. That's a single-shot rifle, ain't it?"

I said it was—and a breechloader, of course.

"Well," said Luke, "I suppose that you hardly never have to take more than one shot at a thing?"

I began to guess that he was joking. Still they all kept all their expressions so well in hand, looking at me so admiring, that I lost that suspicion pretty soon. So I replied that I missed now and then, the same as any man. They asked me how I was on long-distance shooting, and I said that I was pretty good at a 150 and 200 yards.

"Well, well," exclaimed Luke, "that is pretty long range work, all right. I suppose that you have downed a pile of deer and bears?"

I said that I had got a good many deer and bears—the little black bears, of course. They seemed just as interested as ever. How was I to know that every man in that party had downed his grizzly, and that there wasn't one of the lot that wouldn't consider 200 yards almost point-blank shooting at almost any kind of game? I couldn't know. But all those devils were sitting around waiting to work me up to a point and so to make a complete fool out of me.

Luke said casually and slowly: "I know a fine hunter down in the Panhandle that used to practice on little birds. Not setting still, but on the wing. He got so that he didn't need no shotgun when he wanted a mess of birds. He just would step out and collect them with his rifle, y'undestand?"

I would have doubted any man in the state of Maine who had said such a thing, but in this new country I was only covered with awe.

"Why," said the storekeeper as quick as a wink, "I don't doubt but the stranger here could do the job pretty good. He has a hunter's real eye."

"I don't know," said Luke, "but I would be willing to bet a dollar against him."

In a minute they seemed to have worked up a bet on my shooting. I said that I didn't feel like trying my hand, because I was out of practice—by that meaning that I hadn't done any shooting for two days, and that was a long dry spell to me in those times when I lived for the sake of my guns. But they wouldn't take no for an answer. They got me out in front of that store. Yonder was a barbed-wire fence, with half a dozen little gray-brown birds hopping on and off again, flitting around very restless.

The storekeeper said: "You count three to let him get ready. Then I'll throw a stone and scare up those birds, and he can have his shot."

They were all so nervous about it that I was afraid not to try the shot, because they seemed to take for granted that a really good rifle shot would be able to do a trick like this. I lay right down on my stomach and steadied that rifle on my hand and prayed that I might have luck. The three was counted, and the stone was thrown.

There were about a dozen of those little birds, and they did what you've likely seen them do yourself. First they dropped off the top wire and seemed to tumble toward the ground. Then they dissolved themselves into beating wings so's you could hardly see their bodies, and they all picked out different points of the compass and scattered toward them.

In shooting ordinary game, a man gets pretty highly strung, but for trick work like this, you have to have your wits working on ball bearings, I can tell you. I tried to get a bead on that flurry of little nothingnesses. I couldn't. Finally, as I saw them skidding away, I was ashamed of myself and just pulled the trigger blindly.

I lowered my rifle with a foolish grin, not even looking. You should have heard them grunt with pure astonishment. One man, who was too far off to think that I would hear him, said: "Dog-gone me if he *didn't* get one of 'em!"

They stared at me good and hard. I suppose that fool grin of mine must have appeared to them as a mere smile of confidence and satisfaction. For they had seen what I had not seen. One of those little idiotic birds had by chance dropped into the path of my bullet!

The storekeeper was very excited. He got a hammer and stake and drove the stake down on the spot where that bird had fallen. Then he started to write on a piece of clean white pine. "Shot by . . . what's your name, stranger?"

"James Lang."

"Shot by James Lang at forty-five paces, on the wing; witnessed by . . . just you write down your names, boys. I don't want to be called a liar when I tell about this later on!"

They all lined up, very serious, and wrote down their names.

Of course, I gathered by this time that they had been only stringing me at the first and trying to make a fool out of me. What chiefly surprised me was the very great seriousness with which they took this shooting as soon as it was actually done. I could see that there was a difference between bullets in Maine and bullets in the Southwest. In Maine, shooting was just a plain sport.

Out here men shot for a business—or else for the sake of their lives. What every one of those fellows had registered inside of his heart when he saw that bird drop was a bit of gratitude to the Lord that *he* hadn't been standing up to me at that time.

I was pretty busy and pretty silent, figuring out all of this. I passed a rag through the barrel of my rifle while I was thinking it over, because there's no time like cleaning a rifle so good as the time before the burned powders has dampened and set on the steel.

"It don't mean much to him," muttered somebody in a corner of the room. "Look how matter-of-fact he takes it. Must be an everyday thing with him."

Of course, I was matter-of-fact and not proud. I was only mighty ashamed of myself that I didn't have the nerve to tell those men that hit was pure accident. But they started right in making so much fuss and trouble about the thing that I hardly *dared* to confess to them—if you can understand what I mean by that.

They took my shame for indifference, and that just rounded off the picture for them. What they thought about me was that I was one of those terrible men that you read about everywhere and actually meet—a couple of times in your life—in the West. I mean, the "dead shot." Mostly dead shots are dead liars and no mistake. Here and there you'll come across the real thing—a man who seems unable to miss, who keeps his talent bright and free from rust with a couple of hours of practice every day of his life.

Wild Bill, of course, was the great example. He was hero and killer. There has never been another like him; there never *will* be another, because the conditions that he lived in will never be duplicated on the face of the globe. There were others almost as great as Wild Bill—men who could whirl on the heel and in evening light, at a hundred yards' distance, kill with a snap shot from a revolver.

Well, when those fellows saw the miraculous shooting of that little bird, they were certain that it was the coming of another of these heroes of the West. They got reverent right away. The storekeeper wanted to know at once would I come home and have supper with him, because he had a couple of old rifles that might interest me, one of them having belonged to Billy the Kid. And a couple of others put in and would be glad to have me along.

Luke Ridgeway, the tall man who looked enough my style to be a cousin, said that he would be glad to have a chance to talk over a little business with me—just the sort of business that a man with my love of hunting would be glad of.

Considering that I had spent my last penny on crackers and cheese, that sounded good to me. It was with Ridgeway that I went down to the hotel, and I sat opposite him at supper.

IV

THE PROPOSITION

I don't remember all that we talked about, except that he asked me a good deal about Maine and the hunting there. The important part of the conversation sticks in my mind rather than the trimmings.

Before supper was over he proposed that I should go up and hold down his shack in the mountains for a while. He himself was leaving, and he would be gone anywhere between three and six months. In the meantime, he had a little shack on a mining claim on the shoulder of a mountain about five days' packing from Elmira, or about three days' ride. He had a couple of horses up there and a cow that was just fresh. Besides, his cabin was fixed up very comfortable, he said, and he didn't want to leave all of these things without a caretaker. Just now he had an old Mexican up there working for him—a Mexican with a halt in one leg, so that he was pretty sure to be honest for the simple reason that he couldn't very well run away with anything that he stole. Luke Ridgeway proposed that I go up there and camp on that claim of his until he came back, because he had business that took him away. He said he might not be back until six months were gone.

I said: "Suppose that you don't show up even at the end of six months or more?"

He thought for a time before answering: "I'll tell you, Lang. If I'm not back within six full months from today, you can take that cabin and everything in it for your own."

He said that in such a serious, thinking way that I could see at once that he really thought there might be a strong chance that he would not be alive at the end of the six months. That, in turn, made *me* do a little pondering. When a man has a comfortable place and a paying little claim, such as Luke said his mine was, why should he go away for anything from a quarter to a half of a year?

There didn't seem to be much sense in that, especially when he seemed to be running the chance of losing his life while he was away. However, stronger than any doubts that might be floating in the back of my mind were two very tempting facts: that this would be a boss way to get acquainted with this new country—and that I was flat broke. Here was the means of accumulating a small stake. He didn't offer much—only twenty dollars a month. But he pointed out that the cabin was fixed up very comfortable, there was fine shooting all around, and nothing to do except to take care of myself, two horses, and a cow. Altogether, I really couldn't have hit upon a better scheme than that, and I asked him how it chanced that he didn't offer a place like that to some one of his old friends.

"Two reasons," said Luke Ridgeway. "One is that most of the boys wouldn't feel right working for as little as twenty a month. And the other is that, when I saw how you handled a rifle, I just naturally wished that you could have a chance of doing some hunting around that cabin of mine." He looked me straight in the face when he said this. But there was a film over his eye, and I knew that he was lying.

Of course, you say that I immediately quit cold on that job the minute I smelled a rat, but I didn't. No, the danger in that job was simply a greater attraction to me, and all the more because I couldn't guess what it might be. I agreed to travel up into the mountains with him to see the cabin. If everything sized up as well as he said that it did, I would be happy to take up his suggestion. He agreed that was only fair, and he said he was so sure I would like the place that he was willing to invest all the time and trouble of journeying clear back into the mountains to that cabin with me, with the chance that when he got me there his work might be all for nothing.

He loaned me two dollars to pay for a bed and my breakfast at the hotel. I promised to start the next morning.

I spent the evening rousing up as much information as I could about Luke Ridgeway. I figured that anything that I could learn would be worthwhile. It wasn't hard to get people to talk. They had heard about my shooting from the store, and they were glad enough to chat with me. A friendly lot you'll find Westerners to be if you get on the right side of them. The stories about silence west of the Mississippi usually mean that the people are shy and inclined to be suspicious of strangers.

What they told me about my friend Luke Ridgeway was that he had been a prospector for the past ten years. For another ten years before that he had been a cowpuncher. Usually he had been working around that part of the country. He was about thirty-six years old. The time that he hadn't spent around there had been put in south of the Río, for he had made several trips to old Mexico.

As for his living, he struck a fair mine now and then. For the past seven or eight months he had been coming to Elmira occasionally with gold that he took out of an old mine up in the mountains. He paid for plenty of provisions, bought himself a horse and the cow of which he had told me, and all around seemed to be prospering very well. It was suspected that he had struck a very well-paying mine, and that the reason he was making a long trip away from the place was that he might want to show ore specimens and so forth back East in order to get the mine financed on a large scale.

All of the talk sounded fairly reasonable. When I tried to get more particulars about the mine, there seemed to be no difficulty in learning even more than I needed to know. In the old days that mine had been worked by the Indians under Spanish supervision. They had done a lot of tunneling and drifting through the rock. For my part I knew nothing about mines or about mining. I gathered that this was a considerable bit of work in the Spanish days.

Usually where the Indians had mined, they had smelled out every bit of pay dirt. Now and then they overlooked something that was quite good, and this appeared to be one of the cases. Luke Ridgeway, prospecting through the mountains, had taken a look at the old mine about eight months before, after he had been away on a three-years' trip to old Mexico. By chance he had blundered on a vein of pay rock. The result was that he had been churning out money ever since.

When I had heard all of these details about Luke, the mine, and the general history that lay behind the man, I decided that perhaps my first suspicions had been all wrong. Before the next day was over I was sure of it.

Luke Ridgeway was as frank and open as any man I had ever known; he was particularly anxious to have me talk about myself, also keen to see some more of my shooting. I wasn't fool enough to commit myself. On the first evening we went out to see what we could see near our little camp—we were simply riding up—I was on one of Ridgeway's horses—with packs behind our saddles. Before we had gone a quarter of a mile from the place where we had left our horses hobbled, a deer flashed out of some shrubbery just in front of us.

It was a nasty shot—not more than twenty-five or thirty yards away, but there was only one flash at that deer as it got from one covert into the next. However, that was just the sort of work that my Maine shooting had equipped me for. These neat little hand-to-hand shots, as you might call them, are just what a man gets a thousand times while still-hunting through close cover. Fast as that deer ran, the butt of my rifle leaped to my shoulder faster, and I got in a shot. It plunged into the cover while Ridgeway was still barely turning around and unlimbering his rifle.

"A fast try, anyway," he said.

"And a dead deer, too," I said.

He gave me a look that was pretty eloquent, but after what he had seen at the store the day before, he wasn't going to commit himself too far in criticism until he made sure that I was not able to live up to what I had said.

We hurried up to the edge of the covert and we saw at once a streak of red across a bush.

"By gad," muttered Ridgeway, and he was really more impressed this time than he had been before. "Accuracy is one thing, but speed is another! However, I don't think you could have more than scratched . . ."

Here we stepped into a little clearing in the bush. On the far side of it the deer lay—dead. The bullet had clipped right through him, from side to side.

Ridgeway was tremendously excited, and he declared that he had never seen such shooting. What he did not know was that my attention had been called to a little streak moving through the covert in the first place, so that I was more than two-thirds prepared for a glimpse of the deer as it came into the narrow gap. Ridgeway didn't know this.

"That's neater work with a rifle than I ever saw with a revolver. Why do you carry a Colt?"

I didn't say anything. It's pleasant to be admired even to excess. However, when we saw another deer in the distance, and Ridgeway started for it, I gave the deer an unnecessary glimpse of myself and scared it away without Ridgeway suspecting me, because that one deer was enough. I didn't want to have to show myself up in his eyes by missing with a long-distance shot. And miss I surely should have done, because I had not yet arranged myself in relation to the crystal-clear atmosphere of that country.

We had venison that night and carried the best of the meat with us the next day.

It was a grand ride. We were climbing all through the three days, but not climbing fast. There was just a pleasant diversity of scenery. I was busy drinking in the colors of those brown mountains and those green-black streaks and patches of evergreens growing on them, and I was getting my eye used to range finding in this new air.

My system was simply to measure the walking step of my horse. When I knew that, I could tell myself the distance to any object ahead of me and then count his steps to the spot. I was wonderfully wrong, at first. I would have undershot everything. But very quickly I began to get it right again. That, and listening to the tales of Ridgeway about mining, and dodging his efforts to get me to shoot at every buzzard that flew into the sky, kept me busy until we were in sight of the cabin.

V

A Perfect Cabin

Well, when I saw that cabin, I knew my new friend was not a liar about the place, whatever might have been back in his head besides. That cabin was placed in the finest spot that I've ever seen. It was one of those places where you say: "Why doesn't somebody build a hotel here and make a resort? It'd be famous quick."

Yet there never are hotels in those places. They have to stay close to the railroads, and the people that plan the railroads have a sort of a natural gift for finding the ugliest ways across the mountains.

You see there was a cracking big mountain ripping away up into the sky. On a shoulder of it, a quarter of the way up, there was a comfortable meadow, with that cabin in it, a flash of water streaking down beside it, and green trees scattered around through all of the hollows of that big mountainside. On the top was a cap of snow, and all around those mountain ranges hit the top of the sky. You could stand there beside that cabin and keep busy for hours, with eyes traveling faster than an arrow goes, but seeing new things all of the time.

When we got to the cabin, I noticed that the shoulder was a fine meadow, covered with extra fine grass. That little creek stretched its elbows in a pool, very fine and comfortable. And there was the cow—no wild longhorn, but a sleek-sided Durham with a creamy look to her eyes.

I couldn't help saying to Ridgeway: "Look here, Ridgeway, why should anybody in the world want to be a king when he might come out here and build this cabin, like this, and have this sort of country to look at?"

He agreed, saying he knew that I would be happy there. When I got inside the cabin, it was so fine that I just laughed and went around looking at everything, enjoying myself as much as though I had made them with my own hands. Because, if I were to be there from three to six months, there was a good *reason* why I should want to see everything.

There were three good rooms in that place. It was a regular house rather than a cabin. It was built of logs that were trimmed down and leveled by hands that knew their work, I can tell you. There were no chinks and holes between the logs; they hadn't picked out a single tree with a knothole drilling through the heart of it. It was built so that you could get clearance if you stood up and stretched your arms above your head. That's plenty high for any room, and low enough to give you warmth in the winter. That cabin sat right down on the ground like it meant to stay there for a while, and you could tell by the solid look of it that it was going to be a long liver.

There was a bedroom fixed up with four bunks. The two upper bunks would fold up against the wall; the two lower ones were all fixed up with springs and mattresses and everything. Should you want more blankets for the winter, why—just open a cupboard at the side of the room, and there you would find a fine stack of them all ready for you.

A good strong table made of planks about three or four inches thick, with a pair of hurdles to hold it up, was in the room—the kind of a table it does a man's heart good to see. There was no fancy varnishing surface that makes you afraid to leave a cigarette, and it would hold all the magazines and the books you might chance to heave at it. If, by chance, you were to lean back in your chair and rest your heels on the edge of the table—well, where would the harm be in that? Take it by and large, that was about as good a table as you would find, and the floor, too, wasn't made to be worried over by womenfolk. It was made of big rough planks as strong as stone, pretty near. Nobody would bother to scrub that floor. Just give it a good sweeping out, and that would be plenty. If you were to drop a cigarette there and step on it to put it out—why, that was all right. If there was no ashtray handy, which there usually isn't, you could just knock the dottle out of the pipe onto the floor. Nobody's heart would break.

It is queer what a relief it is to get into a house where it is plain to be seen that there never was a woman and there never will be. Why, a good Maine woman would have broken her heart, scrubbing in that house. It would have taken her about six weeks to get that place what she would call presentable. And when she got all through, she would have taken all the joy out of that house for any man.

The living room-dining room was a fine place, too. Its fireplace was one of the kind that don't need a lot of chopping and splitting of the wood. You just take a sapling and bust it in two, and then you could be sure that there would be a way of fitting it into that fireplace. The hearth was made of stones a foot or so across, and set in not too particular, not smoothed off too much. It was so big that it would take a man-size spark to jump all the way across it.

When I saw that cabin I said to myself: "Home! This is home!"

When we passed from the dining room to the kitchen, I saw that the man who built that cabin was not only a mighty fine fellow, but a genius, too. The kitchen had everything that a man would ever want—from a big sink where you could wash a bucket to a big chopping block where you could break up a whole deer in no time. The stove must have been packed in all the way from Elmira. Five days of packing—over a trail that no wagon in the world could ever have lived on for five miles together. It had four legs, and the legs had pillars of stone that they were built into. You could reach under that stove and clean there, but you couldn't move that stove. Not unless you wanted to take it apart and put it together again on the spot—which would be something like throwing away a year of your life! It was the sort of a stove that the boys could lean on—where it wasn't too hot. It wouldn't shake and think about falling down. I never *saw* such an oven! You could handle a whole winter's supply of meat in a single sitting, with a stove like that. It had big potholes in the top and two lids all fitted up with inside rings, so that you could put a small pot next to the fire there. The firebox just made me laugh—I was so happy over it. It had a grate that could be raised or lowered. When it was raised, the box wouldn't hold more than a single, good, big armload of wood. That was enough to cook your meal and heat the water, afterward. When you lowered that grate, you could stack in enough wood to bake bread or cook a deer in that enormous oven. Of course, it wasn't economical. But what difference did that make when you had a whole forest at your back door?

I said that there was a boiler. Yes, sir, the genius who built that cabin hitched a pipe and pump that ran down to the pool. It brought the water up to a tank on the side of the hill above the house. And there was a line running from the kitchen door to the windmill that stood by the tank, to pump up the water, so that you could just stand there and turn it off or turn it on. Did you notice that you never remember about the tank running over until you are warm in bed?

That kitchen would have pleased me if it hadn't had a single thing in it except the stove and hot-water boiler. But that wasn't all. I would be almost ashamed to tell you how many pots and pans there were in that house, all good, honest, unbreakable iron. No tin, no brass, no copper, no aluminum—nothing foolish, but just iron that will blacken up and look more natural and comfortable all of the time. Some folks will never be happy until they have glass things for baking. But I say that a pot of baked beans in a glass dish just looks miserable and suffering. Iron is the boss stuff. And that kitchen was full of it.

If you wanted knives, there was a whole rack stuck full of everything from butcher knives to skinning knives. And are the knives dull? There was a fine pair of grindstones in the corner, one rough enough to work on an axe, and one smooth enough for the honing of a razor.

I put that in for the polishing touch. I just want you to understand that cabin was perfect!

VI

A MOAN IN THE NIGHT

When I got through surveying that cabin, I told Ridgeway that it beat anything for comfort that I had ever seen. I added: "If this cabin had a cellar, it would be a regular palace."

Ridgeway laughed and said: "I don't know what you like in the way of cellars, but maybe you would like to see the sort of a dugout that's under this shack?"

He lifted a section of flooring in a corner of the kitchen—a heavy section that hooked onto an iron ring and worked back on hidden hinges, very smooth and heavy, because that flooring was two and a half inches thick. Underneath, there was a flight of steps, and Ridgeway showed the steps to me with a lantern that he carried. We went down into the snuggest little cellar that you ever saw; it was piled around with things that Ridgeway had had packed up from Elmira—all sorts of canned stuff, jars of jelly and jam, together with a regular all-winter supply of ham, bacon, flour, and such things—which interested me a good deal since I had decided that unless I wanted to do a lot of packing to Elmira and back, I would have to live on salt and the meat that I could shoot in the woods.

There was no window in that cellar, and yet the air seemed fresh, and the walls were not damp. I pointed this out to Ridgeway who admitted that it was queer. He simply said: "This is a mighty porous rock that lies under the house. You never can tell how fast winter will sink away through sandstone and gravel."

Then he took me to the mine, asking me if I were interested in mining—in a way as if he wanted me to say no. So I answered that I didn't see why people wasted their lives mucking away underground when they could have mountains like these to look at, and so many tons of game on foot and on wing. That answer seemed to please him a good deal. The mine was very old and big. He showed me some of the old, narrow diggings that the Indians had made. We even found a remnant of one of the baskets in which they had carried ore up the long, long ladders to the mouth of the mine. What leg muscles those Indians must have had, I remember thinking at the time. But hand labor was cheap for the Spaniards in the New World.

He showed me a little drift that he himself had cut off from a shaft near the mouth of the mine and told me that was where he got his gold. I didn't ask any questions, and I didn't look too close, because I could see that the less interest I showed in that section of the mine the better pleased he would be. No wonder! How could a man go off and leave a gold mine for six months in the hands of a stranger whose honesty he didn't know from the honesty of Adam? I supposed that he had showed me the drift he was working at once, because it would keep me from thinking that anything was made a mystery to me; also, it might put me on my honor more, about not working that drift.

To make that point all the stronger, Ridgeway said: "I'll pay you fifty dollars right now. That's full wages for two and a half months. But if you're to run short of provisions, that money would keep you going. And if I'm gone longer than that time, I'll pay you the other part when I come back and find that you've left everything shipshape."

That was evidently his way of saying that, if he came back and found that I had not been messing around with that drift, he would pay me in full. I jotted that idea down in my mind in red writing, as you might say. I didn't intend to raise any blisters on my hands breaking rock for the sake of gold that I might get out of that vein.

What interested me in that mine was just the large size of it and the way they had tunneled here and there. Now and then you would come to a place where a little tunnel you could hardly creep along would open out into a cavern as big as a room, where they had worked out a pocket of pay dirt long ago. Maybe you would find on the floor of that old cave a broken-pointed pick that had been dumped there 400 years ago!

It was a pretty ghostly trip. When we got out of those tunnels into the open air, I reckoned that it would take a month for me to dry the dampness and mold out of my lungs and out of my mind.

Ridgeway could hardly keep from showing how it tickled him when I told him that. I said: "I should think that, if a man ever got into trouble with the law, he could just walk into that mine and disappear, and it would take a thousand men a year to find him there."

Ridgeway gave me a quick side glance—a regular ripper! Then he said: "Now, whatever put that idea into your head? *You're* glad to get out, aren't you?"

I said that I was, and he said that he believed nobody else would like it much better than I did. However, after Ridgeway went off that evening, taking the old Mexican with him, the thing that hung in my mind was the side glance that Ridgeway had shot at me. You'll often do that, you know—just forget all about a man except one expression of his face. If you step back through your list of acquaintances, you'll find that one of them is grinning, the other fellow is laughing, and the old skinny maiden aunt is shaking her gray head and looking sour. Mostly they are in action. Friends, of course, are different, and you'll see them the way that they really are, changing from one thing to another, happy or sad—and you'll see them, somehow, without any face at all, but just as a sort of a feeling, you know.

Well, the way that I saw Luke Ridgeway was with the devil of suspicion flashing in his eyes as he looked aside at me. It made me mighty uncomfortable; it gave my whole memory of him a very ugly cast.

After he was gone, with the humpback old Mexican, Diego Alvarez, riding along beside him— Diego was the fellow who had been temporarily taking care of the cabin—I sat down to have a pipe and a quiet little think all by myself. Ordinarily you can never think so well as you can when you're alone. I sat out in a rough chair—there were a couple of them under the pines behind the house—and tried to work the problem out.

If Ridgeway could trust that Mexican with the shack for a week, he could trust it to him for six months, it seemed to me. What was there that made me so attractive to Luke as a caretaker? Was it my shooting? Could he pretend that he really cared how much sport I had with a rifle on his place?

Very often a man will take a fancy to you and give you his trust. And you will take a fancy to another fellow and give him your trust, just in a flash. But from that side glance of Luke's I knew that he didn't have any fancy for me; he didn't even trust me. He really didn't like me at all, and he didn't want to have me around. Yet there was a reason that made him mighty, mighty glad to have me in the cabin while he was away!

I decided that I would go over the whole matter in detail, bit by bit, and try to make some head out of it, like a detective. But the first thing I knew, the evening came walking over the mountains, very grand, and here I was letting my pipe go out, just sitting there and admiring the world that I'm privileged to be sitting in.

Have you ever used a microscope and slid the wing of a fly under it? All at once what was just a little film of transparent stuff is now a sort of a miracle, with queer tints of red and blue on it, with wonderful veins running through it, all fashioned as if out of a translucent metal in scales—more beautifully than any human hands could ever work it. That is evening on the mountains—just as though they were put under a microscope, all the stupid, brown monotony and the burned look of too many hot days go away from them. They are magnified into a pure greatness and beauty.

I sat out there for more than an hour, feeling better than a king. Those mountains marched up to me in golden fire and rose, and walked away again in purples and amber and sleepy blue under the stars, until I remembered that I was mighty hungry.

There was only a single spark winking among the ashes of the firebox, but when I shaved a stick of wood into feathers and put it in with a bit of kindling heaped on top, the draft in that stove was so fine and strong that I had a ripping fire cracking there in no time. Taking the lantern down into the cellar, I stood there for a while wondering at the sweetness of the air in that place. However, the food stock interested me more than the condition of the air, just then. I got me a tin of coffee, some bacon, flour, jam, and canned apricots. Then I went upstairs and did some cooking.

To have such good things to work with made me happy. I got the fire to roaring and mixed up some pone for the oven. When that was baking, I decided on a stew. Well, before I got through, I had in that stew dried venison, a bit of the pork, canned tomatoes, celery powder, diced potatoes, onions, and a few green peppers—and dog-gone me if I didn't find even some garlic, which is the most boss thing in the world for making a stew—a stew.

Along about half past seven I started that supper,

and about half past nine I started to eat. It was eleven before I had finished my pipe under the stars and gone to bed. I was happy, I can tell you. I was completely happy. That cooking was about the best time that I had ever had that I could remember. Most women should be in heaven, having all the handy tools that they have to make themselves and their kitchens comfortable. But a woman is not that way; she's not meant to be happy, so long as there is a chance for her to be mean and critical and ornery. A woman would scrub her kitchen floor just for the sake of seeing her husband step on it, so that she could rip into him for making a spot.

But there was nothing in the shape of a woman to bother me up here. Not a sound was around, not a breath was stirring—except the wind moaning very faintly farther up the hillside. I listened to it for a while, and then I closed my eyes and was just about sound asleep when a moaning began to come closer to the cabin. It had me out of bed and standing up in my bare feet with a rifle in my hand. There was no wind that ever lived that could have made a moan like that. Only a heart that was suffering could have made it.

I sneaked to the back door to listen. Yes, that noise was right there at the back door, and there was a little scratching sound under the door! I lighted a lantern and looked. Dog-gone me if there wasn't a little streak of crimson leaking in through the crack beneath that door. With my revolver in my hand, I put the lantern where it would throw a shadow on me, then snatched the door open and presented the gun.

There was nothing outside except a wall of

blackness that sort of fell in on me. Down there at my feet lay a dog, flattening his head against the doorstep, battening his ears down, and whacking the floor with his tail to say that he would be an extremely good dog, if I would be nice to him. Well, a dog can take a hop, skip, and jump right into my heart about as quick as anything in the world. This here was just a common brown-and-tan cur dog with no more spirit than a mouse. I could see that with half an eye, but I couldn't leave it out there. The chief reason was that it was so pitiful and down-hearted; the other was that it had a bullet drilled right through both of its hams. It had dragged itself down here to the doorway. Perhaps it had known the old Mexican and that had brought it here for help. Of one thing I was certain: it was not Ridgeway's dog. There is something in the eye of a man that can love a dog. And Ridgeway didn't have that look about his eye.

VII

TROUBLE AHEAD

When I picked the puppy up, I reached my hands around him and hit a tender place. He gave a yell and set his teeth on my arm, but not hard. He began licking my coat right away to ask my pardon and show that he had meant no harm.

I spread him out on the kitchen table, set my teeth, and cleaned those wounds. It was the worst thing I ever had to do in my life, but there is nothing much surer than that a dog will get an infection in a cut if there is half a chance. When you hurt a person, you can explain that it is for his own good—but when it comes to a dog or a horse, you just have to do what you think is good for them and hope that they may come to understand, someday. I took a rifle ramrod, soaked some cloth in iodine, and then tied that pup so it wouldn't wriggle while I put the iodine through and through its wounds. The yelling that dog did would have raised an army, but then it got so weak that it just lay on its back and rolled up its eyes and groaned like a dying man.

No doubt it would have been better if I had babied that dog for a while and given it some strength with a bit of meat—because it was two-thirds starved. But a man usually will grit his teeth and want to get the worst of anything over in one gulp. If a doctor tells you that one pill is good, you have an idea that two will be twice as good. So while I was iodizing that dog, I did a mighty good job of it, I can tell you.

Well, his tongue was hanging out of the side of his mouth before I got through with him. But when I gave him a smell of the remnants of that stew that I had cooked for supper, he came two-thirds of the way back to life at a single step. He lit into that stew as if he were inhaling mist, not eating solid food. So I just gave him a couple of gobbles, and then took him into the bedroom with me. I put a dish of water in there, but he wasn't a bit comfortable on the floor and kept jerking and whining. Finally, after I hadn't closed my eyes all night, I got up, gave him a cursing, and put him on the foot of my bed. That fool pup just stretched out, gave a deep sigh, and the next moment he was sound asleep.

I was between laughing and swearing, I was so mad to think of how I had lost a whole night's sleep. Yet I was so glad to think that the dog had forgiven me for torturing him, and had only gone to sleep when he got in touch with me.

Pretty soon, it was broad daylight. As soon as I got up and left the room, that dog started howling for me. I went back, swore, and shook my fist at him. He just lifted up his head and sort of laughed at me, as much as to say: "There you are! And I'm mighty glad to see you!"

I couldn't be mad at him, after that. I carried him outdoors, and then I brought him into the shack, put him on a bed of sacks, and left him there while I cooked his breakfast and mine. He kept his head up, watching me all the time, almost wagging his tail off when he smelled the good food cooking. But he didn't whine or yip once—except when I stepped out of the room. Then he set up a yell that made the mountains ring! Confound that dog, he had me going. Just in the distance I walked down to the lake for a plunge, and back again. I didn't stay to dry myself at the lake, but ran all the way to the house with the clothes in my hands, freezing in that cold mountain air.

He stopped his yelling, when he saw me, and I couldn't beat him when he began to whine with joy. I saw that dog was simply afraid to be left alone. The world had used him so badly that he had to be with humans or else break his heart, grieving. It made my heart squeeze up as small as a crab apple with pain to see the size and the make of a dog like that, equipped with no more spirit than this! He was a good, roomy-built dog. I suppose he would have weighed seventy-five pounds. He had a fine, long snout, and teeth good enough for a bull terrier. He had the legs and the body of a good running hound. His hair was short, but there was a good, heavy outer layer of bristle, like the coat of an Airedale, that promised to see him through snowy winters. I suppose that at least a dozen bloods were mixed into the last few generations of his ancestry. He wasn't bad-looking—but there was no heart in him at all.

There were two openings for me. One was to kill the dog and bury it. Then I would be free to go off hunting. The other thing was to stay right there at home and live on dried meat and canned food until those shot wounds were cured.

I decided to kill him, of course. And, of course, I didn't. For two mortal weeks I took care of that dog, until the fool could walk around again. Yes, sir, and, at the end of two weeks, I took my rifle and started out to hunt, with that mongrel wagging his tail, hobbling behind me, whining now and then with weakness and with pain.

I couldn't scare him into stopping that whining. He wasn't in the least afraid of me. Not in the least. Because I had never had the heart to strike him, I suppose. And the contrast between me and the other men that he knew was so great that he just took me for a different breed. All the fool would do would be to put up his ears and waggle his tail when I scolded him. I couldn't help loving him for it.

He was never a crowding dog. I mean, he never took advantage of me, but always wanted to be helpful. He picked up what he learned around me by signs and not by lessons. After supper, for instance, he always saw me pull off my heavy, walking boots and put on some soft deerskin moccasins that I had found in the shack. Before he could walk well, he would come hobbling over to me with those slippers in his mouth as soon as he saw me pull off my boots.

He learned to do other handy things. Every

minute that he was awake, he never took his eyes off my face. No, it was simply impossible for me to teach him with a whip. He learned enough things just out of affection.

The first day we went out walking, we found out that the game had come down to the edge of the meadow, because I had done very little shooting during the past two weeks, of course. Even with a lame dog to cripple me, I got a deer. The dog was prouder of that than I was. He walked around that deer, smelled the blood, growled, and sat down and watched every lick I made in cutting it up. You would have thought that he had killed that animal.

After that, the dog and I hunted every day. I have to admit that it was a treat to have him along with me. He shook the cramps out of his weak hind legs. The wounds had cured wonderfully well; very soon he was running as free as if nothing had ever happened to him.

A month after I got the dog, I found out his origin. I was cutting down a tree for firewood, and the dog was scouting around in the distance when I heard a gunshot and a yell from the pup. He came scooting to me and squatted between my feet with his tail between his legs. His hair was bristling along his back. He was growling and whining all in a breath—a picture of the maddest and most frightened dog you ever saw in your life! I just had time to pick up my rifle and drop my axe, when two men came sauntering along through the trees, one of them with a rifle ready.

He sang out: "Stand clear of that fool dog, stranger! Barney, here's your last day on earth, damn your stupid eyes!" He pulled his rifle to his shoulder.

Barney wanted to run, and he wanted it bad. But when he thought of running, he shivered closer against my leg and then looked up to me to know what he ought to do. I told him to cheer up, and then I said to the stranger: "Look here, if this is your dog, and you want to get rid of him, just leave him with me. I don't mind taking care of him."

He was a mean devil, that stranger. A big, ugly-faced brute, the kind of man you could imagine shooting his own dog.

He said: "Maybe that's kind of you. But I don't want anybody's help. I'll handle that dog myself. I paid my money for him, and I'll have the finishing of him. Won't I, Jerry?"

Jerry grinned and said that he supposed Bill would have his own will.

So Bill told me to stand away from that dog because I was apt to get my shins splintered.

It made me mad. I slung my rifle under my arm and looked Bill in the eye. "Bill," I said, "if you want trouble, I don't mind saying that I'll give you a double handful. Now get out of these woods and get quick. You hear me talk?"

He heard me talk well enough. He made a forward step to show that he couldn't be bluffed.

Jerry read me better. He said: "We ain't so much bent on killing that dog that we want to kill a man along with it."

I was really so worked up that I would have shot—and shot to kill—if Bill had given one wobble to the rifle he carried. He looked me over again and decided that it was foolish to make a great matter out of a dog, so he backed up a little and, from the edge of the trees, said: "I'm not through with you. I'll come back for you, and maybe I'll get the dog, and the man, too!" With that he backed up and got away into the trees.

I couldn't resist the temptation, although it was very wrong. I loosed a bullet through the trees. At the sound and the cracking of the slug through the twigs and branches over their heads, that pair of scalawags let out a couple of yells. I could hear them legging it away as fast as they could run.

But Barney—that was the chief joke. He saw his former boss disappear, and he sneaked out a pace or two toward the trees. Then he gave a growl, and, when the two of them ran away, he tore after them as far as the edge of the trees, as though he intended to run them down and eat them up.

When he got in the shade of the trees, he changed his mind and came back to me, wagging his tail and stepping high. Killing deer and running men were a part of his lifework, to see the way that pup acted. I had to lean on my gun and break out laughing, I was so amused. Yet even while I stood there laughing, I knew that I had the chance of big trouble ahead of me. The brute face of Bill and his sneaking partner, Jerry, promised loads of trouble for me, and I guessed that it would be some time before I should be able to sleep solid through the night.

There was never a guess that panned out closer to a true prophecy.

VIII

BARNEY GIVES THE SIGNAL

By this time, I had been over a month in Ridgeway's cabin. I had come to like it better and better, so much that I began to dread the day when I should have to leave the place. Of course, when you begin to worry about leaving, time flies. The month was no more to me than a week, I can tell you, but what convinced me that I had been for a considerable time in the place was my work with the rifle. I had gained the faculty of hitting off distances, long and short range, very well.

I had grown to like the clear air for shooting. The oddest thing was that I could do a good deal better in the early morning before sunup, or in the late evening just before sundown, when the colored light and the land mist gave the air a density something like that of Maine.

Take it all around, it was a grand month I spent—even though I can look back now and see that I was spending it on the brink of a precipice.

When I think back to those days and remember that odd bargain that Ridgeway had made with me, when I recall some of his odd expressions, it seems that I was a complete dunderhead not to have guessed at all sorts of terrible trouble long before it came. Well, looking backward, we can all be good second guessers.

That day of the meeting with Bill the Brute and Jerry the Sneak, I got back to the cabin and took the precaution of cooking my supper before it got dark. I was ready to close up shop before twilight came and made it necessary for me to show a light. You can trust me that I had no desire to light a lamp by which that precious pair of scoundrels could shoot me. Murder was just their level, and the safer the murder, the better.

When I had the work done up—because it's a lot better to get all the dishwashing done in the evening, and have a clean deck for the morning—I went around and locked up. Another good thing about that cabin was that it had extra strong locks on the doors and on the windows—big locks that were sunk deeply in the logs.

I closed the front and back door and locked every window. Then I made a round of every window in the house, trying the locks all over again. When I had done that, I went back to the bedroom, opened the window there, and went to bed, because I guessed that Barney would give me the signal if anyone tried to get into the house from *that* angle.

Lying awake just long enough to smoke my good night pipe, I thought over the killing of a deer that I had nabbed that morning. I had stalked him over a range of hills farther down the valley; when

I got a chance at him, he was lining out and away across a crest. I just managed to try a snap shot and that shot was a 400-yard guess. I had fresh venison that night for supper. It wasn't altogether luck, either, that shot. So I had something worth dreaming about, and, when I went to sleep, I had just about forgotten Mr. Bill and his friend, Jerry.

I had been asleep a good long while—I found that out later—but it seemed to me that I had barely closed my eyes when I felt a cold, wet nose poked into the palm of my hand. I lifted my head to curse Barney, and then I knew by the shuddering of that cold nose that Barney was scared almost to death, so scared that he didn't dare move or yip. When a dog is as frightened as that, it is time for a man to watch his step.

First of all, I slid the revolver from under my pillow and looked toward the window. That window held a mountain's peak and a half a dozen stars like a little painted picture, but there was no sign of a man's head and shoulders there. Then it came over me that somebody might have climbed through the window and might be crawling toward my bunk across the floor.

That was the most cold idea that ever came to me in my life, I think. I could feel Barney shivering and shaking more and more every minute. That didn't help the state of my nerves any. I pushed myself up on one elbow, inch by inch. One board in the bunk was a little loose, and every time that I moved around in the night, it was apt to slip a little and screech like the devil. Well, this night as I started moving, I cursed my foolishness in not having nailed down that board a long time ago.

You know how it is about some things. You always swear that you'll do something, after you get to bed at night, and then you never think about until you're in bed the next time! I prayed that board would make no noise as I sat up in the bunk. Of course, my prayer wasn't granted.

No, the board slipped and gave a groan, just like a man in pain. I freshened my grip on my Colt, and swung myself up to my knees with a jerk, because I knew that this would bring on a crisis of some sort. Nothing rose at me from the shadowy floor of the room, and there was no squeak of a footfall in the doorway. But all at once, Barney let out a cross between a growl and a howl, and started for the door of the room so hard that his claws slipped and scratched on the floor a minute before he could get himself started.

That scared me for Barney. I yelled at him to come back, but right then he was interested in his own ideas a lot more than mine. He headed out through the doorway, into the kitchen, lickety-split. Then I heard a howl from him—sharp and high as a whistle, not the yelp of a dog that gets a kick and runs away, however. It was the yell of a dog that is hurt but hangs on all the harder. I hadn't expected that much spirit from old Barney, of course, and I was proud to hear that sound.

I told myself that I would find the man and the dog fighting in the kitchen, and that I would put an end to him, then and there. When I got to the kitchen, there was no man either lying or standing there. Barney was a dim silhouette, running around the edges of the trap door to the cellar and whining.

What could have been better than that? I could tell in an instant that I had something trapped down there. Of course, I remembered that cellar was dug out of the solid rock and that there was not a sign of any opening to it except through that same trapdoor. What I earnestly hoped was that Jerry and Bill might both be in that cellar. At any rate, I decided that I would camp in the kitchen the rest of the night.

I put a blind across the kitchen window, so that if one of the pair happened to be on the outside of the house, he couldn't pot me as I lighted the lantern. Then I made myself a light and put a rifle handy, although inside a house there is nothing to beat a Colt that shoots .45-caliber slugs. It knocks you down even if you're not killed instantly. After I had a light, I caught the ring of that cellar door and lifted it just a fraction of an inch, calling down through the cracks: "Bill and Jerry, or whichever one of you may be in the cellar, I want to warn you right now that there is no way out of that place except through this trap door! Now, partners, you can stay in that cellar until you die for the lack of water. Or else you can come up and give yourselves up. If you give yourselves up, just throw your guns up through the trap, here, and then come up, one at a time, and I'll promise that I won't knock you in the head. Does that sound good to you?"

There was no answer out of the cellar, and I sat down to wait for a while, for I figured that they would feel around and light matches until they had convinced themselves that I was right.

Well, I sat there until the morning light began.

Still there was no voice up from the cellar, although I opened the trap door twice and urged them not to make things worse for themselves by trying to hold out on me.

After morning came, I opened up the house. The fresh dawn light made me feel a good deal more at ease and more rested. While I was out of the kitchen, Barney didn't leave the trap door for an instant. He sat there, just whining with eagerness. There was only one wonderful thing about that to me—which was that Barney should have shaken off so much fear of his old boss between the afternoon and the night. Barney was so smart that I decided that just one sight of his former master streaking it away on the run must have decided him that the man was a bluff—and so he was.

Well, when I began to feel better, I decided that the best way to wear out the nerves and the patience of any prisoners would be to let them hear me cooking breakfast. With a great rattling I started a fire, singing and carrying on in great style. There wasn't a peep from the cellar. Then I remembered that there was a lot of canned fruit down there that would give them drink enough to last them for a long time—and enough other kinds of food to carry them along for a year. How could I keep those prisoners down there for any length of time?

This was a new angle on the deal and brought a chill down my spine. I decided that I would have to have it out with them in a little confab, then and there. I propped up the trap door with the bottom of a chair, and I called out to them down there—but that instant Barney squeezed through the gap and plunged down the stairs into the terrible blackness of the cellar!

I gave him up for a dead dog that instant. Then I heard him raving and yelling again. There was only one way to interpret that—my men had got away!

However, a man can't stand by and abandon his dog, even if there *is* danger. So I took my courage in my teeth, so to speak and, throwing open that trapdoor, went down, lantern in hand.

The minute that I stood in the cellar room I saw that it was empty of men. There was just the food supply ranged around on the shelves, or boxed up and lying on that wonderful dry cellar floor. Yes, sir, the two men were gone—if there had been two—and here was Barney, like a little fool, scratching away at an edge of the wall.

Most of that cellar was finished off smoothly, but there was one spot where you could see that the tools of the workers had failed them—or their patience had given out—apparently because the hardness of the rock was much greater at this point.

At this point, the wall projected into the cellar a little, presenting a side like that of a vast, rudely made boulder. *This* was the point where that foolish dog was scratching like a mad thing.

"You little idiot," I said to Barney. "Are you going to tear up a million tons of solid granite to get at them?" Then I had to sit down and hold my head in my hands.

Where *had* my quarry gone? Certainly, if there is any truth in a dog's nose, Barney had heard those men, or that man, retreating in my house after I sat up in my bunk and made the noise. The sound of the retreat had encouraged Barney to trail them into the kitchen. They must have disappeared down the trap—and thence into the cellar. But how could they have faded through the cellar wall? Then I remembered something that had been told to me beside some campfire, about the keen senses some dogs have for spirits. It is said that a dog can tell when a ghost walks near. . . .

When that idea came to me, I stared at the boulder where Barney was still scratching and whining and sniffing with a new feeling. That Barney would have persuaded any man to do something. He ran to me from the place where he was scratching and wearing out his nails on the hard rock. He caught me by the trouser leg.

"All right, Barney," I said. "I'll show you what an awful fool you are."

I went up and got a pick and came back. While I was gone, Barney went almost mad, but, to my astonishment, he would not leave the cellar.

I got the pick ready, gave it a swing, and whanged away at the spot where Barney was scratching. The pick simply rebounded from the terribly hard face of stone.

"You see?" I cried to Barney.

He merely looked up at me and wagged his tail in great pleasure at the thing I had done. He sniffed the spot where I had struck and stood back, looking so expectant that I could not help breaking into a laugh. Neither could I help striking another half-hearted blow. And that light swing of the pick sank to the wood in the solid stone.

IX

More Surprises

Those of you who have done any boxing know how it feels when, after milling around with the other fellow for a long time, you manage to clip your knuckles against the point of his jaw in just that magic place known as the button. Suddenly the big, strong fellow turns limp, staggering before your eyes. Perhaps he falls flat on his face. Not because you have struck him with any very great force, but because you have nicked him on the right spot. It's a queer experience, but it could never stack up with what I felt when I drove that pick home. I knew at once that something was wrong. I had jammed that pick into a hollow in the rock—not forcing it through the solid stone at all. So I heaved at the haft of the pick, and presently I could feel the point wobbling around on the inside of the big stone. I got very excited at this. I jerked harder than before—and suddenly I saw the whole great boulder in front of me quiver and stir.

I leaped for the stairs and ran halfway up to the kitchen level before my pulse rate began to sink toward normal. I had an idea that I had been prying at some vital spot in the foundations, and that I was on the verge of drawing the whole wall down on top of me. But another idea had come to me, a storybook idea. I went back to that boulder, where Barney was still whining and scratching, and I began to work at it and feel it all over. Finally the whole mass gave and turned a little to one side. There was a little click—and now I knew that this was a part of a complicated blind. The side twist of that heavy mass was simply the first part of the necessary combination for opening it. I pressed in with all my might, but the wall was firm. I tugged toward me—and the wall lunged into my face and knocked me down.

So exquisitely balanced was that mass of hundreds of pounds that a child could have swung it back and forth, and revealed what I saw before me as I sat up from the ground again—the long, slanting mouth of a tunnel sinking rapidly down into the earth. I held the lantern before this gap, half expecting to have a shot fired at it from the depth of the hiding place. But there was no sound of a gun. It occurred to me that it was very queer that Jerry and Bill should have known all the intimate secrets of a place like this. If they knew how to escape through this tunnel, they had doubtless entered by the same place. Long hours ago they had gone away and were now, no doubt, discussing methods of doing for me in a new attempt.

I had enough for the time being. Going back to the kitchen in time to save my bacon from burning, I ate a breakfast that had the chief emphasis laid upon coffee—extra black and lots of it. When I had downed the third cup, my spirits were rising again.

I went back to the cellar and started down that tunnel. I had a lantern on which I had arranged a hood. It enabled me to throw just a single ray of light before me, from time to time, to show me the way. And I had a thick piece of cloth wrapped around each shoe to prevent any noise underfoot.

That tunnel had not gone far—always sinking rapidly toward the bottom of the earth—before I began to realize that there was a good deal of similarity between its dimensions and those of the cuts and tunnels that I had seen in the old mine that Ridgeway had introduced me to. I wasn't sure until I came to a great cross-cut. Two separate drifts joined the one in which I was, and, where they focused on mine, there had apparently been a great chamber store with rich ore. At least 20,000 cubic feet of rock had been removed from this single point! Unquestionably this was a section of the mine. I could realize the true vastness of the work that the Spaniards had extorted from the Indians in the old centuries. I also realized that it was madness for me to attempt to follow the trail down this drift. I might simply lose myself in a maze of the underground works, or perhaps walk right into the muzzles of the guns of Jerry and his friend, Bill. So I went back.

Even Barney, who had been sneaking along ahead of me in a most tigerish fashion up to now, seemed to lose all of his interest in the affair as he came into the big chamber where the great pocket of ore had once been removed. He lay down at my feet and remained panting there until I started back, when he readily walked on ahead of me.

I got to the cellar and closed the rock door, securing it by giving it a strong wrenching twist to the side. Then I went back to my rustic chair under the pines to enjoy a doze in the morning warmth of the sun with the sweetness of that purified air around me. Nothing could warm a corner of my heart, and the foul dampness of the great tunnels remained in my soul, as it were, for long hours. I thought again of the deadly side glance that I had received from the eyes of Ridgeway. How could Ridgeway have known and planned upon my meeting with big Bill and his sneaking companion? Finally I decided that I must go for help. Yet how could I go without most signally betraying the trust that Ridgeway had placed in me?

Finally I was very set on remaining in the cabin—no matter what happened, or how many Bills and Jerrys were in hiding for my scalp. If they came and found the shack deserted, they would be pretty sure to pay their attentions to me by stealing whatever they could remove and putting a match to the rest of it. That shack had a personality for me. I would have cared a great deal more about the destruction of that house than the death of almost any man I knew about.

I got some of the bad taste of that affair out of my mouth with a ripping good lunch that I turned in and cooked, very soon—a lunch so good that I thought that the smell of the stew cooking must have been strong enough to draw the sneaks up out of their hiding places even if they were plotting my death at that instant.

Barney was sleepy after that. I opened the trap-door, but he merely yawned at it. That made my own nerves a good deal more steady. I took a nap myself. Then we got up and started on a short hunt. I never had to hunt far, if it were merely veni-son that I wanted. Although I wasn't in any need of venison, having killed only the morning before, still, who could resist the temptation of walking out with a gun in a country like that?

However, the only deer that I beat up was a huge stag that started in the wrong direction when it winded me and came crashing straight to-ward me. When it was three steps away, it saw me with my rifle at my shoulder. It stopped so fast that it almost shook its hide off over its head. Well, I followed that fool stag for a long distance with my rifle, and I didn't fire—I hardly know why, ex-cept that the fear in the face of that poor, scared thing was most awfully like fear in the face of a man. Anyway, I let it go. As a sort of a reward for holding off, you might say, I had a shot at a coyote not ten minutes later.

It's my opinion that the coyote is the wisest thing that lives on four feet. I'm pretty sure that in a country where there is a good deal of shooting done, the coyotes will soon learn to recognize the scent of a gun and the hunter, and follow them for what they may leave behind. Why not? I have seen so many men cut a few steaks out of a deer's car-cass and let the rest go to feed the first thing that comes along.

At any rate, I felt eyes behind me, and, turning sharply around, I got a hard shot at a little gray streak. It hadn't expected me to turn like that, and it jumped sidewise into a bush. But I had it fairly in my sights, and, when it dropped in the bush, it wasn't interested in getting up again. That was a strange rifle shot. When I examined the body, I found that the bullet had cut through its whole body, and come out through the left hip. It didn't leave a large hole where it came out, and that meant that it had remained without spreading, no matter how many bones it had bitten through on its journey. It was a bad pelt, a good deal of the hair off and in a half-mangy condition, so I let the body lie as it was and started rounding back toward the cabin, because I began to feel guilty after even such a short absence as this.

I came back past the mine and looked in at the mouth of it as I went. The shadowy heart of it had a different meaning for me than it had had the day that Luke Ridgeway showed me through the place as far as I wanted to go. I had just stepped back out of the entrance gap in the hillside, and I was taking notice how the mounds of rock—the result of the digging in the mine—that lay around me had been silted over by several centuries of mountain winds, crumbled by the snows and the suns of hundreds of fiercely alternating seasons. Now a skin of soil had gathered, and in this soil the grass had taken root. Here and there, some big boulder thrust its gray knees out into the light of day and would continue to do so for another million years, no matter how thick the dust blew that way in summer.

It does a man good to take note of things like this. The reason is, I suppose, that it makes dying an easier thing by a whole lot. We push our heads above the soil and grow a while, and turn to seed, and drop back into the ground—well, there's nothing so terrible about that. I don't need to be told stories about complicated heavens in order to make me look at death with my eyes opened.

I was still wandering about like that; Barney was chewing a branch of a dead bush that he had taken a fancy to, when all at once he dropped flat on the ground. It didn't take me long to think matters over. I was sort of absent-minded, just then, and that's the best condition to be in to take suggestions quickly, and at the same time take them hard.

I dropped, too, hitting the ground as flat as Barney was himself. Oh, bless that dog and his bad nerves! If he had been a brave pup, he would have stood up and growled. Then the bright idea of dropping for that ground would never had occurred to me. I would have stood up. At the best I would have been able to turn around and get a rifle bullet through my breast, instead of through my back. Yes, sir, for the trigger finger of that murderer was already crooked around the trigger of that gun so hard that he turned the bullet loose even while I was dropping. I heard it bite past me with a whiz. Looking to the side, I saw a man jump behind a tree.

You might say that I *expected* a man.

What beat me was that it was not Bill or his pal, Jerry, that I saw, but an olive-skinned Mexican.

X

A Discovery

You have to remember that my rifle was a single-shot affair. I couldn't waste the bullets trying to scare the Mexican from behind the tree where he was taking shelter at that moment. I dropped that rifle and jerked out a Colt. There I lay on my belly, only wiggling around until I was facing the tree behind which the man had dodged. I might have spent an hour there, waiting for a chance at his brown face.

Here the dog began to show signs of life. He started out and wriggled forward on his belly, very scared, as I could see from the way that he was shaking and hugging the ground, but determined to have a look at the man behind the tree. I had to laugh at that dog, and yet I had to admire him, too. It was what you would have called in a man a fine exhibition of moral courage, because Barney was making himself do things that he didn't want to do, at all. He got around beside the tree, and then it was a grand joke to see him sneak along by inches, sticking his head out and then jerking it back again, as if he were afraid of what he expected to see there. Poor Barney! Well, he finally jumped around that tree—and there was no Mexican bad language in answer. So I jumped up and hurriedly ran in.

The ground shelved down sharply on the far side of that tree. All that the Mexican had had to do was to get down low, on hands and knees, and crawl away. It was only wonderful to me that he hadn't gone to take up a new position among the trees and there pot away at me as snugly as you please. However, he had simply made his getaway. That was a little odd, considering the murderous, cunning look on his face.

I leaned against that tree, feeling weak and sagging at the knees. Yonder was Barney, as busy as a bee, running this way and that, wagging his tail, his nose working down on the ground. No matter how afraid I was of what might be waiting for me yonder among the trees, I had to go ahead. As long as that frightened dog would run the trail, I had to run it behind him.

He worked straight ahead among the trees, keeping pretty much in a straight line and working along fairly fast, while I began to admire his intelligence and surmise that there must be foxhound blood in him.

Just then I passed a bit of soft loam. There I found the footmarks of a man walking straight back along the line that Barney was following. Yes, sir, that idiot dog was running the back trail and not the forward trail at all.

It was too late to start over again, even if he had

sense enough to try the forward trail. So I let him work away. After all, it was almost as worthwhile to discover the back trail of this would-be murderer, as it was to learn where he had taken himself after missing his shot—through no fault of his own.

We worked steadily through the woods, across a clearing and another stretch of forest, and then came whang straight upon the mouth of the mine, but not into it.

Barney stood there on the edge of the shadow, wagging his tail, as much as to say that he would be glad to go on in—if only I would encourage him a little. *I* needed encouragement to go into a place like that. If the Mexican had come out from the mine, he might very well have gone back into it by a circuitous way around. If he went back there now, it would be a sure way of committing suicide to follow that trail down into the darkness.

I was pretty curious, naturally. Finally I went to the shack, got a lantern, and lighted it. Then I hooded that lantern as well as I could and started back. Barney, for the first time, had failed to keep right at my heels. There must have been some bloodhound in his veins. At any rate, he certainly loved a man trail. I found him sitting down halfway between the house and the mouth of the mine.

He was extremely glad to see me, and we went back to that well mouth of watery blackness. I treated myself to a good, long look at the sunshine world around me. I remember particularly taking notice of a silly blue jay, flashing and floating above the tips of the pine trees and scolding some squirrel at a great rate. A mighty peaceful and bright world for a man to leave, of course. Finally

I turned my back on it and forced my steps into the mine.

Using the lantern only once in a while to keep track of where I was going, I pulled aside the hood just enough to loose a single shaft of light. One wink of the light was all that I allowed myself at a time. My head was getting a good bumping on the tops of the tunnels along which we were walking or crawling, for Barney was working at a brisk rate. The ground was damp there in the mine, which made the scent hold clearer. He kept right along, never more than ten steps ahead of me, however. There was not *that* much recklessness in my dog.

Once, I heard the rattle of a rock behind me. It was not imagination; it was exactly the sort of a noise made when a stone stirs under the tread of a man—a grinding, rattling noise all in one, if you can understand what I mean by that. It scared me almost to death. I dropped on my knees and put my shoulders against the damp wall of the drift. Then I called to Barney in a whisper. He didn't need to be called twice. That infernal coward of a dog crouched between my knees, trembling and crowding back against me. Confound a dog like that! A man expects his dog to learn politeness from him, but he reasonably can expect to learn courage from his dog. Any mongrel ought to be foolishly reckless, except when he hears his master's voice. Barney let me keep up heart for both himself and me, which was very hard work.

We waited there for a long time. Just as my nerves began to settle down, and I had decided that there was nothing in the mine, after all, that the noise had been made by a fall of loose rock, Barney would give a start and set my nerves jumping.

Maybe we were there ten or twenty minutes, although it seemed ten times that long before I set my teeth and stood up to get back out of that mine. When I stood up, Barney seemed to think that I meant to go on with the exploration. He started again on that back trail, and shame made me follow him, instead of turning back.

We came presently down to a sharp angling turn of the passage, against the wall of which I thumped myself pretty hard. Then Barney disappeared! I loosed a shaft from the lantern, and I whispered—but Barney was gone. I thought how many stories there are of sudden pits in the middle of a mine—down the abandoned shafts of which a man may drop a hundred feet or more to his death. Perhaps that dog was gone, without a sound.

Then I heard a faint sound just above me as I thought—a sound like a man's breath, suddenly taken as he is about to make a violent effort. I crouched and looked up, raising an arm to shield myself. Then I heard that sound again, but this time, to my great relief, I realized it was the snuff of a scenting dog. I flashed a ray from the lantern, and it struck on the opening where a raise had been sunk in the top of that drift along which we had been working. I climbed up on it, the lantern in one hand and a Colt in the other. The first flare of the lantern light showed me the silhouette of Barney working around on the floor of a little chamber just big enough for a man to work in, keeping on his knees. It showed me the chamber, and a rusty pick on the floor of it, and along the side a streak several inches wide that glittered with a regular embroidery of golden thread.

I know nothing of mining, mining methods or ore, but any child could have told in one glance that this was an enormously rich vein. I knew nothing of the way that veins may pinch out of gold pockets. It seemed to me that the vein there must represent another regular Comstock Lode. I crawled up and unhooded the lantern. Then I sank that pick into the vein and broke off a little chunk of rock. It fairly flamed in my hand, it was so interlarded with the precious stuff. It seemed to me heavier than any rock that I had ever weighed, although perhaps that was just the excitement of the moment. A fever came up in me to tear away at that vein then and there, to pick loose all that I could carry away with me. Afterward, I had a moment of saneness in which I sat down and held Barney by the nape of the neck to keep him from making any noise and disturbing me.

Of course, this was the vein that Luke Ridgeway was working in the mine, and not the sham place that he had showed to me. This was his hidden place that kept him up there among the mountains—not the freedom or the hunting, no matter what he pretended. This was the stuff that he ground up in his little hand mill. No wonder he had been taking out enough to keep himself going. In fact, if he did not have thousands of dollars' worth of that metal hoarded away somewhere near the cabin, I would be very much surprised.

Then there was another difficulty thrown in my way. When he had a treasure like this in his hands, why would he leave the mine and go away? To be sure, he had made certain that I was a greenhorn from a part of the country where gold mining had never been seen; so his secret was fairly safe with me. Yet men do not leave such a thing as that gold vein, unless they have desperate reasons, very desperate—life-and-death reasons.

Another thing popped into my mind, then, with a shock that stunned me. Barney had followed the back trail of the Mexican to this place. That meant that Ridgeway was not the only person who knew about the mine. The Mexican knew, also. That was why he was taking pot shots at me from behind trees. He thought that *I* knew, too. He wanted to remove me from the scene before he went ahead with his operations and began to clean out that vein. That made the whole thing fairly clear to me. Only two points remained to puzzle me. One was that the Mexican had not been able to locate this far-hidden pocket in the old mine, unless he had previous knowledge of it. The other point was that I should have had the coincidence to fall into trouble with the Mexican and Bill and Jerry—one on the heels of the other.

I had the gold fever, sure enough. But I had the will to live just a little bit longer, still. So I pocketed that specimen, and I started back out of that mine, with Barney showing me the way like a regular partner. As I got to the good, honest sunshine again, I didn't pause, I made a way back among the trees and, watching every step of the way, I cut back toward the cabin.

XI

DANGER

The whole place was terribly changed for me. Before, there had been nothing but a lazy good time and general fun, hunting, cooking, and pleasing nobody but myself. When I sneaked back toward the shack on this day, I knew that I would have to live like a condemned criminal until I had settled the Mexican, or until he had settled me. There would be no more easy excursions along through the hills.

Only one thing helped me—Barney. He had been a scared dog all his life, and he had formed the habit of keeping his eyes open and looking around to see what was what. That would help me now. Every third glance I sent at Barney to see what he was doing in the way of registering fear. From that minute on, I was mighty glad that dog was a real coward, afraid of everything in the world except me.

When I got to the shack, I sent Barney in first. He nosed around and looked things over. He came back to me and wagged his tail, showing me that there was no danger in the shack. I thanked God for that dog, again. Then I went in to look things over—not things in the shack, but what I was to do to meet this double danger—on the one hand from Jerry and Bill, on the other hand from the greater danger—that Mexican.

The latter was the main trouble. I had bluffed Jerry and Bill away once, and I might be able to bluff them away again. The face of that Mexican was plain bad and mean and dangerous. He was a mighty nasty fellow. A child could have told that in any language. His little, bright, black eyes with the yellow showing where the white should have been, and his broad, Indian-like features, made me know that he would hunt me down exactly as a Indian might have hunted down an enemy in the old days out in this same country.

Altogether, it was a pretty nasty fix.

I thought of one chance that might be a solution, right away—which was to go back to the mine immediately and find the pocket, and stay there beside the gold, knowing pretty well that, if the Mexican had been there once, he would surely come there again. Perhaps that was the best and the quickest way out of the tangle, and I'm ashamed to say that the reason I didn't take that solution was because I simply didn't have the nerve to go back and wait in the horrible darkness of the mine—maybe for many hours—listening to whispering noises in the distance. No, I didn't have the courage for that. I was never any desperado. There was never a time in my life when I would go hunting for trouble. This was infinitely worse than anything I had ever dreamed of being mixed up with.

I sat in the middle of the kitchen, staring blankly out the window where the clouds were chasing themselves across the sky—all except one little silver bit of cloud—no, that was the moon, just a half moon hanging very dimly in the pallor of that sunflooded western sky. Then I remembered that this would be a moonlit night. That gave me an idea that was just the second cousin to the thought of staying in the mine and waiting for the Mexican. I won't tell you how the idea first came to me, after I noticed that bit of a moon in the sunlit sky. I won't tell you what hours I spent during the rest of the day, sitting there shuddering, telling myself one moment that I would do it, and then telling myself again that it would be too grisly a job.

When the dusk began to grow, I swore that it was better to face the danger, if I could, than to go on living here under the very nose of it. Time and suspense were like a knife-edge, and me standing on the sharpest part of the edge.

In the first dimness after sunset, I built up the kitchen fire, putting in a good load of wood, mostly new-cut, unseasoned, half-green wood that would take a long time in burning. When that firebox was jammed to the top with fuel and the dampers turned down in a certain way, that fire would burn for hours. Then, on the back of the stove, where just enough heat would come to make the pot simmer, I put on a great iron kettle filled with beans, and I dropped in a chunk of salt pork to make the fragrance of that pot seem more natural and homelike.

I put on the teakettle, too, in a place where it would steam, and yet not burn out dry. Then I laid the table with an iron plate, a knife and fork, set out a chunk of bread and a pitcher of cream that I had skimmed on purpose out in the cooling house. I set out a cup and saucer, and I put out a slab of butter. There was a can of jam and a lot of other things, like bottled ketchup, that would make a mountain man, used to pone and bacon and not much else, almost die of joy at the thought of eating them. After that, I pushed the coffee pot onto the back of the stove, where it would steam just enough to keep that house smelling like a restaurant.

When these things were finished off, I went around and closed up the shack good and tight. Except that in the bedroom I left the shutters a little bit open, so that a man could squint in and survey the whole room. In the kitchen I left the western window just a bit open so that the western wind, which was blowing pretty steady after sunset time, would wag the curtain back and forth and give a man a chance to look things over inside.

There was the shack looking as though it were all prepared for the night with an enemy to take thought of on the outside. The two loopholes were arranged so that, if a man glimpsed in through those places, he would see that two of the rooms were empty—everything all set out and a meal steaming hot on the stove. It would look as though I had just stepped into the living room and might be back any minute. A man might wait right there at the kitchen window—or at the bedroom shutter—with his rifle ready.

When these things were all ready, I opened the trap and went down into the cellar with the dog and the lantern. With that hooded lantern, after I had opened the mouth of the tunnel, I started off down it.

It was a damp, miserable job. For one thing, I had a pretty good chance of getting lost in that mine. Because I didn't want to starve to death, I had put some dry bread in my pockets. But I had no water—and if the oil burned out in the lantern before I had found my way out. . . . Well, it made me feel like the first day of school when I thought of that—sick and empty in the pit of the stomach, I mean. But I was too desperate to stop. That murdering face of the Mexican was worse than a living nightmare, and I wanted to get him bad.

I plugged ahead. When I came to the big cross drifts, I stopped for a while, pretty much tempted to turn back. At last I was able to force my way on through it. I took the right-hand drift and plugged away. For a long time we kept going down. Then I came to a place where the timbers had broken— from rotting away in that underground dampness, I suppose. The passage was completely jammed before me. I went back and took the left-hand turn. Now I walked for more than an hour, winding up and down, back and forth, crawling more than I walked. When I did walk I had to bend over. I made up my mind that night that the life of a miner must be worse than any other life a man can lead.

Only by chance I came out right in the end. I took a right-hand instead of a left-hand turn. In another five minutes I saw the broad, white face of the moon hanging before me in the black of the tunnel. When I came out from the mouth of the cave and into the sweet, open air of the night, Barney was glad of it, too. He did a sort of war dance. But he was a pretty silent dog—except when he was left alone—and I was never gladder of his silence than I was on this night.

After that, I cut away through the trees, determined to keep to cover all the way to the shack, if I could, because that moon shining through the thin mountain air was almost as bright as the sun. I put out the lantern and went along pretty slowly, because I did not want to make any great noise.

I hadn't gone a quarter of a mile from the mine when I saw a little red eye watching me from the ground a short distance away. Then I got the smell of wood smoke—just a thin drift of it. That gave me a new idea—to sneak up and find the Mexican, perhaps at his own campfire.

I slipped along, therefore, as quiet as you please. It must have taken me half an hour to cover the distance between the spot where I had seen that campfire for the first time, and the place itself. It was under a great tree that I could see clearly from the top of the cabin. I can remember that big tree perfectly because of its queer, lopsided outline. I had paced it off twice. It was just six hundred and twenty yards from the cabin—what you might call a good healthy long-range shot from *any* man's rifle.

When I came closer to the little red eye of the fire, I saw that it was a final ember of a fire that had been put out—or all out except this spark of life. About the time that I discovered this, something jumped up and went scuttering and scampering away through the brush—something no bigger than a weasel. Its presence there told me that the man who had built that fire couldn't be anywhere near. I lighted the lantern and looked over the spot. It was easy to see why an enemy of mine would select this spot. I have said that I could see the top of this tree from the roof of the cabin. A man who climbed to the very top of this monster could see the cabin almost to the ground.

Whoever my friend was, he had probably cooked a meal here as soon as the light of the day was dim enough to keep the fire smoke from showing where he was. This one spark had escaped, and I put my heel on it.

By the spot I found the heads and skins of two little squirrels. One thing interested me a lot more than anything else about that spot—both of those squirrels had been shot very neatly, and right through the head. I have done my share of good shooting, as I have said before, and I have seen others do their share. Men who bag tree squirrels with bullets placed as accurately as that are not grown on every bush. It made me turn cold and then boiling hot—to think of this cool devil squatting out here under his look-out tree and cooking his squirrels, as he made ready to go in and do to me what he had already done to the squirrels.

XII

TREASON

I headed back for the cabin at a faster rate of speed, for I felt strangely sure that I had bagged my bird, at last. I would almost have sworn that I would find the broad-faced Mexican waiting outside the cabin. So I was fairly reckless and paid no attention to danger on any hand. Going straight on until I saw a light from the lantern in my kitchen shining through the western window, I stepped into clear view of the house, my rifle in my hand. I was fairly sick, because I had no lurking silhouette of a man there before me. Instantly I suspected that my elaborate trap had failed completely.

I turned Barney loose ahead of me, and, when I waved him along, he cantered up to the back door and stood there, wagging his tail and sniffing. I didn't need any more complicated message to assure me that the cabin was empty. If there had been the scent of a stranger in the place, Barney would have scooted back to me with his tail between his legs.

Hardly caring what happened, I tramped on, while a dozen shots could have been taken at me from any of the neighboring trees. I got to the cabin and threw the door open. There I found the place was empty, indeed—a good deal emptier than I had guessed. On the table there was only a scrap left of my loaf of bread; the bean pot had been heavily called upon; the can of jam was entirely empty!

Oh, I had had a visitor, well enough. The trouble was that I had stayed away too long. If I had been half an hour—or even ten minutes earlier—I might have nabbed him. Now all that I had of him was a scrap of paper, one edge of which was secured by the weight of a plate. On the paper there was scrawled in large letters only two words:

Gracias.
Mañana.

Or, translating them: Thank you. Tomorrow. Well, I could translate them a little more freely than that and get out of them a meaning with a great deal more vigor in it. "Thank you for the meal. Tomorrow I will call again, or shortly after tomorrow, and then I'll finish you off."

Now that I had a relic of this enemy of mine to study, I sat down and pored over it—after I had closed the shutters and made the house impervious to the eye of a spy. I decided that the hand that had scrawled out those letters so swiftly and fluently must be the hand of a fairly well-educated man. Most Mexicans do not waste their time on good writing and reading. If they can scratch a signature, that is culture enough for one short life. This fellow wrote easily. What was still more important—he wrote with a pen. Now, since there was no ink in the cabin, he must have carried his ink with him. I knew that a fountain pen among Mexicans was about as much to be expected as an aureole on the head of a Wall Street banker. Here was an educated Mexican, then, who shot squirrels through the head when he went about to collect his supper, and who was now bent on putting a slug of lead through my head so that he could enjoy the profit of that little vein of gold ore without any hampering from my hands.

It increased my worry a great deal. You expect that a fellow without any foolishness may be clever and cunning, but you don't expect him to have the patience of a thinking man, and you don't expect him to work out matters so carefully. He makes more mistakes in big things, but fewer in little ones. I felt that I was up against a stronger man than myself, to say nothing of whatever danger there might be from Jerry and Bill in the background of this affair.

Altogether, that was a miserable night that I spent in the cabin. I was glad when the dawn came. It didn't make me get up. It simply gave me enough feeling of safety to make me fall into a short, deep sleep.

I was up, however, not more than an hour after the sun had showed his face. I started my fire for breakfast, and then it occurred to me that I would like to have a look at that tall tree at the foot of which the stranger had eaten his supper. I took my rifle out and around the house, therefore. When I was on the farther side—away from the big tree—I climbed up the wall, which the bigness of the curve of the logs made an easy thing. I managed from the roof to see that tree very distinctly, just as you see a tall man standing head and shoulders above a crowd.

When I squinted down the barrel of my rifle, the first thing of importance that I saw there was the dimly silhouetted figure of a man in the branches. It gave me a shock. There was my quarry—and I knew that tree stood 620 yards from the house—too far for him to expect trouble from me, surely. You have no idea how small the body of a man appears when it is 600 yards away. I got my bead automatically at 600 yards. Just as I was raising the gun a hairbreadth to make an allowance for the extra twenty yards—aye, or half a hairbreadth—the bad luck of the man in the tree made him start to climb down. In doing that, he came out from the partial screening of the branches, and, as he stood on a branch, the morning sun shone full against him.

Having lived by day and dreamed by night of marksmanship, it did not take me long to get my bead and touch that trigger. The next instant, the spot where he had stood on the branch was empty.

He might have jumped down from that place, or he might have been knocked down, but there is a queer instinct that always tells a hunter whether or not he has hit the target. That instinct told me that I had made a bull's-eye, and no mistake.

I was off the roof of that house as though the ground were water, or else as though I had wings.

Then I streaked it through that forest with Barney running at my heels—as though he understood perfectly that this time *I* would show the way while he followed. A mighty sensible dog he was.

In a minute I came out near the tree. There I remembered that I would have to use some caution in approaching what might be a wounded man, and what was sure to be a man with a gun in his hands. So I came around in a quick semicircle and came upon the big tree from behind. Very lucky for me that I had done that, because, crouched in some brush ahead of me, not twenty yards from the tree itself, a man with a rifle at the ready was waiting for me.

I was so excited in the hunt that my own gun came to my shoulder automatically. There would certainly have been a dead man in the brush in another instant if I had not luckily chanced to notice that the back of this crouched fellow's neck was not olive brown at all, but red tan.

Instead of shooting, I kept my head, and said: "Look behind you, stranger!"

He gave a sort of groan and said: "Don't shoot, Lang!"

I knew that voice, and, when I saw the face that he jerked around at me, I knew the man that owned the voice. It was no other than Ridgeway himself!

That was a fair staggerer for me. It went sickly through my mind that I was not only fighting open enemies but that there was treason in my own side of the camp, which made it no even fight. He dropped his rifle and stuck his hands up above his head.

So I put my own gun at the ready and said: "Get

up and come out of that, Ridgeway. And mind what you do with your hands. I trust you just the way that I would trust a snake!"

He said: "I'd come and willing, Lang. But I can't very well move. Your bullet drilled straight through my leg. I'm about gone. Who would have dreamed that even *you* could shoot like that?"

There was no need to disillusion him. There was no need to tell him that I had twice paced off the distance to that tree so that I had a good deal of a bulge on it in the matter of target shooting. I let Ridgeway think what he pleased. Now I saw that what he said was no doubt true—about the wound, I mean. His face was white, and it was turning whiter all the time. It gave me a queer feeling, I can tell you—to think of a man sitting there and bleeding to death while he waited for an enemy to come along. I took out my hunting knife and kneeled down. It was not pleasant work. The minute that I got close to him, I saw his wicked eyes working at me, while he computed his chances. So I stopped those unhappy thoughts by taking his revolver and his knife away from him.

He started to say: "Look here, Lang, you don't think that I'm really any enemy of yours?"

I broke in: "I'm busy, and just now I don't want to waste any time in thinking. All that I want to do is to get this fixed."

"That's pretty fine of you, Lang," he said. "I want to explain that the reason I was sitting here in the brush with my rifle was that I didn't know what. . . ."

"Shut up!" I said. "I can't work and listen all at the same time. Sit tight and keep still, can't you?"

I cut away the leg of his trouser, and, when the wound was open to the air, I made a tourniquet. Then I made an outside bandage out of his shirt. With that finished, I took his guns and even his knife and started away. The way that he began to carry on was a shock.

He cried: "Don't leave me here without a gun, old-timer! Don't leave me here. He'll get me sure!"

"Who'll get you?" I snapped at him.

"The greaser!" he said.

"You know about him?" I asked him.

"How could I help it? And. . . ."

I turned my back on him. "If you know that," I told him, "you're a rat for not having given me warning." I walked away and left him, although he stayed there yelling after me until it occurred to him that his noise might tell a third party, if there were one nearby.

I heard his voice drop to a moan.

XIII

'IT'S MANUEL!'

That fellow thought I had gone away with no intention of coming back to him. Sometimes I think that you can judge a man's heart by the suspicions he's capable of having of another man. I can't help thinking that Ridgeway was the sort of a man who would have been capable of just that sort of a thing. Back in Maine they wouldn't leave a wounded man to die—even if he were poison. I got one of Ridgeway's horses and fixed a packsaddle on its back. Then I came back to the brush, and I found that poor Ridgeway had burrowed farther back into shelter.

He was so glad to see me that the tears came into his eyes. *That* helped me to see how mean he was, and how ornery. I made no remarks, because, no matter what he said or did, I had my duty by him that I had to perform.

I got him into the saddle with a good deal of

trouble, because he was turning weak now, and getting faint and limp. Just as I would heave him onto the saddle, he would roll halfway off and come heavily into my arms. What with his weight and a dancing horse that didn't like the proceedings a bit, I was pretty well worn out with about ten minutes of this foolishness. At last I managed to get him fixed and started back for the cabin.

When he found that I had stayed with the job, he opened his eyes a little and smiled at me—a sort of a "God bless you" look. I felt more kindly toward him not because I figured that he was any less a rat, but because I had been doing something for him. You invest a little trouble in another fellow and it is always sure to make you like him—and usually sure to make him dislike you. That's one of the queer things in this world of ours.

I got Ridgeway back to the cabin and unloaded him from the horse. Just as I got him dragged off the saddle a waspish noise hummed past my ear. Something flicked right across my face. What had struck me in the face fell down at my feet—a thin slice of leather that had been clearly ripped away by a flying rifle bullet. I didn't have to ask the horse to go for shelter. He gave a jump and a kick and was gone as I yanked Ridgeway back through the doorway into the kitchen. As I slammed the door, another bullet came combing through, just exactly breast high. On top of that bullet there was a yell of rage out of the woods—a devilish screech of disappointment.

Being shot at was no joke or pleasant party, but hearing a human being let out a screech like that— not a bit human, you understand, but like the squeal of a mad ape—well, that was worse. You could not imagine that man being afraid of the dark. You could almost imagine him seeing better by night than by day. Altogether, I never heard a daylight noise that gave me more the horrors.

It brought Ridgeway back to his senses for a minute. He gasped out: "It's Manuel!" Then he fainted again, but not from the loss of strength, you can bet.

I worked for a good hour after that, cleaning the wound and soaking iodine on it until Ridgeway yelled for mercy. Then I loosed the tourniquet a little, put on a fresh bandage, and got him fixed up in a bunk. He was so thoroughly scared, after hearing that devilish voice out of the morning and the woods, that he begged me not to leave him for a while. I had to go hungry for a whole hour and sit there and hold his hand. He was like a sick child, weak and shaking.

After that I was allowed to go back and fix breakfast. I gave him a little, and, after he had eaten, he fell into a sleep. I sat at the door of the bedroom and ate my own breakfast, none too comfortable. Little use as a sick man was—nothing but an encumbrance, of course, and much as I had reason to doubt and despise this Ridgeway, still with a devil like Manuel hanging around on the outside, it was a comfort and sort of fortification of the soul to have another man in the house there with me.

He babbled and talked away a good deal in his sleep. Then he dropped into a quieter rest, remaining sound asleep that way until long after noon. It was wonderful to watch him change as he lay there. You could tell for yourself that sleep is the finest thing in the world to build a man up. I could see his color get clearer; his cheeks no longer sagged; the straight set came out of his mouth very fast.

When he opened his eyes about one o'clock, he was looking, clear and straight, at me. His head was so level that he remembered everything that had passed, and he started to say something about it. I headed him off and told him that he could wait until he was a lot stronger before he did any talking. Not that I wasn't anxious for him to begin, but I was still itching with anger, feeling that, if I waited a little longer, I might cool off a bit and be more my real self.

He ate a pretty good lunch, and, when evening came, his appetite was fine for supper. It was simply beyond believing how quickly that man was recuperating. He had one of the best constitutions ever made and the strength of a pair of devils.

By the time his supper was put away, he begged for a pipe of tobacco, and I didn't really see how a good smoke could be harmful to any man, so I let him have it. He puffed away very heartily, enjoying himself fine.

After all of that, and, when I had cleaned up the dishes, he called to me, and, when I came in, he said: "Will you listen to me now, old-timer?"

I said that I wasn't ready to listen to any explanations.

He said: "Well, let me have a Colt, at least, will you?"

That was rather a facer for me. While I rested an elbow against the jamb of the door and looked back at him, he said: "I tell you, Lang, that fellow will find a way to get in here. The minute that he knows that I'm in this cabin, he'll simply go mad until he gets at me. Believe me when I say it, because I know him for sure."

He said it with the sort of emotion that convinces you more than the words do.

I said: "How was it that he didn't get at you when there was not even the wall of a cabin between you and him?"

"He didn't know where I was, then. But he knows now, and he'll be sure to come at me. Look here, Lang, I can guess what you have in your mind. The way I've acted seems queer. Almost as though I had had it in for you. But now you hear me talk. I raise my hand and I swear to God that I never had the least idea of lifting a hand against you. It never came into my head to shoot you down . . . the way you shot me down."

"I didn't know it was you," I told him. "At that distance, the face of one man is a good deal like the face of another. You know that I didn't intend that shot for you."

"That doesn't keep me from lying here on the flat of my back," he said.

"It didn't keep you from trying to murder me from the brush when I came up with you," I said.

Then he yelled at me: "You fool, how could I guess that it was you who fired? I thought it was Manuel, and that I'd have him snaking around through the trees after me. It didn't occur to me that anybody in the world would be able to shoot like that . . . except Manuel!"

He flared this out at me in a sort of a rage, but that rage wasn't very convincing, somehow. Deep down in my heart I knew that he was lying, and that he was putting on that pretended anger just as a bluff. That didn't make me like him any better, when I hated him already. So I told him that it wouldn't do. I was pretty simple, but I was not a fool.

I said: "There is something crooked about the way in which you've treated me. You know it. I'm not idiot enough to trust a gun in your hands!"

It was astonishing to see how white he got when I said that.

"Look here . . . Lang . . . old partner," pleaded Ridgeway, "do you think that even if I had anything up my sleeve against you, that I'd be mad enough to lift a hand against you so long as I lie here helpless, on the flat of my back . . . not able to help myself against that devil, out yonder?"

That was fairly convincing, you'll have to admit. I went back into the kitchen and smoked a pipe over the idea—the pipe being a grand way to help you when you have to think. When the pipe was down toward the dregs, I decided that after all there was a good deal of truth in the last things that Ridgeway had been saying. I went back to his room and gave him a Colt. As his hand closed over it, he grinned like a starving man who sees food and drink just before him.

"Now sit down, old-timer," he said, "and listen to me yap, will you?"

I only said: "I can't do it just yet. I wouldn't open my mind and listen to you in the right way. It wouldn't be the least use for you to talk to me."

"We've got to come to an understanding and work together, if we're to stand him off," said Ridgeway.

"How bad is he?" I asked.

"I'll tell you just this much . . . he's so bad that I left this cabin because I was afraid that I might have some sort of trouble with him. . . ."

I shouted in a fine rage: "You mean to say that you knew he was here before you got me to . . . !"

"Wait a minute, man," Ridgeway said. "All that I mean to say is that I was afraid he might show up. But I figured that all of his spite would be directed at me. How could I know that he would hand this grudge on to another man?"

There was a real feeling of truth behind a part of this, at least. I listened and couldn't help believing.

"All right," I said, "and now tell me what good you can do for me, while you lie there on your back?"

"I can watch this window and this side of the house," he answered as quick as a wink. "And that's something. That's a good deal when you have a fellow like Manuel against you."

"Yes," I admitted, "but. . . ." Here I broke off, listening sharp. I could hear a faint groaning out in the kitchen. At first my hair stood on end, because the sound was *inside* the house—not from the outside. "What is it?" I whispered.

"It's Manuel," Ridgeway whispered, whiter than ever. "No matter what it turns out to be, his hand is in it."

XIV

THE PLAN

When I started for the kitchen, I was walking slowly. You can depend on it that my mind was working, when I heard that same subdued, bubbling sort of a groan again. I knew that old Barney was stretched out on the floor of that same kitchen, and, if there were any harm to the windward, it was strange that he did not give me some signal of it.

When I got to the kitchen door, I found Barney standing with his head turned toward the big water boiler that was the chief comfort in the house. He had his head cocked to one side, watching, and, when he saw me, he didn't move his eyes toward me—just acknowledged me with a little lowering of his ears and a waggle of his tail.

Then I heard the groan again, deep and strong, and with the humming sound of pain in it. This time I spotted it, too. It came out of the hot water boiler. I turned on the tap at the bottom of the boiler, and held a bucket under. About three quarts of boiling water and a hundredweight of steam came ripping out.

Then I saw how that devil Manuel had struck at us in our little fort, the cabin. He had simply shut off the water supply. When I thought of what a fool I was for not having considered this possibility before, I wanted to laugh. I didn't. It was a good deal too serious.

I thought of the stove next. If I didn't want the heating pipes to melt, it would be a fair idea to put the fire out, and that was what I did. I put that fire out and had a fine demonstration of how much a fire can smoke when the doors and windows are shut. That kitchen was white with smoke before I finished. But it was better to have smoke in it than bullets. So I kept the windows down.

Then I went in to Ridgeway and started to tell him the news, but he didn't give me a chance.

"There's one thing plain," he said, "we can't go on living in this house without water. And, along with that idea, there is another . . . we can't carry water into the house while Manuel is out there with his rifle, waiting for us to appear."

I looked at him, amazed. He hadn't had a word from me about what had happened, and he had had to figure out everything just by the sound of the escaping steam and by the smoke that he had smelled. I called that brains. Right then and there I decided that if Manuel were as bad as he was brainy, he would have a hard time beating this same Luke Ridgeway of mine. I determined that any suggestions he could make would be the ones that I would want to follow.

I didn't say anything, then, just nodded at him. I

sat down and lighted a smoke, and he smiled and nodded back at me as much as to say: "Now you're showing a lot of good sense. I can do the thinking for the pair of us." He appreciated himself, right enough.

While he closed his eyes and began to think, I waited. Every now and then he would open his eyes with a start and stare at the ceiling, and then he would close them again and shake his head, dismissing something that had suggested itself to him. That seemed very queer to me. The only idea that I had was to leave the cabin by way of the tunnel through the mine. But although that way might serve for me, it would never serve for Ridgeway himself. But there was more in the wits of that fellow than I could ever dream of. He went on thinking matters over and shaking his head from time to time. At last he said: "If Manuel were a fool, we could work this matter out. But Manuel *isn't* a fool. And there's the trouble. I've got to get hold of a thing that will pull the wool over the wisest rascal in the world."

"Will you tell me what he's done to you, or you to him?" I asked Ridgeway.

"It's too long to tell," said Ridgeway.

It was plain to me that it wasn't the hardness of the telling that stopped that rascal, but because there was at least as much on the side of Manuel as there was on his own side. However, I couldn't waste time on such ideas as this. I had a pretty good idea that Ridgeway had brought me up here to a trap of which he hadn't warned me, and which he was pretty sure might be the death of me. How that would serve his ends, I didn't know. But I *did* know that Manuel had shot at me from hiding twice, and, although I was no hero and no man-fighter—although I had shot at a man for the first time in my life that same day—still I was in a heat to get at that infernal Mexican.

So I said: "I'd like to have just half a minute alone with Manuel to settle things, but the coward would never give me a chance."

Ridgeway gave me that ugly side glance of his. It was so plain wicked that it scared me worse than a leveled gun.

"Don't you worry about Manuel," he said. "He'll murder you from behind a tree, but he'll also shoot you in a fair fight, because he's that kind of a Mexican. Now if you mean what you say, about wanting to meet Manuel face to face, I'll arrange it for you."

What a rat that Ridgeway was. I couldn't help putting in: "Look here, Ridgeway, as far as I can make out, you and this Manuel, the man-eater, ain't the best friends in the world. How does it come that you want me to take the chance of get-ting my head blown off? After that happens to me, won't Manuel come in here and just cut you into small pieces, and you there on the flat of your back, unable to help yourself?"

That suggestion made him close his eyes and turn white, he was so sick. But there was some-thing else in his mind that didn't make him sick at all—something that pleased him a lot, because it sent the color back into his cheeks and made a sort of an evil, laughing light show in his eyes.

"Why, Lang," he said, "you don't understand what faith I have in you. I've heard a great deal about this Manuel and the way that he can shoot. But I've seen you shoot and I've *felt* you shoot!" He laughed, but there was an ugly ring in his laugh. It was easy enough for me to see that he wasn't telling his whole mind to me. What the other half of his thoughts were I couldn't guess.

Suddenly I said: "Ridgeway, what makes you want to get me killed?"

He tried to brazen it out and appear hurt and shocked by a suggestion like that, but he couldn't manage the trick. Because although he talked loud enough, yet at first he blanched and winced as that shot of mine went home.

Then he began to say: "Why, old-timer, what sort of a skunk d'you think that I am, to get a man to . . . ?"

I shut him up, then. I couldn't stand to listen to him lie and try to pull the wool over my eyes. I had to show him that I knew he was *partly* a dog. I said: "Look here, Luke, is it because you understand that I've found the real vein in the mine?"

Well, sir, that fetched the man. He gasped and propped himself straight up in the bed on his elbows.

"*You* found it!" he cried. "How could *you* find it?" Which was a sort of polite way of saying: "How could a fool like you find such a thing?"

I only grinned at him. "The dog took me to it," I said. That, in a manner of speaking, was the truth, although, of course, it was the least important half of the truth. I enjoyed that moment a lot, sitting there and seeing Ridgeway eating his heart out with doubt and curiosity and suspicion. Such thoughts and feelings make a man's face a pretty fair copy of the devil's, and that was just Ridgeway's look.

Then he lay back in the bed and closed his eyes, for fear that I would see *too* much in his face. However, there was no point in torturing a wounded man, particularly because I knew that I could never squeeze more than simple lies out of him, and that I would get no nearer to the truth of this matter by telling him what I knew.

"You know it, too?" muttered Ridgeway at last. I can tell you that there was iron in his voice.

"Aye, and Manuel knows it," said I, "and when three people know the same secret, you may as well say that the world knows it."

"As for Manuel . . . yes, that's bad," said Ridgeway. "But you *should* know I took a liking to you right from the first. But I wanted to have you up here for a while and try you out before I told you the secret. . . ."

"The secret of your six-months' trip," I suggested to him pretty dryly. He gave me one of his quick, side-ripping glances. But I put right in. "Let's not talk like a pair of fools. There's one important thing that I want to do. You've acted in a queer way, Ridgeway . . . just what harm you've tried to do me, I don't know. But I've heard the bullets of Manuel whistle around me on two occasions, and that's all that I want of that. I want to get at him, and you say that you know a way for that. So tell me what the way is, and I'll be done with you for today."

He gave me a grin that put the devil in his eyes again, like a shadow. Then he said: "All right . . . here's my scheme. It's not very complicated, but it might work. My idea is that all that keeps Manuel from closing in on you is that he doesn't know how badly wounded I may be. He doesn't know whether I'm lying pretty near to death or whether I'm up and around now. He doesn't know how I got hurt, most of all. If he had been near enough to see that, he would have had *both* our scalps when you ran out to take a look at your bag. Which was a pretty foolish move, between you and me, partner. For what Manuel saw was you taking care of me, real brotherly. And there you are. Now, son, what I propose is to have you drag me out to the kitchen. Out there, I'll make a noise . . . I'll sing . . . and start up a fire. That will make him think that *you're* there, of course. So, he will focus all of his attention on the back of the house. But while I'm doing that, you sneak out the *front* of the house and begin hunting for him. Or, if you want him to hunt *you*, just loose off a gun and he will quick enough realize that it's the wounded man who is hobbling around in the kitchen . . . y'understand? He'll go gunning for you!"

"Meaning that he would prefer getting me to tackling you?"

"Meaning that he would rather attack a man in the woods than a wounded man in a house with strong walls like these. Besides, he don't know how badly I'm wounded."

Well, I studied this over for a while. I didn't like it, in a way, but I couldn't put any finger upon the exact thing that was wrong.

Finally I said: "Just let me know, will you, how you are going to manage to move around, with a leg such as you have to handle?"

He only laughed in my face. "This is for my life," he said. "And for my life I could manage to go a mile . . . dead easy." He said the last of it through his set teeth, and I believed him. He had enough willpower to serve for a whole army.

I didn't wait to understand any more whys and wherefores. I just got ready for what was to come. I looked to my Colt, and I looked to my rifle. That was just a matter of form, because I always kept those guns in tip-top shape.

"Ridgeway," I said, "I'm going out to try to kill a man, or to *get* killed. All I have to say is that I understand, if I get my share of the lead that flies, where I meet you again will not be in heaven. You're a bad man, Ridgeway, and I know it. I just got to tell you that before I leave, because I don't want you to think that you've pulled the wool across my eyes!"

He didn't answer. He just closed his eyes, because he didn't want me to see what was in them. Then I helped him out into the kitchen, and he sat down by the stove, where the two windows didn't look in on him. Right away he began to make the noise he spoke of. He began to sing in a voice that was not very musical, but that was louder than the braying of a donkey.

Me, I started for the front of the house, right then. I was almost glad when I had my head outside of that cabin and under the honest sun again, even if I were to get a bullet along with the clean air.

XV

SOLUTION

That part of the scheme of Ridgeway worked fine. I managed to get to the edge of the pine woods. There I leaned back against a tree, not mindful of the pitch that I could feel soaking into my shirt between the shoulder blades. Then I decided that the best way was just as Ridgeway had said—to let the Mexican know that I was there and let him come after me, if he had a mind to. I fired the rifle, and, as I reloaded it, I knew that I had begun a duel that would last until either the Mexican or I was dead.

Not a very pleasant feeling, of course. I knew that fellow was poison, partly from what I had seen of him, and partly from what Ridgeway had said about him. Still, I was glad to be out there where we could fight the battle, fair and square.

I had a good place, with a thick hedge of trees around me, and I waited there, only stirring enough to peer out between the trunks every now and then. The most tiresome, heart-breaking, nerve-racking work that was ever invented. I could realize for the first time what a deer feels when it lies wounded and hears the hunters coming.

Then Barney, who had remained there wedged up against my heels all the time, began to loosen up. He yawned, stretched, and came around to look me in the face and waggle his tail. It made me mad, at first. Then I told myself maybe Barney was right. Why should I kill myself with nervousness, instead of with bullets? I decided to hunt the hunter.

That hour had played me out so that, when I started walking, I was as weak and giddy as though I had been sitting up all night at a card table and drinking plenty of black coffee to keep going. However, a little still-hunting did me good. That was my own old game from the Maine woods.

The difference between hunting a deer and hunting a man is that one of them is armed with antlers and a sharp pair of ears, and the other is armed with a revolver and a brain. Which, after all, is not such a big difference as you might think.

I circled slowly around that shack, keeping pretty deep in the woods, until right behind the shack where Barney froze onto a trail. I sneaked over and took a look at it, but I couldn't make anything out of it. It was his nose and not his eyes that was talking to Barney. He followed the trail until he came to a damper place and there I saw the print of a great big naked foot. My Mexican, right enough. You couldn't imagine any white man going barefoot over that sort of rocky country, not even if he wanted to be as silent as a snake in his movements.

Barney went ahead, silent. Just wagging his tail when I patted his back and whispered to him that he was a good dog. He worked that trail out of the edge of the woods—and then he followed it right straight at the kitchen door of the shack!

I tried to tell myself that I was mad, or else that this was an old trail showing that Manuel had sneaked up to the house the day before. But instinct told me that Barney was dead right, and that the Mexican was right there in the house that minute—waiting for me. *That* was an ugly minute, if you'll believe me.

What I did was the strangest part of all. Before I knew it, I had blundered out behind Barney into open view of the shack. Once I was in the view of it, I kept right on traveling—not even crouching, but walking upright. That was a sandy soil, muffling the footfall. There was no dead grass; it was short and green and kept close-mowed by the cow, because that fool cow preferred the pasture around the house—she was too lazy to walk any distance for her dinner.

That was why I managed to get up to the house without a sound of me being heard. The reason that I kept on going forward—well, I don't know what it was, unless it was that I was too afraid to turn back, once I had started, and partly, too, that there was a grisly picture in my mind—caused by the silence of the house—of big Ridgeway lying dead on the floor, with his throat cut from ear to ear, and the Mexican kneeling over him and going though his pockets.

I got up to the back of the house—and Barney ran the trail to the kitchen door and began to sniff and to scratch there. My heart stood still. I was close enough to reach the cabin wall in about two steps, and I dropped on my knees there as I heard a voice whisper loudly in the kitchen: "What the devil is that? Ah, the dog."

"Only the dog," said the softened voice of Ridgeway.

Much as I detested him, and much as I was horrified to find that he was in there talking in a friendly way with the Mexican, still I was glad to hear that voice of his and know that my vision of his death had been a lie.

"Not so loud," said the other. "Where the dog is, there will be the master."

"Don't worry," Luke said, "because Ridgeway is sure to be out there in the pines, sitting tight, no matter where his dog may roam around."

"There is still an hour or two before evening," said the Mexican. "But when the shadows begin, then he will think of the cabin, and he will try to come back . . . and then I shall do as poor Waters would like to have me do . . . and as this *Señor* Ridgeway deserves. Does he not deserve it . . . to speak honestly?"

"The dog ought to die under the knife . . . bullets are a pile too good for him," Luke said. "Why, this Ridgeway is a regular wolf!"

"I know," said Manuel. "Waters used to tell me . . . a sneak. And a wolf is a sneak. Making other people take the dangers . . . the way he left you here in this shack . . . after he dragged you out of your bed . . . oh, I shall handle this Ridgeway. . . ."

When you hear another man's name saddled on your shoulders it's usually a little irritating, but when you have the name of a fellow like Ridgeway, with himself sitting by, calling himself names, and making it hotter for me every instant. . . . Well, I was half wild. I kneeled there, trembling and fingering my Colt's butt. I've often had people gasp and ask me if I were not too much afraid even to stir. No, I can tell you frankly that, although I'm no hero, I got too angry then to have a bad nerve in my body. I'm not proud, but I'm too good ever to be a Ridgeway.

"But how did you have a chance to get acquainted with Waters?" asked Ridgeway.

"They put us together on the same gang, breaking rocks on the road, and then in doing a lot of easier work. While we were doing that, we got to know that we were from the same section of the country. Finally Waters told me how Ridgeway had railroaded him into jail. Waters is a pretty good man, *señor*. Stupid, but pretty good. I liked him, and when he told me how Ridgeway lived on his money and how Ridgeway got from him the secret of the rich vein, and then how Ridgeway. . . ."

I couldn't stand it any longer. I was savage toward both of them—Ridgeway, who had saddled his identity on me, and the Mexican who had tried twice from ambush for my life. I stepped to that door and jerked it open, and, sticking in my head, I yelled: "You greaser dog . . . here I am!"

Oh, he was a cool fellow. But when you're hunting a man, you don't expect him suddenly to open your door and call your name. I didn't think of it at the time, but, as a matter of fact, I suppose that I did the only thing that could have saved my life.

Manuel was simply paralyzed. He whirled around, and I let him have it with the Colt. I missed him, and the bullet hit the stove with a terrible clangor. Before I could shoot again, he had flashed his gun out and taken a crack at me. Because of his shaken nerves, Manuel missed—oh, just by an eighth of an inch. The man who tells you that a miss is as good as a mile lies, because I've dreamed about that eighth of an inch ever since.

I didn't miss with my second shot. Manuel had dropped for the floor—a snaky but a deadly way of revolver fighting, because it gives the other fellow a smaller target to shoot at, and it gives you a steadier hand for the firing. But Manuel needed a fifth of a second more to put in *his* second shot. That fifth of a second was nowhere to be had, because, just as he dropped to the floor, I let him have the second chamber of that good old Colt.

Manuel flattened out and lay still. The bullet had hit him in the back, near the base of the neck. It remained in his body, after it had smashed up most of him. I turned him over on his back, and he opened his eyes at me.

"God did not hear my prayers," Manuel said.

"You fool!" I yelled at him. "*There* is your man . . . *that's* the real Ridgeway. . . ."

He knew that I knew he was dying, and that there was no point in a lie. He writhed up his lips like a dying dog and tried to drag out his second gun to kill Luke, but I held his hand. After that, he lived about ten minutes altogether. He didn't do a great deal of talking, but there was enough said for me to get the story pieced together before he died. Most of it you have gathered yourself.

Ridgeway had been down in Mexico for three years, and, while he was down there, he ran into

Waters, a fellow who had been in prison and made an escape from an Oklahoma penitentiary. Waters told him a yarn about a rich vein in that abandoned Spanish mine in the Southwest. Ridgeway and Waters finally decided to take a try at it.

They were to sneak over the Río and go north. When they got to the mine, Waters was to show the vein to Ridgeway. Then Ridgeway was to buy the tools and so forth, and he would make all the trips to town for provisions, while the fugitive, Waters, remained in the mine and worked there until they had gutted the pocket or fairly opened up a great vein. Then he would take his half, and drift south again, leaving Ridgeway to manage the mine.

That was the way that they started. When Ridgeway found out how rich the vein looked, he lost his head. They took more than $5,000 worth of metal out of that mine in eight days, working it very clumsily. Ridgeway decided that he would take a try at that mine all by himself. That wasn't hard to do. He simply turned stool pigeon and gave word about Waters to the police. They made a night call, scooped in Waters, and Ridgeway was left with a lone hand to play.

In prison, Waters became a friend of this Manuel and made him hot with this story of a betrayal. Finally the end of Manuel's sentence arrived. Before it came, however, word had leaked out in the prison that Manuel intended to put the wrongs of his prison friend right—he had allowed the police to get hold of the talk. The police, in turn, had passed along a friendly hint or two to Ridgeway, because a stool pigeon has to be encouraged for the good of the profession.

That was about all that I got out of Manuel before he died, except that his last words were a prayer that I would send Ridgeway after him.

Of course, the whole point was that in prison Waters had no photograph of Ridgeway. He could give this Manuel a good description of a tall, bony man, over six feet, with heavy bones and weighing around 200 pounds. Every one of those details fitted in with myself as well as it did with Ridgeway.

That scoundrel was clever enough to guess that the Mexican would have to work by a mere description. When he spotted me in the store at Elmira and saw me do the shooting, he got his grand idea. He would hire me to take care of the cabin, and, when he disappeared, he would hang about in the offing.

In the meantime, the Mexican would arrive, find in possession of the cabin a man who looked like the mine stealer. One of two things would happen. Either the Mexican would kill Lang and feel that his mission was executed, or else Lang would kill the Mexican, which would be the best of all. From the shooting which he had seen me do, Ridgeway was willing to bet on me. Most of all after I brought him down out of the tree.

In any case, his own skin would be safe.

And, confound him, his skin *was* safe!

I took care of him until he was able to navigate. Then I drew down the money that he owed to me, and I left the cabin. Ridgeway was the most surprised man in the world because I didn't shoot him while he was helpless, lay the blame on the Mexican, and say that they had fought each other to the death—a story that the police would have been perfectly willing to believe—knowing as they did what was in the mind of the Mexican when he left the prison.

It was the Mexican, evidently, who escaped that night through the trapdoor, not Bill and Jerry. They were probably intimidated by my ready rifle, for I never saw them again.

You may be sure that Barney never lacked a home as long as he lived. Good old Barney!

I should like to say that Ridgeway died soon, and died unhappily. This being a true story, I have to tell the truth. That rat left the West and went into Missouri, where he bought a good farm and married. When he died five years later, he left his widow and two children mighty well provided for. If I were to let real names leak out, those children would be mighty surprised to learn that their good dad was really a scoundrel.

Why did he leave the West?

That was because that fine vein turned out to be only a very shallow pocket. The Indian miners had missed something—but not much.

Bill and Jerry I never saw again—but Barney is still with me, not over-spry, but loyal.

If it had not been for my talk with Cobden, I would never have gone West. And if I *had* gone West, I should not have carried along that silly passion for range finding. If I had not had that practice, I should never have known the range of that big tree—or shot down Ridgeway—or in so doing untangled the whole problem.

You see how everything pieces in together, pretty neat?

Besides, I would like to draw a little moral out of this story. I would like the youngsters to see that anything that a man learns to do *really* well may prove to be the saving of him. Even if it's no more than the ability to guess distances.

MAX BRAND®

THE GOLDEN CAT

John Jones has never courted trouble. But his partner
Rourke seems to draw it in spades—like when he agrees
to escort a group of tenderfoots to a remote hacienda in
the Sierra Negra. First they have to get an ornery old
invalid, his beautiful daughter, her dandied-up fiancé
and the rest of their entourage over some of the rough-
est terrain in the country. Every day, they risk their hides
to protect their party against the vicious bandits who
roam the area. But as they journey on and the murder
attempts continue, it appears the most dangerous enemy
might just prove to be one of their own.

Dorchester Publishing Co., Inc.
P.O. Box 6640   ___5699-2
Wayne, PA 19087-8640 $5.99 US/$7.99 CAN

Please add $2.50 for shipping and handling for the first book and $.75 for each additional book.
NY and PA residents, add appropriate sales tax. No cash, stamps, or CODs. Canadian orders
require an extra $2.00 for shipping and handling and must be paid in U.S. dollars. Prices and
availability subject to change. **Payment must accompany all orders.**

Name: _____

Address: _____

City: _____ State: _____ Zip: _____

E-mail: _____

I have enclosed $_____ in payment for the checked book(s).

CHECK OUT OUR WEBSITE! **www.dorchesterpub.com**
_____ Please send me a free catalog.

MAX BRAND®

PETER BLUE

Peter Blue was one of the most feared gunmen in the West. But now he's holed up in a small shack, hiding from the world. For he doesn't want anyone to know about the bullet that's destroyed his right hand, his gun hand. He realizes it won't be long before he's found and another man comes to challenge him. After all, he's made plenty of enemies in his lifetime. But he's determined to be ready for them—with the fastest left-handed draw they've ever seen. If only he can get his fingers to stop trembling and his aim to hold true...

RIDERS OF
THE PURPLE SAGE
ZANE GREY

Zane Grey's masterpiece, *Riders of the Purple Sage*, is one of the greatest, most influential novels of the West ever written. But for nearly a century it has existed only in a profoundly censored version, one that undermined the truth of the characters and distorted Grey's intentions.

Finally the story has been restored from Grey's original handwritten manuscript and the missing and censored material has been reinserted. At long last the classic saga of the gunman known only as Lassiter and his search for his lost sister can be read exactly as Zane Grey wrote it. After all these years, here is the **real** *Riders of the Purple Sage*!

PAUL S. POWERS
DESERT JUSTICE

Sonny Tabor leads a rough life. Wrongfully accused of a string of murders, he has a price on his head and is relentlessly pursued by the law. The four novellas in this volume, collected for the first time in paperback, showcase riveting action and high drama as Sonny is forced into a life of continual flight and constant danger. In one story, he's left handcuffed to a lawman in the middle of the desert without food, water or horses. And in another, he's captured with an outlaw and sentenced to hang. Sonny is desperate to prove his innocence—but that means he'll have to live long enough to find the real killers.

CHASING DESTINY

STEPHEN OVERHOLSER

Thousands of dollars stolen. A man murdered on his own ranch. The crimes were enough to form a posse hell-bent on vengeance and ready to shoot at anything that moved. When their bullets caught a fugitive square in the face, they didn't spend much time identifying the body before pronouncing the man guilty. But some folks in town don't believe the real culprit is six feet under. Some folks think the real murderer is hiding out, still counting all his gold. But they'll have a lot of dangerous hard work ahead to prove whether they're on a fool's errand or...*Chasing Destiny*

Dorchester Publishing Co., Inc.
P.O. Box 6640
Wayne, PA 19087-8640

_____5728-X
$5.99 US/$7.99 CAN

Please add $2.50 for shipping and handling for the first book and $.75 for each additional book. NY and PA residents, add appropriate sales tax. No cash, stamps, or CODs. Canadian orders require an extra $2.00 for shipping and handling and must be paid in U.S. dollars. Prices and availability subject to change. **Payment must accompany all orders.**

Name: _____

Address: _____

City: _____ State: _____ Zip: _____

E-mail: _____

I have enclosed $_____ in payment for the checked book(s).

CHECK OUT OUR WEBSITE! www.dorchesterpub.com
_____ *Please send me a free catalog.*